78

DEATH
BY
DISSERTATION

DEAN JAMES

SILVER DAGGER
M Y S T E R I E S
An Imprint of The Overmountain Press
JOHNSON CITY, TENNESSEE

Note to the reader: The events described in this book take place prior to those related in both *Cruel as the Grave* and *Closer Than the Bones*.

Book design by Cherisse McGinty

Hardcover ISBN 1-57072-266-8
Trade Paper ISBN 1-57072-267-6
Copyright © 2004 by Dean James
Printed in the United States of America
All Rights Reserved

1 2 3 4 5 6 7 8 9 0

This book is most humbly dedicated with respect, gratitude,
and affection to Professor Katherine F. Drew,
whose example of professionalism and integrity
I shall always strive to emulate.

ACKNOWLEDGMENTS

I would like to take this opportunity to offer my thanks to a number of people who contributed in important ways to this book. First, to the fine folk of The Overmountain Press who were willing to give it a chance, especially to Beth Wright and Sherry "Eagle Eye" Lewis; second, to my dear friends Megan Bladen-Blinkoff and Patricia R. Orr, who suffered through far too many drafts of the manuscript but never complained; third, to Chief William F. Taylor of the Rice University Police Department for cheerfully answering my questions about his department; fourth, and finally, to the history department of Rice University, circa 1981-1985, which gave me the opportunity to realize my dream. I can only hope that setting a mystery in a fictionalized version of the department won't cause them to regret it!

C H A P T E R · 1

I WAS CONVINCED graduate school was the lowest circle of Hell in the *Inferno*, but Dante discarded it as too terrifying for his readers. My particular corner of hell was a seminar room half full of dedicated medievalists; and slouching in a stuffy seminar room on a beautiful October afternoon, even for a nonathletic slug like me, was hard work. Especially when I was having to listen to Dan Erickson babble on and on about the absolutely riveting number of horses Charles Martel had had in his army when he defeated the Muslim invaders at Poitiers in A.D. 732. That was a heck of a long way away from 1991.

Dan was one of those intense, incredibly focused students that professors enthused over publicly but secretly wished to throw to a pack of salivating, feral dogs. And that would be definitely mild in comparison to the fates devised by fellow students. Everyone has had a "Dan" in class: the earnest face that follows the professor's every word, every gesture; the neatly word-processed papers, always a few pages over the maximum, turned in a week early; the hand ready to fly, the moment his brain has formed a question. Was Dan the reason I was spending all this time in graduate school? Was I going to spend the rest of my life, post-Ph.D., teaching Dan-clones, or, worse maybe, the ones who *didn't* care? Perhaps, being a college professor might approximate Dante's view of Purgatory. Lord only knew, then, what Paradise might be.

I listened to Dan burble on about the eighth-century French climate, the physiology of the horse, and something about horses' diets, then promptly tuned out. This was one day in Professor Julian Whitelock's seminar on the early Middle Ages that I wouldn't have a question to pose after the reading. It was Whitelock's fault, forcing Dan to present a paper so close to the date of his dissertation defense. To pay the professor back, I'm sure he found his most boring one.

I avoided the eye of one of my fellow students as Dan waxed ever more enthusiastic. Maggie McLendon, sitting across the table from me, had her lips clamped together, trying not to laugh. Her expression dared me to keep a straight face. If she so much as winked or smirked at me, I wouldn't be able to resist laughing myself.

Sitting next to Maggie was Rob Hayward, whom I had known since childhood. He cast an amused glance my way. I was probably glowering at him. Most of the time I affected bored disinterest when he was around, though he was as handsome and charming as ever. I didn't have as much control of my wayward hormones as I thought. Which, of course, made me even angrier at him, and at myself.

Nearly two months into the semester, I still found it hard to believe that Rob was here. I had thought—and prayed—that he was out of my life forever. My worst nightmare had been realized that day in late August when I walked into the history office and saw him chatting casually with the department head.

Maggie had caught on to the tension between me and Rob, but even though Maggie and I were good friends, I wasn't ready to confide the history of my tangled relationship with Rob, nor the depth of my feelings of betrayal and anger. My stomach clenched, and I ground my teeth. I took a deep breath and forced myself to relax. I couldn't let him do this to me every time I saw him or thought about him.

Maggie frowned, eyes on me, and I smiled at her, even as Dan babbled on toward the blessed conclusion of his paper. I glanced around the table to see how others were reacting.

Charlie Harper, Rob's roommate, sat next to me, and he shifted in his chair as Dan finished and looked expectantly around the room for questions and praise. Charlie had the most acid tongue of anyone I'd ever known, and I waited, with some relish, for him to unleash it on Dan.

But Julian Whitelock well knew Charlie's proclivities and was out of his chair before Charlie or anyone else could frame a question. "Thank you, Daniel," he drawled. "That was a *most* fascinating examination of an *under*-researched aspect of the life of Charles Martel. I do believe I have a new appreciation for the horse after hearing your paper. And we all appreciate your taking the time to contribute to this seminar when you are so busy preparing for your dissertation defense." Whitelock's cultured South Carolina accent remained carefully neutral. Judging from the glazed look in his eyes, he was exerting every vestige of Southern charm he could muster.

The quirky thing was, Dan was apparently a favorite of Whitelock's. If he put work onto his favorites, I was glad to be one of the students he merely tolerated. I knew I was damned already to a "B" for the course, no matter what I did, and I saved myself a lot of sweat and heartache by not toadying to the professor.

"I'm afraid, Daniel," Whitelock continued, "that we won't have time to entertain questions for your paper today."

Dan seemed as relieved as the rest of us, and he grinned slightly as he put his paper away. Smiling, Whitelock urged the group to give Dan a round of applause. Amidst the halfhearted clapping, the professor cast a venomous glance around the table.

A fit and fierce sixty years old, he had a patrician face and long, thick white hair, which gave him the air of a Southern grandee. He never wore white linen suits or panama hats to class, but it didn't take much imagination to see him that way. His accent, I was certain, he exaggerated simply because he knew it annoyed everyone. The ever-present dollop of venom in his voice didn't help much either.

"Now," Whitelock announced, "Charles is going to read us a short paper, a preliminary to the work he'll present in full to the seminar in two weeks."

I looked across at Maggie and rolled my eyes slightly. She responded with a wry smile, then settled her face into an expression of intent interest. She was so adorable when she was serious, and I could have easily fallen in love with her, except for one problem. She was straight, and I was gay. If only she were a man, she would've been perfect. Though I didn't dare tell *her* that. Oh, well. I wasn't in graduate school to fall in love and have a mad, passionate affair, anyway. I avoided looking at Rob.

Beside me, Charlie cleared his throat noisily, opened his file folder, and began to read. I glanced down to see how many pages he had and found only a thin stack. *Good,* I thought. *Maybe this won't take too long, after all.*

Charlie Harper was a very good historian. His problem, though, was that he didn't write well. His sentences were long and complex, which wasn't so bad if you were reading them. Listening to them, however, and following Charlie's logic required an effort of concentration that I simply couldn't make at the time. He had a deep and pleasant voice, though, and I let the sounds flow by without taking in the meaning of the words.

Instead, I continued my survey of the room. The other two attending the seminar were women, and one of them was a stranger whom Whitelock had not bothered to introduce. An attractive blonde of about forty, dressed in an expensive business suit, she had watched the proceedings with a face schooled to hide her thoughts. I noticed something familiar about her, but my memory refused to track down the resemblance.

The woman seated next to her I did know, though not all that well. Selena Bradbury, also blonde and maybe five years younger than the other woman, wasn't enrolled in our seminar either. She had finished her courses several years earlier and was now completing her dissertation. I thought I'd heard that she was to defend the coming week, but I couldn't remember.

Frankly, Selena could be a tad intimidating. Her nickname among the older grad students was the "Ice Queen," and, true to form, she had made no move to warm toward Maggie or me. Whitelock was the only person for whom she manifested any regard, and her attitude toward him was hard to fathom. She had attended our weekly seminar three times, and she asked excellent questions. Most of the time she sat quietly, watching, with those ice-blue eyes that could freeze you, like the ninth circle of Dante's Hell.

Evidently I had been woolgathering during Charlie's brief presentation, because I caught only one sentence before he turned over the final page and looked around at his audience.

All at once I felt an air of tension in the room. Rob's face had scrunched up into a question mark, and Maggie's face had gone completely blank, but Whitelock's face had turned the shade of a ripe tomato. What had I missed? For the next seminar I was going to have to bring a Diet Coke so the caffeine would keep my mind working.

I watched Charlie. Through his dark beard and moustache I could see him grin, seeming to offer a challenge of some sort. What had he done now? I waited and wondered. No one spoke.

Whitelock struggled to his feet, the color in his face subsiding. "That's all for today." For a moment he sounded like he came from New York City instead of Charleston. From his place at the head of the long table, he turned and stalked toward the door. Over his shoulder, he threw the words, "Mr. Harper. My office."

Once the professor was gone, Charlie looked around the room and laughed. "The master calls. Excuse me, folks." With a casual air, he bundled his papers into the folder and left.

A few seconds later we all heard the slamming door of Whitelock's office just down the hall. Heads together and whispering, Selena and the oddly familiar stranger walked out together. Dan trailed forlornly in their wake.

"What gives with Charlie and Whitelock?" I asked Maggie, trying to ignore Rob. "I wasn't paying any attention to what Charlie was saying, so what's going on?"

"Andy Carpenter," Maggie said, grinning at me, "how could you not have been listening to one of Charlie's magnificent orations on Frankish history?"

"It's all Dan's fault," I retorted. "He destroyed whatever powers of concentration I might have had, with that paper on medieval Frankish horseshit, or whatever it was."

Rob snorted. "It was horseshit, all right."

"It's exactly the kind of academic research that makes the Republicans in Congress want to cut funding for higher education," I said.

"I think even the Democrats would have trouble justifying this," Maggie laughed.

"I suppose," Rob said with a sly smile, "Whitelock is so politically neutered— or do I mean neutral?—that it doesn't matter to him."

It pained me to have to agree, so I just ignored him. I asked my question about Charlie's paper again. "What about it made Whitelock so angry, Maggie?"

"As well as I could follow Charlie," she replied, "I *think* he was trying to show that Whitelock was misguided, at best, in that article he wrote a few years ago on kingship in Merovingian Gaul."

For the life of me, I couldn't remember what the professor had said about kingship in Merovingian Gaul, though I had waded through the article twice the previous month, trying to make sense of it. Whitelock's prose was no better than Charlie's.

Rob sighed. "I don't know why, but Charlie seems to have it in for Whitelock lately. I mean, today he practically called the guy a fool in front of all of us. How does he expect to get the man to direct his dissertation?"

"Well, he's *your* roommate!" I said rudely. "If you don't know, then how the heck should any of us know?"

Charlie had been in the program for a year longer than we had, though he and Rob had known each other in their undergraduate days. Having Rob in the same program with me was bad enough, but when he moved in next door with Charlie at the start of school, I was almost ready to head back to Mississippi and trash my dream of getting a Ph.D. in history.

"I don't know exactly what Charlie is doing," Rob answered, with heavy patience. "You might have noticed, Charlie doesn't listen to anyone. He follows his own drummer."

Rob was right about that. Charlie wouldn't be beaten into submission by Julian Whitelock. Charlie came from a wealthy family, and our professor respected nothing so much as money.

"Well," I said, standing up, "no doubt, Charlie will come out the better. Some people have a talent for treating other people like shit and walking away clean." I looked straight at Rob as I said it.

He stood so quickly, his chair overturned and fell with a loud bang. "And some people can't seem to do anything but act like jerks all the time, no matter—" He stopped in mid-sentence and looked at me with a weary expression, his anger cooling suddenly. "Oh, just forget it." He grabbed his backpack and stalked out.

Maggie frowned at me. "Are you happy with yourself now?" The ice in her tone would have chilled the Sahara. "You finally got a reaction out of him, after taunting him for two months. Was it what you wanted?"

I looked at her defiantly. "You don't know him the way I do. He has a temper like you wouldn't believe."

"You're right, Andy," Maggie observed as she stood up. "I don't know Rob all that well, but I do know you. And I think you're acting like a jerk, whatever he may have done in the past."

That really stung, and I had nothing to say as I followed Maggie out of the seminar room. I was about to offer a conciliatory remark, but as we neared Whitelock's office, we could hear raised voices inside.

Abruptly Whitelock's door opened, and a smiling Charlie appeared. "*You*'ll see whose ass is in a bind, believe me," he said before pulling the door shut with an emphatic click.

Then Charlie saw us, and, not a bit bothered that we had overheard him, his grin widened. "Somebody's going to murder that bastard one of these days." He marched off down the hall, laughing to himself.

C H A P T E R · 2

THE DISAGREEMENT with Maggie left me feeling out of sorts. I didn't want to admit that she was right, because I had been deliberately baiting Rob to see how he would react. I didn't want to examine my motives, because I'd have to think more about how I really felt. *Not* something I was ready to get into.

As Maggie and I walked down the stairs one flight to the floor where our carrels were located, she didn't seem to want to talk about Charlie's nasty comment. I retrieved what I wanted from my carrel, right next to Maggie's, and bade her good-bye. She nodded in response and settled down in her own carrel, busying herself with a book. I wandered off, knowing that by the next time I saw her, a thaw would have set in.

On the way home I decided to make a couple of stops. The first was at a trendy deli on Montrose where all the yuppies, guppies, and buppies gathered to eat. At four in the afternoon, the place wasn't busy, and I was able to get my sandwich and potato salad without having to wait as long as usual. I stuck my food on the floorboard, out of the sun, and swung the car on down Montrose toward Westheimer and my second stop.

On a graduate student's budget, I had to take my entertainment where I could find it. Sometimes I felt like I spent my entire life in two places: my apartment and the library. Every great once in a while, I splurged and went to a movie. Occasionally I visited Houston's Museum of Fine Arts, when admission was free, or the Menil Collection, where they just asked for donations. Bookstore crawls were the best, though. I often lusted over books I couldn't afford, but wandering through a bookstore was a good, free way to break the monotony of my daily routine.

I found a parking place alongside the building that housed Houston's biggest gay and lesbian bookstore. I hadn't been by since the semester started, and I was in the mood to browse. Not to mention the fact that there were always some good-looking guys cruising the shelves. I wasn't in the market, but I sure didn't mind surveying the produce.

A quick glance through the magazines convinced me I hadn't missed much in the previous two months. No interesting fellow browsers, either. I moved on to check out the nonfiction section, with the same results.

Maggie's birthday was coming up, though, and I decided I could find her an appropriate card here, one with a scantily clad hunk and a suggestive message inside. Naturally I had to look at all the possible choices before I found just the right one.

At the checkout counter, I smiled pleasantly at the clerk as I paid for the card. Just behind him sprawled the counter where you could order various caffeinated beverages and good, fattening things to eat. Dan Erickson stood there, his back to me, fastening an apron around himself.

I absentmindedly accepted my change from the clerk while I watched Dan, who was engrossed in taking an order from a couple of older men. They cast appreciative glances at his blond good looks.

When did Dan start working here? I wondered. The pooh-bahs in the history department frowned upon part-time jobs because graduate students were supposed to concentrate on their intellectual work, not physical labor. Things like food and rent had to be paid, though, and Dan wasn't the first grad student to need a job while finishing a degree.

More to the point, however, why was he working in a gay and lesbian bookstore? He was, as far as I knew, straight, and this seemed like an unusual environment for a straight man to choose for employment.

I wandered around to the other counter and got in line behind the two flirtatious customers. I stood with my head slightly turned, and Dan focused his attention on the men in front of me. He still hadn't spotted me. Their supply of banter exhausted, the guys took their coffee and cake and retreated to a nearby table.

I stepped up to the counter. "Hi, Dan."

His eyes widened when he saw his waiting customer.

"Fancy meeting you here," I said. "Are you joining my team?"

"Andy!" he said, staring at me. He expelled a breath. "I guess I should have figured on running into you here sooner or later." He hesitated, glancing over his shoulder. "Look, can I talk to you for a minute? If you want something, let me treat, okay?"

"Okay," I said, curious about what Dan wanted to confide. Besides, I could stand a bribe. I ordered a latte and a piece of cheesecake, one of my weaknesses.

"I'll join you in a minute," he said, and I found a table in the corner.

While I nibbled on my cheesecake and sipped my latte, Dan helped a couple of women who had wandered up to the counter. Once he had filled their order, he conferred briefly with a manager-looking guy in a bright purple shirt, which showed off a highly buffed physique. Dan gestured in my direction, and I affected not to notice while the manager stared at me. He nodded, and Dan patted him on the arm. I wouldn't have minded trading places with Dan right about then. Maybe he would introduce me. I smiled at the thought.

Dan pulled out the chair across from me and sat down. "I don't have long," he said, "but I thought I ought to explain what I'm doing here."

I wiped my mouth with my napkin and sat back in my chair, watching his earnest face. *Why the sudden need to unburden himself to me?* I wondered.

This happened to me all the time on airplanes. I invariably had a seatmate who decided, for whatever reason, that I was Ann Landers or Dear Abby incarnate, and I ended up hearing all about the lives of people I'd never met before and, frankly, never wanted to see again. I guess I looked too much like a big, cuddly teddy bear (or so I'd been told). Maybe if I shaved half my head, got my nose pierced, and dyed my beard blue, people would leave me alone.

"You don't owe me any explanations." I nobly tried to ignore my rampant curiosity. "Though I do appreciate the snack."

Dan waved that away, and I settled in to listen. "I know you must think it weird," he laughed self-consciously, "to find me working in a gay bookstore."

"Just because you work here doesn't necessarily mean you're gay," I answered.

"Exactly!" He smiled in relief. "I mean, they prefer to have gay staff here, and I don't guess it hurts to let them think I am, right?"

I set my cup of latte down with a bit of a thump. "Look, how you represent yourself to these people doesn't concern me in the slightest. That's between you and your conscience." I did find the notion irritating, but he could be inside the closet, behind the wallpaper, and just couldn't admit to himself why he really wanted to work here.

"I know, I know," Dan said hurriedly. "It's just that I needed the job, and this seemed like a good place." He hunched his shoulders and leaned closer. "I mean, it's not like any of the history department faculty will wander in anytime soon, right?"

"Probably not, unless some of them are hiding something," I said pointedly, though Dan seemed not to catch my meaning. "Are you worried they'll give you a hard time over having a job?"

"Yeah," he admitted. "They know that I'm teaching part-time at H.C.C."—Houston Community College—"but that's acceptable, since it means I'm getting teaching experience. But I've only got a couple of classes this semester, and I needed some extra money."

"Dan, you can work as many jobs as you like, and I couldn't care less."

He didn't seem to hear me. "It's just that my younger brother is in college now," he continued, "and money is tight back home. I'm the eldest, and my mother needs all the help she can get."

I remembered hearing that his father had skipped out when he was pretty young. Dan grew up in a rough neighborhood in Boston, and he worked hard to get to graduate school. I could sympathize, since I'd paid my own way to the luxurious life of advanced education.

"Dan, I don't think anyone in the department would begrudge you anything; we don't all have trust funds and rich parents to fall back on."

He grinned. "You got that right!"

I sighed inwardly. He was quite attractive. Maybe he needed some help getting out from behind the wallpaper?

"We can't all be Charlie Harper," I said, and Dan's face immediately clouded.

"No," he said shortly. "And I wouldn't want to be, even for all that money."

"By the way," I said, changing the subject, "that sure was an . . . um, unusual paper you presented this afternoon."

He grimaced. "Julian insisted. I'm incredibly busy getting ready for my dissertation, not to mention my interview with Harvard."

I nodded. We all knew that Dan was up for a postdoctoral fellowship. He managed to work it into the conversation whenever possible. "How's that going?" I asked, willing to be polite as I remembered why Dan wasn't as attractive as I had been thinking. "Isn't that coming up soon?"

"Yeah, I have about two more weeks, and then I'm off to Harvard."

"Any idea what the competition's like?" I asked, before he could launch into all the details I'd heard several times before. "Do you know who the other candidates are? Frankly, I'm surprised that Selena Bradbury hasn't applied."

He frowned. "I'm pretty sure she applied, but I don't know if she's made the short list. I haven't heard who else has been selected for an interview, though Julian did hint to me that I might find myself competing with at least one more of his students. I guess he was talking about Selena."

"Could be," I agreed. If the contest was between Dan and the Ice Queen, he probably had an edge because of his gender, but Selena was pretty formidable academically, and she might be just what the guys at Harvard wanted. "Good luck, Dan."

"Thanks, Andy," he said, standing up. "Thanks for letting me explain," he added. "I guess I'd better get back to work."

"Well, don't overdo it," I cautioned. I couldn't help myself sometimes. There may have been more to this Ann Landers thing than I was willing to admit.

He grinned again. "Are you done? If so, I'll clear this off."

"Sure." I nodded. "I've got to get home anyway." I picked up the bag containing Maggie's birthday card.

"See you later," Dan said, walking away with his hands full.

I knew I couldn't make it home without going to the bathroom, so I visited their facilities before I left. As I was coming out of the hallway, I looked across to see a familiar face coming through the front door. I stopped, frozen where I stood, peering out from behind the doorway.

What was Rob Hayward doing in a gay bookstore?

C H A P † E R · 3

ONLY A GRADUATE STUDENT would consider a lecture *relaxing*. But after my deli-sandwich dinner, that's exactly how I entertained myself. I drove back to campus just for the pleasure of listening to one of my favorite professors speak on her specialty, women in Victorian England. Dr. Elspeth Farrar, despite some eccentric notions, was one of the university's most distinguished history professors. I had taken two of her courses the previous year, enjoying her fascinating lectures. I'd heard much of that night's topic in greater detail in one of her classes, though I had to admire the way she tailored the material to entertain and instruct an audience that consisted of a wide variety of people—students, professors, and interested public.

After she concluded her talk, Dr. Farrar answered questions from those in attendance. Idly I gazed over the crowded lecture hall, recognizing a number of familiar faces. About four rows ahead of me and to my left, I saw the history department's senior secretary.

I doubted that Azalea Westover had a sincere interest in Victorian women. For a modern, single, working woman, Azalea had some old-fashioned notions about women's roles in life. Then again, maybe she *did* have an interest in the Victorian age. Whatever her own interests, she was smart enough to play the academic political game like an Olympic medalist. The next day, I was certain, the history department chairman, Putney Puterbaugh, would hear some bright remark on the night's lecture to let him know Azalea had been her usual supportive self.

As I watched, Azalea dipped her head sideways to whisper a remark to her companion. I caught a glimpse of the companion's profile as she turned to respond. The profile revealed strong, attractive features in a face that was familiar. She had attended our seminar that afternoon, and she was a graduate student, too, I finally remembered. I had seen her only a couple of times before on campus. What was her name? Margaret Wilford—the name finally came to me. I had heard someone refer to her rather cattily as a drone, because she had a reputation for being a very hard worker. Despite this, the professors sometimes complained about students like her, because she had the audacity to work for a living while completing her dissertation. Like Dan Erickson, in a way. Imagine the concept—life in the real world and a dissertation, too. I shuddered.

On the other side of Margaret sat her companion of the afternoon seminar. Unlike Margaret, Selena Bradbury remained in the academic world and lived on a stipend supplemented by teaching freshman history for the university. I had never suspected that she was a crony of Azalea's, but she, Margaret, and Azalea were all whispering merrily while Dr. Farrar answered questions. It was probably good that the Ice Queen had friends, but, judging by Azalea's presence, I couldn't say much for Selena's selection. The three blonde heads together, the color of their hair nearly identical, made an unusual sight.

My eyes continued roving. A row behind the three women, on the left, Rob Hayward and Charlie Harper were whispering back and forth, while Maggie McLendon kept poking Charlie in the side in a futile attempt to get him to hush. While I watched, trying not to laugh—because hushing Charlie at full steam could be just about impossible—Maggie gave up the attempt, snatched up her backpack, and stalked out of the lecture hall. Charlie and Rob didn't even see her leave, they were so involved in their discussion.

As members of the audience continued to ask questions, none of them terribly interesting, I decided to follow Maggie's example. I wanted to retrieve a couple of books from my carrel before I headed home for the night. I caught up with her in front of the library.

"Oh, hi, Andy," she said, relief in her tone. She preceded me inside. "I was afraid for a minute that it was Charlie, and I've had enough of him for a while."

"What is it this time?" I inquired with sympathy, as we rode the ancient elevator up to the fourth floor. She had definitely thawed since the afternoon, and I decided not to bring it up, unless she did.

She groaned. "You know Charlie. He kept making snide remarks all the way through Dr. Farrar's lecture. Rob and I tried to make him shut up, but I left my spare roll of duct tape at home."

"I doubt even duct tape would work on Charlie's mouth," I observed as we threaded our way through the dimly lit stacks toward our carrels in the back of the building. "The vitriol from his tongue would corrode just about anything."

Maggie tilted her head up at me and laughed. "That's why I like you, Andy," she said, and I had to smile in return. Her face, normally so serious, lit up when she smiled, and she was a lovely young woman. "No matter what he does or says, Charlie doesn't seem to have much effect on you. I wish I could ignore him the way you do."

I shrugged as we rounded a corner and came to our carrels. "Disinterest is the only real proof against Charlie's barbs. Nothing irritates him more than my treating him like he's the most boring person I've ever met." I grinned. "That's the only way I've gotten through the past year and two months as his neighbor."

"At least you're not his roommate," she pointed out. "Just imagine if you were in Rob's place."

"As far as I'm concerned, the two of them deserve each other." I slammed my backpack down on the desk.

Astonished, she peered at me around the corner of her carrel. "Andy, what on earth is the matter with you?"

"Sorry," I muttered. "I'm just tired, I guess."

Her lovely face framed by her long auburn hair, Maggie looked at me for a moment. She moved out of her carrel and stood next to mine, watching me the whole time. I grinned at her sheepishly.

"Andy, I've known you for over a year now, and we're pretty close, or at least I thought we were. But since this semester started, I've been wondering. You've been in a pissy mood for over a month." She frowned at me, like someone scolding an unruly child. "What is it with you and Rob? I mean, what *was* it with that scene this afternoon? You're like a sore-tailed cat in a roomful of rocking chairs anytime he opens his mouth. If you don't want to tell me about it, I can understand, but surely you realize that your feelings are pretty obvious. And not just to me, either."

Suddenly enervated, I sat down at my desk. My animosity toward Rob could cause me problems if I wasn't more careful. I had to get over this. I took a deep breath, exhaled slowly, then looked up.

"You're right, Maggie. I've probably been making a fool of myself, and I can't afford to do that."

"I don't think any of the professors have paid much attention, Andy, if that's any comfort." She grinned at me, suddenly relenting. "Most of them seem oblivious to us most of the time. But the other grad students have probably noticed. It's a fairly small group, and the gossip will be going strong before too long. As it is, some are already uncomfortable with your openness about your sexuality."

"I know that," I said.

"Don't let those idiots get to you! There are all sorts of petty jealousies and competitions here. You wouldn't believe some of the stories my father has told me about his students over the years." Maggie's father was head of the English department at the university. "The point is, don't create trouble for yourself."

"Thanks," I said, and I meant it.

I had sensed, the first time I met her, that having her friendship could be important to me. I needed a friend like her. She seemed ready to march into battle on my behalf. Though she was obviously curious, she wasn't going to force me into any confidences I wasn't ready to make.

"I've known Rob since we were children," I said, "and there are some . . . past incidents between us that I'd just as soon forget." I grinned. "Though, obviously, I'm not doing too well at it."

"Whatever happened between you in the past," Maggie said, watching my face closely, "you need to put behind you and concentrate on the present. Graduate school is hard enough without adding emotional trauma."

"Very good advice, Miss Landers."

"Don't laugh at me!" She frowned, a bit irritated. "I hate it when you get flippant for no good reason."

"I know, and I apologize. I didn't mean that the way it sounded." I was tempted to confide in her about seeing Rob in the bookstore that afternoon. He hadn't seen me, since I had waited until he was out of sight before scooting out as fast as I could. "One of these days, after a couple of margaritas, I'll tell you the whole sordid story."

"It's a date." She flashed me a grin and went back to her carrel.

I pulled a couple of books I needed from the shelves of my carrel, and Maggie retrieved what she needed from hers.

"Shall I walk you out to the parking lot?" I asked. "I just have to check these out"—I brandished my books—"and I'll be ready."

"Before that, though," she said, "do you have time for us to run upstairs? I want to check my mailbox in the lounge. I forgot to check it this afternoon after the seminar."

"Sure." I followed her up a nearby staircase.

We stepped out into the dimly illuminated hallway on the fifth floor, home to the history department and the history graduate students' lounge. The nearest ceiling fixture was several feet away, and the doorway to the lounge was shaded in darkness. A brightly colored poster from a previous year's exhibit at the Houston Museum of Fine Arts covered the glass portion of the door, now closed. A thin line of light shone from beneath the door. I twisted the knob and walked in, Maggie close behind me.

". . . really threatened you if you didn't stop?" someone was saying. That someone was Rob, and he was speaking to Charlie. From the scowl Charlie tossed in our direction, I supposed Maggie and I had interrupted a private discussion. Charlie's tanned face had flushed dark red, whether with annoyance at our intrusion or with anger over something else, I had no idea.

"Well, if it's not the gorgeous Miss Maggie McLendon, the feminist hope for medieval history!" Charlie sneered. "*And,* Mississippi's answer to Charles Homer Haskins, Andrew Carpenter. Shouldn't you two be somewhere memorizing Pollock and Maitland?"

At first I thought it was leftover spite that he hadn't been able to expend on poor Dan that afternoon. But no, I decided, this was his normal, endearing personality.

While Maggie rummaged in her mailbox and did her best to ignore him, I stifled a yawn and replied languidly, "Oh, I expect I'll have it memorized about the same time you finish plagiarizing Sir Samuel Dill for your dissertation."

Maggie looked up, grinning, from the mailboxes. I laid my books on a table and poked my hand in my own mail cubbyhole.

Charlie stared back at me, momentarily bereft of speech, a peculiar expression on his face. He looked almost disconcerted. I smiled smugly, congratulating myself.

"Oh, come on, guys," Rob said. "Not tonight, Mama's got a headache."

Looking at the two of them, I wondered—not for the first time—how Rob could stand sharing living space with Charlie. Both came from good ol' Southern families, like me. In temperament, however, they were very different. Rob, russet haired and green eyed, sported a trendy Van Dyke. Tall and well-built, he had a genial disposition that masked a volatile temper. That had always worried me, because I never knew when he might erupt. When he did, you'd better get out of the way. Charlie, dark and glowering, reminded me of childhood imaginings of a demon, though he, too, had an attractive face. His short, neatly trimmed beard contributed to the slightly demonic appearance that his acerbic nature indicated.

What did Rob see in Charlie that the rest of us couldn't? How did Rob manage to room with him without smacking him over the head twelve times a day? I hadn't the foggiest notion.

The Rob I had known had had difficulties dealing with a gay male friend, and I just couldn't figure out his relationship with Charlie. Maybe after what I had seen that afternoon, they were a lot closer than I had expected. But that would mean Rob wasn't straight after all, and past experience had taught me otherwise. Or maybe he had gone in the bookstore to buy a present for a gay or lesbian friend. I was thoroughly confused, and I resented Rob for making me feel this way. I avoided looking directly at him, and he ignored me.

Deflated by my comment for only a moment, Charlie turned his attention to

Maggie. "Well, what did you think of your favorite loony's lecture tonight?"

"That's not fair," she retorted. "It was an excellent lecture—what I could hear of it over your rude remarks, that is!"

"Well," Charlie drawled, his South Carolina background more evident in his voice, "she does manage to sound compos mentis in public, I grant you, but any scholar who thinks that Queen Victoria wrote pornography in her spare time just isn't all there. The sooner she's retired, the better off this department will be."

I considered intervening, but this was a fossilized bone of contention between Maggie and Charlie. Anyway, Charlie did have truth on his side—up to a point. Dr. Farrar was obsessed by the idea that the epitome of nineteenth-century virtuous repression wrote pornographic novels in secret. The professor even claimed that a duke of her acquaintance had shown her several examples of the queen's literary ventures. She rather cannily refused ever to say just *which* duke, however.

Charlie smirked while he watched Maggie struggle to reply.

Ready to leave, I tugged on Maggie's arm, pulling her toward the door. I gave in to impulse as I went out into the hall. "You really have to stop taking those lemon-juice enemas, Charlie. They've soured your whole disposition."

Rob's unrestrained laughter mixed with Maggie's as she and I headed for the elevator.

On the way out to the commuters' parking lot, I listened to Maggie's complaints about Charlie. I nodded vaguely from time to time and let the words flow right past me. I'd heard pretty much the same lecture from her at least twice in the past two months. Her litany ended by the time we reached the parking lot, and I watched her drive off before I unlocked the door of my aging Plymouth. As I pulled out of the parking lot, I realized I had left my books in the grad lounge. Damn!

Well, I wasn't going back for them now. I'd retrieve them the next morning, though I hadn't planned on spending much time on campus the following day. There went my schedule! I wouldn't be able to stay at home and read. Since I lived close to campus, I was hoping I could get things done and not mess up my morning, after all.

In about ten minutes I was home, parking my car in the driveway of a comfortable, if slightly shabby, duplex in the area of Houston known as Montrose. Situated roughly between the Rice University area, the ritzy River Oaks, and downtown Houston, Montrose was a convenient—and colorful—section to live in. Heavily populated by gay Houstonians, the area was much like any other residential section of Houston. In a city with deed restrictions but no zoning, you might see an adult bookstore or a topless bar across the street from your house. You might also find tree-shaded streets and plenty of attractively renovated houses. Apart from the fact that I didn't feel like a minority in that part of town, I enjoyed living in Montrose, with its own character and eccentric charm.

I shared one half of the duplex with another history graduate student, Larry Mitchell, straight and, thankfully, with no hang-ups about having a gay male roommate. He was off on a research trip to the Southern Historical Collection in Chapel Hill, North Carolina. Rob and Charlie occupied the other half, a fact I tried to ignore. In the two months Rob had lived there, he stayed out of my way.

Once inside the front door, I leafed through the mail and found the new issue of the *Medieval Quarterly*. I scanned the contents, noting with some surprise that Julian Whitelock had published an article, his first one in years. I was curious, especially in light of what had transpired in that afternoon's seminar, but I decided I could wait until the next day to explore the delights of "The Role of the Bishop in Merovingian Gaul."

I dropped the journal on a table in the living room and sat on the ratty old couch. Most of the furniture was courtesy of the Salvation Army sale room—all a little worn, but still serviceable and sometimes comfortable.

I wasn't in the mood for serious historical prose, and besides, the books I needed were still on campus. I decided to devour a treat I had picked up earlier in the week at Murder by the Book, the specialty mystery bookstore in Houston. I had a date with a Margery Allingham novel I'd never read; Whitelock and his bishops weren't going anywhere. Murder always seemed like a relaxing alternative to graduate school.

Some hours later, tired but still laughing at Campion and Lugg, I put down my book and stumbled off to bed.

The alarm went off at a disgustingly early hour, six-thirty. At the best of times, I was not a morning person, but I usually forced myself to get up and get going. If I stuck to my schedule, I got things done. I stumbled into the shower, luxuriated in the hot water for ten minutes, then reluctantly got out. Soon after, dry, wearing underwear, and nearly awake, I went downstairs for my breakfast, a can of Diet Coke and three prefab sausage biscuits.

When the food was warmed by the microwave, I went back upstairs to my bedroom. I switched on the TV just in time to catch the opening sequence to "Bewitched." I waited anxiously as the scenario unfolded. As soon as Marion Lorne appeared, I relaxed. Any episode with Aunt Clara automatically meant a good one.

I dressed quickly over the closing credits of the show. If I hustled, I could get to the library when it opened at 7:45, retrieve my books from the grad student lounge, and return in time for the next episode of "Bewitched" on another of the cable channels. Then, I could get to work and and not be cranky all day.

On campus in record time, I kept a close eye on my watch. I walked up to the front door of the library, and thankfully for my peace of mind, the person who opened the library was right on time. I scurried inside and to the elevator. The clock on the fifth floor read 7:48 as I stepped out. I turned down the corridor toward the grad lounge, and as I approached, I could see the door ajar, but the light inside the room was off. Consuelo, the cleaning woman, seemed to be behind on her normal routine. The door was usually wide open and the light on by the time the building was unlocked.

I pushed the door open and flipped the light switch. As my eyes adjusted to the bright light, I saw my books still on the table in the corner where I had left them. Straight ahead of me was another table which held a small statue and a thick book with a familiar symbol emblazoned on its spine. Could it be?

Momentarily distracted from my goal, I stepped closer to examine the book. Yes, it was the one I had been looking for earlier in the week, Sir Frank Stenton's *Anglo-Saxon England*. The library's online catalog had informed me that the book was checked out, but not, of course, who had it. Maybe I could leave a note inside the book, and the current user would let me have it soon. Stenton's book, otherwise known as the bible on Anglo-Saxon England, was at the top of my reading list.

As I reached toward the book, my gaze skittered to the right, and I noticed a man, his back turned to me, asleep on the vinyl-upholstered couch. Hesitating over the book, I decided to turn off the light and grab up my books as quietly as I could, but something about the man's position didn't look quite right. His head was bent forward at a strange angle, so I stepped closer to investigate.

When I stood over him, I saw what I hadn't been able to see before. The back of the man's head was matted with blood. The length and thickness of his hair had kept the blood from dripping off the couch onto the floor. Instead, the blood had collected in a small dark pool beneath his head. As I touched the body, which by now I realized was lifeless, I recognized him.

Someone had bashed in Charlie Harper's head.

C H A P T E R · 4

JUST THE DAY BEFORE, Charlie had joked that somebody would murder Julian Whitelock. Now Charlie was dead.

Or was he? I had to make sure. I moved a little closer. Bent over him, I stood irresolute for a moment, then my stomach started doing somersaults. Yes, Charlie was dead—he wasn't breathing. Eyes riveted upon the body, I took a step away from the couch, willing myself not to throw up all over the floor. I had to get out.

I sensed a rush of movement behind me. Before I could turn, hands hit me hard in the lower back and I was pushed against the couch. Struggling to avoid falling on the body, I grabbed the couch with both hands, but my momentum was such that I couldn't avoid bumping the side of my head against the wall. At least I didn't break my glasses. They were knocked only slightly askew.

As I tried to maintain my balance over Charlie's body, I turned my ringing head to catch a glimpse of the person who had pushed me, but no one was there. Then I heard the click of a door—probably the door to the stairway across the hall.

My head began to ache from the force of the impact. Who could have been hiding in the room? I backed away from the couch, noticing that the commotion had caused Charlie's body to roll farther into the couch. Hearing a faint sound, I turned to find Consuelo right behind me. Small and plump, her hair an improbable shade of blonde, she stared in wide-eyed surprise at the congealed blood and the body on the couch, while I took several deep breaths to steady my jangled nerves.

"*¿Que has hecho*, Andy?" Her English normally was good, but in times of stress, she turned to her native tongue. Now her face was pale, and she looked at me with suspicion. For a crazy moment, I felt like laughing. Charlie had pissed me off plenty of times, but I invariably chose verbal, not physical, retaliation.

I answered Consuelo, without thinking, in Spanish. "*No he hecho nada,* Consuelo." To reassure the woman, I asserted again in English, "I didn't do anything. Someone else did this. Did you see anyone running out of this room just before you came in?" As I spoke, I herded her into the hall and pulled the door almost shut behind us. I wanted to get away from the horror on the couch.

"No, but I think the stairway door slammed when I came around the corner," she replied, her words slow and considered. "Was there somebody here when you came in?" She looked relieved at my claim to innocence.

I nodded as I rubbed the small of my back. "While I was bending over to see who the . . . body was, someone came from behind and pushed me. By the time I turned around, whoever it was had gone—probably down the stairs. He's out of the building by now, or else hiding somewhere in the stacks." The whole incident puzzled me, now that I had the chance to think about it with a head that no longer rang. "I suppose it could have been the person who killed Charlie"—my stomach flip-flopped again at the thought—"but it looks to me like Charlie's been . . . dead . . . for several hours at least. The, uh, body was cold." I shuddered at the thought of having touched his body.

"Charlie? Charlie Harper?" Consuelo asked sharply, then muttered something in Spanish which I didn't completely catch. The word I did hear sounded like one of the vulgar ones that could have gotten my high school Spanish teacher into trouble for teaching us.

"Why didn't you find the body when you cleaned in there this morning?" I asked.

She looked at me with suspicion, as if my question contained some sort of trap. "I didn't clean in there yet. I was running late this morning because my husband forgot to set the alarm clock."

"Then I guess Charlie has been here since last night."

"I'll go call the campus police," she offered.

As Consuelo departed, I remembered something I had seen just before she startled me. I wanted to examine the room again before anyone else appeared. I opened the door carefully, trying to avoid smudging possible prints.

What had to be the murder weapon stood on a table directly across the room from the door: a small but heavy brass statue of a slender young man, fashioned to commemorate a fund established by the family of a graduate student killed in a car accident several years before.

Resisting the urge to throw up, I didn't look at the dead thing that used to be Charlie. Instead, I stared down at the table and the statue upon it. I frowned; something didn't seem right. What was I missing? I saw as I went closer to the statue that a few strands of brown hair were caught in the nameplate on its base. The plate was fastened with small brass nails, and it was around one of these that the hairs had caught. I stared at the hairs briefly before my feet started itching to get out. As my mother might have said, my head knew better but my feet couldn't stand it. I backed out of the room, pulling the door, once again, almost shut. My natural nosiness had had enough of the scene of the crime.

As I looked up from my uneasy guard post at the door, two campus security officers came hurrying down the hall toward me.

"You the one found the body?" The short man, balding and fortyish, barked the words at me.

The officer's taller companion said, "I'm Porter, and this here's Quigley. Where's the body?"

"In here." Indicating the door, I stood aside to let them enter. Though I introduced myself, they didn't appear interested in me. I trailed into the room behind them.

The two men stood shoulder to shoulder, staring down at the body. After a moment, Porter turned a stunned face toward me. "You know this guy?"

I nodded. "Charlie Harper—one of the graduate students in the history department."

"The investigator who'll handle this is on the way. As soon as he gets here, he'll want to talk to you. I think it'd be better if you wait somewhere else. Someone will come and get you."

"Right," I answered with some relief. "I'll be in the history department office." I left the two of them whispering in front of the door.

Stopping short, I groaned. My books were still in the grad lounge! Who knew when I'd be able to get them? Well, there went part of my reading program for the semester. Not to mention my morning schedule.

Then I was ashamed of myself. Charlie had been murdered, and I was worried about getting behind on my reading. But it just showed how self-involved one could become in graduate school. Any number of professors in the department might think that the sun rose out of a certain part of their anatomy, but that was their delusion. A murder in their midst would shake things up a little, though I doubted some of them would even notice. After all, it was *only* a graduate student who had been killed.

Charlie might have been a colossal pain in the neck when he was alive, but that didn't mean we could shrug his death aside as if it didn't affect us. He had probably been killed by someone we all knew, and that was frightening. And *that* thought ought to shake up even the most self-absorbed in our midst. Suddenly, I was very angry. Charlie had been irritating, and perhaps even malicious, but I couldn't think that he had deserved murder.

Still deep in thought, I collided with someone as I turned the corner of the hallway.

"Andy, I'm sorry, I wasn't watching where *you* were going," Maggie growled as she backed away, holding an armful of books. Like me, Maggie was not a morning person. Her natural charm didn't surface until at least 10:00 A.M. "Are you okay?" she asked in a tone that warned me I had better say yes.

"Oh, I'm fine." Then I spoke before I thought about it. "Especially considering I just discovered a dead body."

Whoosh! Maggie's books hit the floor.

"Sorry," I said sheepishly as I stooped to help her gather them together.

"Honestly, Andy, you and your sense of humor." She glared at me.

Uncomfortable now, I shook my head. "That wasn't intended to be a joke. I wasn't thinking too clearly when I told you that, but it's the truth."

Her big eyes got bigger, and she leaned against the wall to steady herself. "Oh, no!" she said, the fear raw in her voice. "Who?"

"Charlie." I reached out, just in case, to catch the cascade of books I was anticipating, but Maggie kept a tight grip on them.

She stared at me. "Oh, no," she said again, her voice slightly steadier. "Just yesterday he was joking about someone murdering Julian Whitelock." She caught her breath. "Was Charlie murdered?"

"Yeah. Someone bashed him on the head with that stupid statue."

"I can't believe it." She wagged her head back and forth in disbelief. "Who would murder him?"

"Murder! Who's been murdered?" a voice demanded harshly from behind me.

I turned to see Azalea Westover a few feet away. Her short, compact body was nicely proportioned, and her blonde hair curled around an attractive, cherubic face. The look of angelic innocence was spoiled, however, by Azalea's very prominent teeth, which were large enough to keep her lips from meeting except when she talked.

I remembered a remark of Charlie's about Azalea. "Just take a look at her," he had said, "and you can get an idea of what would happen if Bugs Bunny left his condoms at home when he screwed Shirley Temple."

Cruel, yes, but also accurate—vintage Harper. Charlie had been known for quick and caustic remarks, which were always funny to those who were not their targets.

"Well, who's dead? What happened?" Azalea repeated her query, and I realized I had been standing there, staring at the woman like a dimwit.

I finally found my tongue. "It's Charlie Harper, Azalea. I found him in the grad lounge this morning when I got here."

She drew herself up to her full five-five and tried to frown—although, with her pearly whites, it was difficult. "Well, Andy, what happened? How do you know it was murder?"

Breathing deeply to control my temper, I responded through clenched teeth, "Someone hit him on the back of the head. I don't imagine he did that to himself."

Azalea smiled, offering an impressive display. "Well, well, the little bastard finally bought it, huh? I always thought he'd get what he deserved."

I wanted to slap her and, in fact, came close to it for poor Charlie's sake, but I didn't want to have to answer an assault charge, no matter how justified.

"My goodness, woman," Maggie sputtered, "I didn't think even *you* could be such a coldhearted bitch!"

Well, our Azalea retreated a step on that one, while I resisted breaking into a cheer. Maggie was the one graduate student Azalea appeared to be afraid of, because Maggie's dad was reportedly next in line to be Dean of Humanities. Azalea, political little soul that she was, tried her best to stay on Maggie's good side.

Azalea, without any comment, turned and walked back the way she had come, toward the department office. No doubt to get on the hotline to Putney Puterbaugh, who would probably live up to his nickname, "Pooter," and fart around, getting in everybody's way, causing mass confusion, as usual. McLendon, one; Westover, diddly-squat.

Maggie stared after Azalea with a look of intense distaste. "I'd love to pull every one of that bitch's teeth with rusty pliers." She spat out the words. "She must have forty of them."

I groaned as I thought of something. "Rob doesn't know about this yet. I wonder whether I ought to call him, or if the police would get me if I did."

Maggie shrugged, unconcerned about the niceties of police protocol. "There's not a whole lot they can do, I guess. After all, it's natural to spread the news." She headed for the office. "Let's go see what Azalea's stirring up, and maybe we can use one of the phones there without having to wage battle over it."

Wage battle put it succinctly, I thought. Normally Azalea refused to let students use the phones in the history department office, unless it was on behalf of one of the professors.

I followed Maggie down the hall. The more I thought about the situation, the more uneasy I became. The consequences of Charlie's murder were beginning to sink in. Until the murder was solved, we'd all be weighing one another's words and actions, looking for something suspicious. Campus security officers occasionally found transients in the library, but they didn't often prove violent. It was possible, I supposed, that some stranger had murdered Charlie. His bitchiness could goad someone, mentally unstable in the first place, into an attack—I could imagine that quite easily. But I hadn't spent countless hours reading mysteries for nothing. The killer had to be someone we all knew.

My mind flashed on the thought of Whitelock as the murderer. Surely even he wouldn't kill a graduate student just because he had been ridiculed in front of other students.

Maybe Azalea had done it, I thought maliciously. She hadn't shed any tears over the news, and I considered her capable of just about anything.

Uttering an old Irish blessing against goblins, I entered the office at Maggie's heels.

As soon as I walked in, I was the center of attention. Azalea's junior coworkers, Lindy Carter and Thelma Williams, both in their early twenties, were saucer-eyed with excitement. They surrounded me, edging Maggie out of the way. I backed up into the corner and plopped down on the couch with Lindy on one side and Thelma on the other.

Both Lindy and Thelma were fond of me, because I had this strange habit of treating them like real people. Amazingly enough, they seemed to appreciate it. Azalea sat behind her desk, trying to set herself apart from her coworkers' vulgar curiosity, but I was willing to bet that her ears were standing at attention to catch every tidbit possible. She wanted the information as badly as they did, but she didn't want to ask me for any more details and risk another howitzer blow from Maggie.

Selena walked in then, and a jittery Thelma broke the news to her before I could stop her. The Ice Queen's eyes narrowed for a moment while I watched her. I thought she would pretend not to be interested, but then she, too, urged me to tell what I knew.

I couldn't avoid telling them what I had discovered, so I tried to make it as clinical and dispassionate as possible, for their benefit as well as my own. I kept my speculations about the murder weapon to myself, because I didn't want to blab *everything* before the police got going on the case. I was also trying to keep the image of Charlie's body from reappearing so clearly in my mind. In the midst of my description, a voice boomed out from behind me.

"What the hell is going on here this morning? Some idiots in a police car nearly ran me down when I crossed the street in front of the library."

Without even turning in the direction of the doorway, I identified the speaker, both by the volume of the words and by the tart diction of their delivery. Whitelock had arrived—loaded for bear, as my mother would say, just like always.

Since the women seemed speechless, I found the task of breaking the news once more my responsibility. I stood up and took a few steps toward the professor. At six-three, I towered over the man, who was at least a foot shorter than I. Did I mention that Whitelock didn't much like me?

His patrician features were pinched in fury. He ran a hand in agitation through a thick mane of white hair. "Well?" he demanded. "Answer me, Carpenter."

"Well, sir," I replied, frowning, "I'm afraid something pretty bad has happened. Charlie Harper was murdered in the grad lounge last night."

The color drained so quickly from Whitelock's face, I thought he was going to faint.

C H A P T E R · 5

I STUCK OUT AN ARM to catch Whitelock, just in case, but he held himself to stiff attention after a moment of weakness. Selena moved forward to offer support, but he brushed her away also.

I decided not to bother shielding his sensibilities from the truth. "I found Charlie dead in the grad lounge this morning, sir. Somebody bashed his head in."

Ignoring the gasp that came from either Lindy or Thelma, I concentrated on watching Whitelock's face. This time, I thought I detected the twitch of a nerve under his left eye, but he let nothing show.

He turned to Azalea. "Should any person in an official capacity wish to speak to me, I shall be in my office, Miss Westover." He then marched out.

Cool was one word for it. Though, if my advisor heard similar news about me, I hoped she might at least have the decency to express public regret at my passing. From behind me, I heard a snort of disgust. Such was Maggie's comment on Whitelock's behavior.

Azalea had busied herself with her word processor, and Lindy and Thelma had disappeared, no doubt to spread the news. I watched Selena hurry out after Whitelock. *Good luck playing the ministering angel!* I thought. Shaking my head, I returned to the couch, where Maggie had made herself comfortable, to ask her whether she still thought I should call Rob. Before I could speak, we heard a commotion at the door.

Imagine a skinny, pear-shaped being with matchstick legs and a mop of fuzzy gray hair atop a face that belongs to a perpetually bewildered chipmunk. Putney Puterbaugh, august chair of the history department, had arrived. Somewhere, in the back of my mind, Judy Collins started singing "Send in the Clowns." When life didn't come with a soundtrack, I supplied my own.

Pooter, as we called him not so affectionately, got hysterical easily, which made you wonder why the rest of the faculty voted him in to the job as department chair. Maybe they thought he could do the least amount of damage as an administrator. Which just showed how practical-minded most of *them* were.

I groaned, and Maggie, trying not to laugh, poked me in the ribs.

"Andy, Andy, Andy," Pooter gabbled at me, Azalea holding on to his arm and trying to slow him down. "Oh dear, oh dear, oh dear, what are we going to do? What are we going to do?"

I groaned again in my head as I stood up and tried to reassure the poor guy. "Dr. Puterbaugh"—thank goodness *Pooter* hadn't rolled off my tongue—"please try to calm down. The campus police have the situation under control, and I'm sure they'll get to the bottom of this before long."

Pooter moaned, and Azalea went into the brown-nosing Nightingale routine that she did so well.

"There, there, Professor Puterbaugh," she soothed. "Why don't you come to your office, and I'll fix you a pot of your favorite herbal tea. That will help you feel better. Just come with me." She gritted her teeth and started towing.

Pooter stopped dithering, thankfully, and allowed Azalea to drag him out of the room. I sank down on the couch with Maggie. One look at her face, and I burst out laughing. Unable to restrain herself any longer, she started howling too. Then, realizing that this was not the most politic time to be caught laughing madly, we both shut up.

"Lord," Maggie whispered to me, "that poor man is such a fool."

"Yeah, they should call it the 'Pooter Principle' instead," I responded, then almost started laughing again.

Maggie gave me another poke in the ribs, because Azalea was glaring at us from the doorway. I shut up, but I glared right back, daring her to say anything. She then decided to ignore us and marched over to her desk.

Maggie rolled her eyes at me and picked up one of her books to thumb through. I needed to stay until the campus police wanted me, and Maggie wasn't about to miss anything, so we remained on the couch.

A tall, slender black woman in uniform then walked in the door, looked around, and headed straight for me. "Officer Williams," she informed me. "Are you Andy Carpenter?" she asked, consulting the notebook in her hand.

I stood up. "Yes, I am, Officer." My stomach started a gymnastics routine.

"Relax for a minute," she responded. "I need to stay with you until Lieutenant Herrera, the investigating officer, gets here." She gave me a keen look. "I suppose it's too late to ask whether you've been talking about what you saw."

The dismay on my face gave her the answer she had obviously expected.

Though I could tell she was irritated, Officer Williams nevertheless grinned. "That's the way it happens, sometimes." She shrugged and asked to see my driver's license and student ID.

As she copied some information from them, I realized that the police would check to see whether I had any kind of criminal record. Lovely thought. There weren't any blots on my escutcheon that I could remember, so I didn't worry about it.

The officer returned my license and ID, and I subsided gratefully onto the couch, suitably chastened. Good grief, as many mysteries as I'd read, I knew better than to go blabbing my mouth to everyone, but I couldn't resist the temptation to be the center of attention. At least, I comforted myself, I hadn't said a word to anyone about my observations of what looked like the murder weapon. Except to Maggie, that is. And I couldn't possibly suspect her!

Officer Williams, with dispatch, collected the names and addresses of Maggie, Azalea, Lindy, and Thelma. Then she stood silently beside the couch, her presence ensuring that no one talked about anything, much less the murder.

I thought about what I had noticed in the half hour or so since I had found the body. Whitelock's reaction to the news of Charlie's death had been unusual. Under normal circumstances the man vented his emotions the way rabbits gave birth. Why, despite the shock of the situation, had Whitelock been nearly speechless on this occasion? What was he hiding? Something was strange, and I had an uneasy feeling that things were going to get stranger.

In about a half hour, Quigley—or was it Porter?—stuck his head in the door and gave a sign to Officer Williams, and she ushered me into the hall.

I followed the two of them to one of the smaller seminar rooms that the campus police had commandeered. Officer Williams disappeared as I entered the room, and a handsome, dark-haired man in a slightly rumpled suit, his tie loose, stood and motioned me to take a seat across from him.

In clipped tones, he introduced himself as Lieutenant Rafael Herrera of the university police department. Mid-thirties, I judged, and a little tired right then, but still he managed to give me a thorough inspection. Was it my imagination, or had the air conditioning failed yet again in this room?

He explained that he would be taping the interview, and another man prepared a tape recorder, set it down on the table in front of me, and switched it on. After announcing the date, time, and my name, Herrera wasted no time before plunging right in. "You found the body, right?"

My stomach contracted. "Right." Gosh, did my voice squeak like that all the time? I tried again, willing up those hormones. "Right." Good, at least an octave lower. That ought to impress the guy.

Herrera just looked at me, his dark eyes patient. Sensing the man's temper might fray easily, I got down to business. I gave him a concise report of the events of the morning. I stumbled a bit when I told him about being pushed against the wall and disturbing the body.

"What happened after you got pushed?" Herrera's eyes narrowed as he asked. His mouth, framed by a thick, black moustache, set into a hard line, and I had the uneasy feeling he thought I might be making things up.

"For a minute," I replied, "my head was ringing from bumping into the wall. Then I think I heard a door close—probably the door to the stairs across the hall. The person was most likely in the room when I got there, then he pushed me to keep me from seeing who he was."

"You said 'he.' How do you know it was a male?"

I frowned, thinking about it. I could almost feel the hands on my back. "I don't *know* that it was a man, but my impression is that the hands were pretty big. But that's all I've got to go on, I'm afraid."

"Did you see anything which might help identify who it was?" Herrera's mouth relaxed, and so did I. Maybe he had decided to believe me.

"Not a thing."

"What happened next?"

I continued my account, concentrating hard on remembering. When I finished, Herrera nodded, apparently satisfied. Then he asked what I had touched in the room. I thought about it and gave him the brief list. Now was the time to mention that I had gone into the room a second time, but my nerve failed me. I just wanted it to be over.

"Did you know the victim very well?" Herrera asked. So much for getting out of there.

I shook my head. "Not really. I've known him for about a year, but we weren't particularly good friends. We didn't have much contact outside of classes."

"Can you think of any reason why someone would kill him?" Herrera's voice, fluid and soft, was soothing, despite the tenseness of the situation, and an occasional vowel revealed that Spanish was his first language.

I struggled to remember the question. Ah, why would anyone want to kill Charlie? How about vicious, cutting remarks? How about a personality like an arrogant prima donna? Instead, I said, "Well, he wasn't the easiest person to get along with. He had a sharp tongue, and he didn't spare very many people." I shrugged. "Other than that, I'm not sure why someone would want to do this to him." Funny, I found it difficult to say the word *kill*.

Then it hit me. The night before, Maggie and I had stumbled into the middle of a conversation between Charlie and Rob. What was it Rob had said?

The effort of memory must have registered in my face; Herrera was quick to pick up on my confusion. "Have you thought of anything else?"

Reluctant to try to explain something that might not add up, I nodded. I told him about the previous night, and he immediately was interested in Rob.

"Where can I get in touch with Mr. Hayward?"

"Actually," I said, trying to remain casual, "they both live"—I stumbled over the verb—"right next door to me."

"The victim was your neighbor?" Herrera verified, and I nodded. "And you say you didn't have much to do with him?"

"Just because he lived next door doesn't mean we were best friends. The apartment is in a good location, it's reasonably priced, and I didn't have the luxury of choosing my neighbors when I moved in."

I replied with some asperity, but Herrera seemed satisfied. He asked me for the address and wanted to know if Rob would be at home.

"I don't know what his schedule is," I replied. "He could already be here, or he could still be home."

Herrera stood up. He was a couple of inches shorter than I but more solidly built. He must have outweighed me by about thirty pounds—and most of it muscle, I bet—he looked like he worked out regularly. I didn't want to have him annoyed at me.

He thanked me, then explained that I would have to come to the campus police office, if I was willing, to sign my statement and have my fingerprints taken for purpose of elimination. I assured him I would be *delighted* to cooperate. With that, he dismissed me.

The air in the hallway was noticeably cooler, and I felt my head ease a little. I went to the bathroom and wiped my face with some cold, wet paper towels. Peering nearsightedly into the mirror, I assessed my features from the point of view of a homicide cop considering a suspect. After deciding that I could do a better job with my glasses on, I took another look. Average face, no real distinguishing characteristics; thick, short, dark blond hair; matching beard; brown horn-rimmed glasses, slightly oversized, through which gleamed sea-blue eyes. I felt I was entitled to one poetic touch in what was otherwise a catalog of sadly ordinary attributes.

Whether or not I looked like a homicide suspect was another question. As I well knew from the hundreds of murder mysteries I had read, the person who discovered the body was often high on the list of suspects. But was real life—or real crime—anything like a book by one of my favorite mystery authors?

The men's bathroom in the history department, I decided, was not the place to contemplate such philosophical matters—although some madcap persisted in writing graffiti in Russian on the walls of the stalls.

Out in the hallway, I almost knocked down Elspeth Farrar, the professor whose lecture I had attended the previous night. The poor woman tottered as if she was about to fall, and I reached out to steady her.

Dr. Farrar brushed my apologies aside, along with my hand, insisting that she was okay. Then, peering up at me, she asked, "Whatever is going on down the hall, Andy? I do believe I saw someone in a police uniform milling about."

I was surprised she asked, because usually she ignored what went on around her. That didn't mean she couldn't be observant when she wanted, but most of the time her head was stuck in the nineteenth century.

"Well," I said, not wanting to be the bearer of ill tidings yet again, "I'm afraid something pretty bad happened here last night." I hesitated for a moment. "Somebody killed Charlie Harper in the grad lounge."

Dr. Farrar responded with nothing I had expected to hear. "I must say, it's about time someone put that vermin in its place."

Then she turned and walked away.

C H A P T E R · 6

WHAT AN EPITAPH for Charlie! "Vermin" was probably as close as Dr. Farrar would come to a four-letter word in conversation. Much of the time she talked like a character in a Victorian novel, and I wasn't sure her vocabulary included many words outside a Victorian dictionary, despite her bizarre notions about Queen Victoria's secret writings. Charlie hadn't always been discreet when expressing his opinions, particularly about what he viewed as professorial incompetence. I was sure word had gotten back to Dr. Farrar, somehow. My money was on Azalea Westover.

Home, I decided, was the place I most wanted to be. I had plenty of work waiting for me, not counting the two books sequestered in the grad lounge, and if I hung around, people would pester me for information. The grapevines on campus were as efficient as those at any university, and with Azalea as the Head Grape, it wouldn't be long before the whole campus had the story. I could catch up with Maggie later and talk more about the situation.

Downstairs, I flashed a smile at Mary Catlin, who, in lieu of an electronic surveillance system, checked backpacks and purses for purloined library materials. She waved me through with a friendly smile, the same way she did when I had an armload of books she didn't take time to examine. Such faith she had in me and my innocuously innocent face; it paid to know people in the right places.

During the short drive home, I unwillingly thought about Rob. Though it pained me to admit it, I was worried about how he would react to the news. As far as I knew, Rob was Charlie's only real friend and the one who would feel the loss most deeply. Charlie was just too hard to get to know, too prickly to allow anyone to get close to him. I was angry over the unfairness of his death, and regretful for the denial of promise yet to be fulfilled, but I would not grieve for him.

I didn't want to break the news to Rob; I quailed at the thought of confrontation with Lieutenant Herrera after he found out what I had done. But since I had known Rob practically all my life, I felt I should do something for him in this instance, even though I still harbored feelings of resentment toward him for actions and omissions in the past. The tragedy of Charlie's murder made me realize that some of my own perceived grievances were not so compelling after all.

When I pulled into the driveway on my side of the duplex, I saw Rob's car on his side. *What am I going to do?* I wondered as I got out of the car. *Do I tell him or don't I?*

Just then another car pulled up in front of the house, resolving my dilemma. Lieutenant Herrera had come to question Rob. That seemed rather fast. I would have thought they'd spend more time on campus, getting the lay of the land first.

My stomach again performing gymnastic maneuvers worthy of Houston's own Mary Lou Retton, I unlocked my front door and nodded at Herrera and his companion. As I closed the door behind me, the lieutenant was waiting for a response to his knock.

I flashed back on what I had seen in the grad lounge that morning. My head started throbbing. I headed for the refrigerator to get a Diet Coke and some aspirin, then I returned the living room and settled in my favorite chair.

Sipping the Coke helped quiet my stomach but did nothing for my head. The aspirin needed time to work. The mid-morning sunlight streaming through the front window made the whole room feel warm and humid. I wanted to get up and turn the air-conditioner down a few degrees, but the electric bill would be high enough without that. I sat still and tried to cool off, while my mind hopped around like a Chihuahua on speed.

I worried about Rob and his reaction to the news. I also wondered what the police would think about his relationship to Charlie. I didn't know for sure, but I thought Charlie was gay. I was open with him about my sexuality, but he had never said anything to me about it. The fact that he hadn't used it as an opportunity to deride me made me think I was right. Would Herrera draw conclusions about Rob and Charlie because they shared an apartment and lived in Montrose? He might even think Rob killed Charlie for some reason. If he thought they were lovers, that is. Rob probably wouldn't waste any time letting Herrera know how hetero he was. At least, that's what I would have thought before seeing him in the gay bookstore. Now I wasn't so sure.

The phone rang then, and I welcomed the distraction to my paranoia. "Hello," I said, a little wary.

"Hi, Andy. It's Dan."

"Hi, Dan. What's up?" This was the first time he'd ever called me. What on earth could he want?

"I should be asking *you* that." He laughed nervously. "I just heard about what happened this morning, and I thought I'd check on you."

"Well, it wasn't an experience I'd necessarily like to repeat," I said, "but I guess I'm all right now." *But I'm a little nonplussed,* I added silently, *because I never figured you, Dan, for the kind of guy who goes in for ghoulish details. I mean, you don't even read mysteries!*

Living in Texas for several years had taken some of the Boston twang off Dan's voice, but not all of it, especially in times of stress. That was evident now. "I'm glad to hear you're okay, because finding something like that would be rather disturbing, I should think."

I took a sip of Coke before replying. "It *was* disturbing, but I think Charlie was more disturbed than I." I didn't mean to sound waspish, but I couldn't quite figure out what he wanted to know. To tell the truth, Dan was a bit on the pushy side. Though friendly, he was always pretty determined to get what he wanted.

"I should be feeling more regretful, for Charlie's sake," he said hurriedly, alert to the tone of my voice. "But, geez, the guy could be such a prick. If you'd been around him longer, you'd know what I mean. Still," he went on, more reflectively, "that's no reason for bashing him on the head. If it were, half the faculty would be dead by now."

"I can't argue with that." I tried to keep the distaste from my voice. "People kill for the damnedest reasons sometimes, and I'm sure the police can sort this one out." *I hope,* I added to myself.

"You're right," Dan said. "Guess I'd better let you go. I've got to get back to work. I have some last-minute details to tie up before I hand in my dissertation to the committee."

He sounded reluctant, as if he'd like to pump me for further details, but I didn't offer him any encouragement to linger on the line. I wished him good luck with his dissertation. I hadn't even taken my hand off the receiver before the phone rang again.

"Hello," I said, more warily than before. As soon as I heard the caller's voice, I knew I should have just let it ring.

"Heavens, Andy, why'd you bash his head in?"

I groaned; I should've unplugged the thing right then.

"Well, Bella," I replied, trying to keep my rapidly fraying temper under control, "I suppose I could ask *you* the same thing."

Bella Gordon—history graduate student, former fashion model, and daughter of the Honorable Frank Gordon, mayor of Houston—snorted. "Charlie was a creep most of the time, but I didn't have any reason to do it."

"Right," I replied, loading as much sarcasm into my voice as I could, "so you got your tame commando to do it for you."

It never paid to be subtle with Bella. The woman had the tact of a cactus. There wasn't much of the dumb blonde about her, though, except perhaps her penchant for seemingly endless conversations about any subject under the sun. She had never met a silence she couldn't fill. Despite her semi-constant yammering about inconsequential things, she had what it took to be a good historian.

She snorted at me again. "Bruce wouldn't dirty his hands like that."

Bruce Tindall, Bella's "tame commando"—that was Charlie's epithet, by the way—had been hired by Bella's father to protect the light (or scourge, depending on your point of view) of his life. The Honorable Frank had run a successful election campaign on his promise to curtail drug trafficking in Houston, and despite the spectacular lack of success of his program, he insisted that his nearest and dearest needed twenty-four-hour protection from the drug lords he supposedly had offended. "Killer Bruce"—yet another of Charlie's epithets—was the man on the job.

Bruce seemed to be a nice guy, considering that he had to put up with Bella all the time. He was about my height and had similar coloring, but there the resemblance ended. A thirty-five-year-old ex-Marine, he was solid muscle and looked like the star of a martial arts movie. Maggie had more than once told me how gorgeous he was, and I had to concede that I wouldn't mind trading bodies—but not jobs—with him. I also, as the saying goes, wouldn't kick him out of bed, though he wasn't my type.

"What do you want, Bella?" I sighed loudly into the receiver. Maybe she'd take a hint. I should have known better. Nothing ever seemed to faze the woman.

"Details, of course, you idiot," she replied. I could hear the affection in her tone. "I wanted to make sure *you* were all right, Andy," she continued, her voice all honeyed concern.

"Well, I'm fine," I said. Then I sighed again; I might as well give in, or she'd come over and sit on me till I told her what she wanted to know. If, somehow, Lieutenant Herrera found out, then I'd let *him* deal with Bella.

I rapidly sketched the pertinent information, and at the end she seemed satisfied. She expressed concern again when I told her about being pushed by the mysterious stranger in the grad lounge. Finally, after promising to call her the minute—ten years from now, maybe—I knew more, I hung up and switched on the answering machine. For once it might prove useful; they did tend to work better when you actually turned them on.

I went to the front window and peeked out. Herrera's car, still in the street, meant I wouldn't find out anything more for a while. I refused to think about what another talk with him might entail. Instead, I went to the kitchen and began cleaning up a couple days' worth of dirty dishes. I couldn't concentrate on reading now, despite my earlier plans.

My thoughts were jumbled as I cleaned. Now that the horror of my morning discovery had retreated somewhat, I was becoming intrigued by the puzzle of it. Who could have hated Charlie enough to kill him? Maybe treating the whole thing as a game would keep those memories of the dead body at bay. I could only sit on the sidelines and speculate, though. I didn't think Lieutenant Herrera would welcome any attempts on my part to play Jessica Fletcher.

Nearly an hour later, after I had dropped into my chair for a brief respite from cleaning, the doorbell rang. Again I peeked out the window; Herrera's car was gone. I opened the door to admit Rob.

He looked awful. He was pale, and his eyes were suspiciously red. He walked into my living room and collapsed onto the couch.

"Come in," I said sarcastically and pushed the door shut. This was the first time Rob had ever come next door. In the past, I had taken such great pains to let him know how unwelcome he'd be, I was surprised to see him, even now. I wasn't sure what to say.

"Looks like it was pretty bad with the police," I said after a moment, using my great gift for stating the obvious.

He gave me a funny look. "You don't know the half of it."

He rubbed a hand across his face, then suddenly started laughing. Alarmed, I made a move toward him, thinking he might be going into hysterics, but he just waved at me to stay where I was.

Rob inhaled deeply before he spoke again. "Looks like I'm gonna be number one on the Suspect Hit Parade."

"Why?" I asked, genuinely surprised. "What possible motive could you have for murdering Charlie?"

The words sounded harsh, even to me, but Rob barely winced. He stared at me, and I found it impossible to tear my eyes away from him.

"Apparently someone told the police that Charlie was my lover."

I laughed scornfully. "And they believed it? You—Mr. Straight Arrow—and Charlie? You gotta be kidding!"

Rob sat there, frozen.

"Now, if someone told me you had beat him up because he was gay, that I might believe. But his lover, no way." I watched his face. "Is that it, then? Did you bash his head in because he tried to seduce you?"

Rob flushed. "Okay, I deserved that, I guess. I owe you that much." His face twisted in pain. "Andy, please sit down, and let me talk to you. This is important, and you've got to let me explain."

"Where the hell do you get off!" I shouted. "I don't have to let you do anything, after what you did to me." I could feel my fists clenching. I wanted to hit him, to strike out physically, the way he once had.

The doorbell rang.

CHAPTER · 7

I TOOK A DEEP BREATH and backed away from Rob. He watched, frustrated in his need to unburden himself to me. The doorbell rang again. I continued to the door, ready to tell whoever it was to go away.

Maggie had her hand at the buzzer when I pulled the door open. "Hi, Andy. I hope you don't mind my coming over like this," she said as she walked inside, not having noticed my glower, "but the minute I finished my class, I thought I'd check on you." She paused when she saw Rob, obviously upset, sitting on the couch. "My goodness, Rob, are you okay?" She looked back at me, realizing that I, too, was upset. "What's going on?"

I wanted to throw up. I didn't want to face dragging out my dirty laundry, even in front of someone as sympathetic and understanding as Maggie. Not here, not now. But I seemed to have no choice.

I collapsed into my chair, watching both of them. "Rob told me, just now," I said, my voice flat, "that the police may suspect him because he was supposed to be Charlie's lover. I said it was more likely that he bashed him on the head because Charlie tried to seduce him." I snorted derisively. "Like anybody would really think Rob's gay, despite the fact that he visits gay bookstores."

His head snapped up at that, and he started to speak, but Maggie beat him to the punch. "And why are you so surprised, Andy? You didn't realize Rob is gay?" She laughed. "Didn't your gaydar go *ping*?"

In other circumstances, involving someone else, Maggie's honest incredulity and my own blindness might have been funny.

I watched Rob's face and said, "It did once, about ten years ago. On that occasion, I was informed in no uncertain terms that I was wrong. And, moreover, that I was disgusting and perverted and filthy and that I should stay the hell away from him. Plus, I got a few bruises as a souvenir."

"Geez!" Maggie whispered, and she sank down onto the floor, right where she had been standing, and looked at us.

Rob faced me. "I doubt there's anything I could ever do," he said, his eyes compelling me to listen, "to make you understand how profoundly sorry I am for what I did to you. I have no excuse. All I can say is that I reacted out of ignorance and fear. The blame is mine. You dared me to be honest about how I really felt, who I really was, and I couldn't face it. I freaked out on you."

For an uncomfortable moment, I saw not my living room of the present, but the old hay barn on my father's farm. An afternoon ten years earlier, when I was sixteen and Rob, seventeen. Wrestling in the hay after a long day's work, playing the way we had since we were toddlers. Suddenly, the touch of flesh on flesh held a different meaning, no longer playful, but charged with a new and breathtaking electricity. A long, lingering kiss, shared in surprised understanding. Then, horribly, the naked fear and panic in his eyes. Finally, the hateful, corrosive words and the physical blows.

"So you've finally come out of the closet?" I said venomously, snapping into the present. "And now that's supposed to make everything hunky-dory? You're queer, at long last, and I'm supposed to be happy about that?" The nausea had passed, and I felt possessed by a cold, clear rage.

Rob flinched from the mockery in my voice, but he blazed right back at me. "Geez, Andy, give me a break! I was seventeen years old, I grew up in rural Mississippi, and I didn't know anything about being queer, except that it was wrong. How did you expect me to react?"

He took a deep breath and continued. "You scared the hell out of me. I thought I had hidden those feelings from everybody. I freaked out when you kissed me, and because I liked it, I thought I was one of those filthy perverts the preacher used to talk about."

"Don't you think I was scared, too?" I demanded. "I gave in to an impulse because, for once in my life, it felt like the right thing to do. And then I felt like the gates of hell had opened up, just for me, when you reacted like that. I didn't deserve that, and it took me a long time to realize it."

"I didn't know you were still so bitter. Though why I'm surprised, I don't know." Rob shook his head. "I still see your face—the hurt and the pain—that afternoon, and sometimes I can't sleep. I've wanted so many times to talk to you about it these past two months, but I could never find the words, or the right time. I thought that running into each other all the time here in graduate school would make it easier, but you've made your feelings clear. You never have a conversation with me; you either say something rude or start some harangue.

"I don't expect you to forgive me, Andy. I wish that you could, but I know, more than you may be willing to admit, what I did to you. To a lesser extent, perhaps, I did it to myself as well." His eyes pleaded with me to understand.

"What is that supposed to mean?" I asked, looking away from him.

"It took me a long time to face the truth, but when I did, I realized I hurt someone who meant a great deal to me, someone who had been a part of my life for as long as I could remember. I pushed away someone whose affection, concern, and support. . . . Oh, the hell with it!" Rob said wearily. "I might as well say it, I don't have anything left to lose." He took a deep breath. "I hurt the person I loved most in the world, the one person who glimpsed the real me and didn't turn away in disgust. I'll never stop wondering what a difference that would have made, if I hadn't been such a fool." He was crying, the tears flowing silently down his face.

"Damn you!" I said, as I, too, started to cry. I wanted to beat him and scream at him for the ten years of heartache and doubt, the sleepless nights and the daydreams. Hating myself for the daydreams, but unable to expunge him from my memories. A while back, I'd been involved in a relationship that lasted three years, but Rob was always there, like a ghost at the wedding. I had never gotten him completely out of my system, despite what he had done to me.

"I'm sorry, Andy, there's no point to this." He stood up. "I'll get out of here."

"No, wait!" I said, reacting before I thought about it. I paused. I didn't know what I wanted. My anger drained away, leaving me dazed. I looked around for Maggie, but she had disappeared. "Don't go yet. Please," I said as I got up and stumbled for the kitchen.

Exhausted, Rob sat down on the couch again.

Maggie was in the kitchen, crying quietly. She grabbed me when I came through the door and hugged me until I thought I wouldn't be able to breathe again. "Oh, Andy," she said, "I never imagined this. Are you gonna be okay?"

"I honestly don't know," I told her, disengaging myself from her arms. "I feel like I've been hit by a bulldozer." I went to the sink, laid my glasses aside, and started splashing my face with cold water. Then, feeling slightly more coherent, I dried my face with some paper towels and peered nearsightedly at her.

"What are you going to do?" she asked.

"Geez! I don't know." I rubbed my eyes. "I feel like getting in my car and driving away and not coming back. I don't think I can face him day after day, in class after class."

"Yes, you can," she said, her voice clear and strong, her tears forgotten.

I put on my glasses and stared at her. "What makes you so sure?"

"You didn't work hard for four years, teaching high school history, scraping and saving every penny to attend graduate school, to give it up because of this."

That's what you got for confiding in so-called friends. They used your words, threw them back in your face, when you tried to weasel out of something.

"Thanks a lot," I told her sourly.

She smiled patiently at me. "Andy, I know you're hurting. You're bewildered and don't know what to think. I'm not sure what I'd do in these circumstances. Frankly, you have every right to be pissed at him, now and forever. But you know what?"

"What?"

"He does care about you."

"Oh, really? And what makes you the expert?" I wasn't sure I wanted to hear her response. Couldn't I just make her—and him—go away and get out of my life?

Maggie ignored my rude tone. "I've noticed him watching you. A lot. I don't think he's aware of how much he does it, but it's one reason I was sure he's gay. I didn't realize that you two had known each other so well, but I could tell that he had strong feelings for you. He's a lot more vulnerable than you think, and he's risked a lot, telling you what he did."

"Oh, you think so?" I definitely didn't want to hear this.

"Yes, I do think so. Andy, don't you see what he's done?" She was almost pleading with me. "He's reversed the situation of ten years ago. He's exposed himself utterly to you. He has no defenses left right now, and if you turn on him, the way he did on you, he won't blame you. A lot of people wouldn't. But you'll always have to wonder what might have been."

"And so you think I can go out there, kiss and make up, and we can ride off happily into the sunset forever?"

Maggie smiled at my derision. "Maybe. Maybe not. There's only one way to find out."

I shook my head. "I can't handle that kind of risk right now." I fought the rising tide of panic in my mind and in my gut. "I can't go through that again."

"But you won't be alone this time. I think Rob is prepared to risk just as much as you are, and at least this time, you'll have the home-court advantage, so to speak."

"Spare me the lame sports analogies, please." I frowned at her, even while a certain organ did a flip-flop or two.

"When you get that sarcastic with me, I know you're starting to feel better." She had the nerve to grin at me.

"Bitch," I said, without rancor.

She took my hand and led me out of the kitchen. "Yeah," she replied, "and you're the one who told him not to leave."

As we came back into the living room, Rob looked up, hope naked in his eyes. He stood, and I held out a hand to him. I simply meant to shake his hand, but he, perhaps willfully, misinterpreted the gesture and threw his arms around me instead.

The warmth of his body coursed like an electric charge through me. I returned his hug, almost by reflex. I had to admit that he felt good in my arms.

I let go of him, and he understood. He dropped his arms and moved away. His eyes bored into mine.

"Can we start over, maybe?" he asked, his voice husky.

I nodded. "I'll try, but I can't promise anything more than that. Let's work on being friends, okay?"

He smiled. "At least you're talking to me."

"You may have cause to regret that."

"I'll take a chance."

"Good!" Maggie said briskly. "Now that we've done the drama-queen bit for the day"—Rob and I both threw her a look—"suppose you tell us, Rob, what the police had to say to you? Why did they think you and Charlie were lovers?" She sat down on the couch and patted the space beside her. Rob sat down, and I got comfortable in my chair.

"Someone in the history department told the good lieutenant that we were," Rob said flatly.

Maggie and I looked at each other and said simultaneously, "Azalea!"

Rob nodded wearily. "That was my guess, too. I know the woman despised Charlie, and she doesn't seem to have much use for me, either, though I haven't the foggiest idea what I've ever done to piss her off."

"She knew you and Charlie were sharing an apartment," Maggie said. "That was enough."

Rob shrugged. "I guess so."

"So how did Lieutenant Herrera broach the subject with you?" I asked. "Was he accusatory?"

"Not at first," Rob answered. "He started off in a mild way. But the more we talked, the more insistent he became that I was deliberately misleading him about the true nature of my relationship with Charlie." He shook his head. "I kept insisting that we were friends, roommates who shared the expenses, but Herrera just kept pushing at me. He didn't seem to believe that two men in Montrose could live together and not be spending all their time in the sack."

"Did *he* say that?" Maggie asked, appalled.

"Yes, more or less," Rob said.

My hands clenched in my lap. Herrera had been polite to me. But now that he knew where I lived, he'd probably take the same tone with me if he questioned me again.

"I even offered to take him upstairs and show him our separate bedrooms," Rob went on, "but he wasn't interested. I could tell he didn't believe me. Or else he's intentionally misunderstanding the whole situation. I think he's found his chief suspect, and he doesn't want to look any further."

"But what motive would you possibly have had for killing Charlie?" Maggie asked. "It makes absolutely no sense to me. You told me you and Charlie weren't lovers, but I'm not sure how you can prove that to anyone else!"

Rob smiled sadly. "I did love him, in a way, as a friend, because he was the first person I came out to, five years ago. You'd be surprised how supportive and, well, almost tender, he could be. He cared about me, and he did his best to help me, even though he was ambivalent about his own sexuality. He could be nasty to almost everyone else, but he and I had a different kind of relationship. I didn't try to make excuses for him. I know he could be awful, but I cared about him in spite of that."

Maggie seemed willing to accept everything Rob said at face value, but I'd known him longer, and I wasn't completely convinced. There was something hard to read in his expression when he denied having a physical relationship with Charlie.

Nevertheless, Maggie and I were both moved by his simple declaration of feeling for his friend. Charlie had been a difficult person to like, even to tolerate on occasion, and I doubted he'd have a more feeling or compassionate eulogy than the one Rob had just given him. I looked at him with a newfound respect. If he was being completely honest, he had most definitely changed, and I had to make myself realize it. I, too, had changed in many ways in the past ten years, and in my blind rage at Rob, I had denied him the capacity to grow and learn and to mature.

"Since I knew Charlie better than anyone," Rob said, "and because everyone seems to think the two of us were having a relationship, I think I'm going to be an attractive suspect for the cops." He took a deep breath. "And then there's the fact that we had a big argument a few days ago, and more than one person must have overheard it."

"What did you argue about?" Maggie asked.

Rob looked at her; he wouldn't look in my direction. "I don't think the subject of the argument is all that important. What *is* important, from the police's point of view, is that I was just about ready to haul off and hit him, when someone walked in. Charlie could be a jerk, and he made me really angry that day. We were in the grad student lounge, not the best place to have an argument, but, of course, he probably did it on purpose, just to provoke me."

"Oh, Rob," Maggie said. "Did you say something stupid like, 'I could kill you'?"

He leaned back against the couch and closed his eyes. "Of course I did. You and I know that it doesn't really mean anything, but it's the kind of stupid thing you say when you're upset. And it won't be long before the police collect that little tidbit and come talk to me again. It's not bad enough that someone I cared about has been killed. There's all this other stuff to deal with, too."

Watching his face and the defeated slump of his body, I wanted to do something to help him, in spite of my reservations. Deciding to go with my heart and not my head, I reached over and squeezed his arm. "Maggie and I will stand by you. You didn't kill Charlie, and they're not going to be able to charge you with it and make it stick. If we have to, we'll figure this out ourselves."

Maggie echoed my words. As she spoke, I realized that this was what I had been thinking all along. Ever since reading that first Nancy Drew book when I was ten years old, I'd had a hankering to play detective. Reading hundreds of adult mysteries hadn't changed that notion. I had always been curious about people and what makes them tick. That's why I became so interested in history. I wanted to know more about people who've been dead for more than six hundred years.

Rob cheered up slightly. For the first time, his smile looked hopeful. "Well, then, where do we start? I owe Charlie that much."

I leaned back in my chair and tried to appear as if I knew what I was doing. I looked to Maggie for assistance, but she wrinkled her nose and left me to pole the barge alone. "We should start with a motive," I suggested, "although the police will probably start with opportunity. Who had a motive to kill Charlie? Admittedly, he made a lot of people angry. The things he would say sometimes and then get away with, just because people were afraid of him." I shook my head, remembering. "But that's not enough to kill him. So what other reasons could there be?"

Rob's face clouded over.

"What is it?" I asked.

He hesitated. "I think Charlie was blackmailing somebody."

Blackmail! The word reverberated in my mind. Rob waited warily for a reaction from Maggie and me. Charlie could be loathsome, but blackmail was farther than I thought even he would go.

"Who was he blackmailing?" I asked.

Manifestly uncomfortable, Rob shrugged. "This is kind of hard to explain, partly because I haven't had time to think it all through, but I think Charlie could have been blackmailing several people."

"Why do you think that?" Maggie asked.

"This is where it gets complicated, I'm afraid." His face scrunched up as he organized his thoughts. "There are probably a few things neither of you know about Charlie. He wasn't easy to get close to." Rob paused, sensitive to his understatement. "I felt sorry for him. He didn't know how to make friends, with his attitudes and that godawful acid tongue."

"But you, at least, got beyond that with him," Maggie said.

He nodded. "Yeah, I did. When we were undergraduates together, even though he was a couple of years older, Charlie told me enough about his so-called family life that I could understand why he was like he was. His parents are wealthy, and he was the youngest of four sons. The other three all took business degrees and went into the family's businesses, but Charlie was always the one who was different—a gay, liberal, brainy type from a conservative, wealthy Southern family.

"He came out to them when he was about eighteen. They had sent him to an exclusive prep school in Boston, and I got the impression from Charlie that something happened that forced his hand while he was at the school. He was never comfortable with being 'out,' though, and he never talked publicly, as far as I know, about being gay. If you cornered him, he might admit it, but most of the time, he just ignored the subject." Rob shook his head. "I went through that stage myself, but Charlie was still stuck in it.

"Well, when Mom and Dad and all the big brothers discovered that baby Charlie was a faggot, all hell broke loose. For about a year, Charlie said, his life was sheer misery. Then, one of his grandmothers stepped in and somehow made the family see a little more sense, at least so they could get along. When Charlie decided he wanted to attend graduate school, after failing miserably at working in the family's businesses, they finally gave in. After all, even they had to admit that being a college professor was respectable. And, of course, the fact that he was several states away didn't hurt," Rob observed ironically.

"Charlie never seemed to be short of cash," I commented, "unlike the rest of us. It must be nice to have a rich family."

Rob laughed. "Charlie didn't need the fellowship he got to pay for his education. His monthly allowance was incredible. You should see his expensive computer system. And a fancy CD player, a VCR, and a video camera you could have used to film *Gone With the Wind*."

When Rob stopped to take a breath, an idea surfaced, and I expressed it aloud. "But if he had a wealthy family and a generous allowance, he surely wasn't blackmailing for money, was he?"

He sighed and shook his head. "I don't think money was that important,

because the people I suspect were his targets can't afford large sums of money."
He paused. "No, what Charlie liked was the power trip, getting an edge over
someone. That was the part of Charlie I disliked, and he knew that, so he tried
to keep what he was doing from me." He splayed his hands in an interrogative
gesture. "I don't know why, but I was the one person he actually tried to have a
real friendship with."

I wondered whether Charlie might have fallen in love with Rob, but now
wasn't the most tactful time to ask.

In an effort to console him, Maggie said, "You may never be able to explain
these contradictions to yourself, Rob. Hold on to your memories of your friendship, and keep that separate from whatever else Charlie may or may not have
done."

Rob seemed comforted by Maggie's words. "I suppose you're right," he
sighed. "But the situation's a real bitch."

I nodded in commiseration, and Maggie squeezed his arm. I moved the conversation back toward motives for murder. "Rob, what proof do you have that
Charlie was blackmailing someone?"

He rubbed his forehead with both hands before he answered. "That's the
problem, Andy. I don't have anything substantive." He clenched and unclenched
his hands in his lap. "Everything is impressionistic, subjective."

"Well," I said, "if you can put your impressions into words, perhaps I can
help you decide whether you're right."

"Okay, here goes. Do you remember hearing—right after the semester
started, at our first department meeting—that Charlie had a paper accepted for
the annual conference of the *Societas Historiae Francorum*?"

I nodded. "It was a big surprise. He crowed about it for a week."

Rob leaned back into the couch once more. "Well, you know they never
accept submissions from graduate students, and Charlie said some things which
led me, in a vague way, to conclude that his good fortune was a little more than
that. One thing he *didn't* make known was that Julian Whitelock was on the
committee that selected the papers that year."

"And you think that somehow Charlie coerced Whitelock into making sure
his paper was accepted?" This I found hard to believe.

According to graduate student lore, Whitelock's reputation for contrariness
was legendary. No one, not even the university president, could persuade him
to do anything he didn't want to do. Sometimes the man seemed to think he
lived in the period that he taught, acting the part of one of the strong-willed
Merovingian kings who usually got murdered for their pains. But then, Whitelock was a pretty big noise in the S.H.F., more or less the dean of the American

school of Frankish history, so if anyone could get away with it, he could.

"Yes," Rob asserted. His face had taken on a determined look I had once known well. Perhaps he knew more than he was willing to reveal at the time. How else could he be so positive? "Whitelock and Charlie were two of a kind in certain ways, it seems to me. They were always butting heads over something, and I think Whitelock would have tried to get Charlie kicked out of the program because they had such a hard time getting along. But Charlie was the most talented student Whitelock had had in a long time, so he was willing to put up with him."

I still had doubts. "But what could Charlie have known about Whitelock that was worth blackmail? The end, in this case, must have justified the means for someone as ambitious as Charlie, because, in his field, giving a paper at S.H.F. is quite an achievement. What," I asked again, "could Charlie have had on Whitelock?"

"From the remarks Charlie made at the time, I think he knew something about Whitelock's private life which could cause a big scandal. I'm not quite certain what it was, but I think it had something to do with his sexual tastes." Rob's nostrils flared in disgust. "Charlie said something obscene, which I won't repeat, about how Whitelock got his jollies, and believe me, if Charlie was right, Whitelock does *not* want it known."

This wasn't the kind of thing I cared to know about someone's private life, but if we were going to figure out the puzzle of Charlie's murder, we were going to have to wade through the muck, whatever our feelings. "What do we do next?" I asked. "Do you want to talk to the police about your suspicions?"

"No," Rob replied, almost violently. "I tried to broach the subject with Herrera, but he just laughed at me. I can theorize all I want, but he's not going to pay any attention until I hand him some physical proof." He ran a hand through his hair. "I need to look through the apartment. The police went through Charlie's room and took a couple of his notebooks. But I have a feeling they've missed something important, and I'm going to check out my suspicions."

"Sounds like a good idea," I told him, "but be careful. You don't want Herrera accusing you of tampering with evidence."

"I'll be careful," Rob promised. "And while I'm looking, there's something I'd like both of you to do. Have you received your copy of the most recent *Medieval Quarterly* yet? Charlie's came yesterday."

I nodded. "So did mine, but I haven't had a chance to read it. I did notice Whitelock has an article in it."

"I haven't read it either," Maggie said. "I wasn't in the proper masochistic mood."

Rob spoke quickly. "That's the article you should read when you have a chance, and see if anything about it strikes you as odd."

"Okay," I replied, baffled. What could an article in a scholarly journal have to do with Charlie's murder?

Rob stood up. "I'm pretty whacked out right now. And I've got an afternoon class that I'd better start getting ready for."

Maggie stood and gave him a hug. I rose and held out my hand to him, and he clasped it warmly. Our eyes met.

"Thanks," he said. "I'll see you later." His eyes offered some sort of promise, but I didn't want to interpret it.

Maggie followed him, and when they were gone, I leaned against the front door. Overwhelmed by the morning's events, I couldn't think what to do next.

I looked at my watch. Well past one, and I hadn't had lunch yet. My head was throbbing. If I appeased my empty stomach, my head might feel better. In search of sustenance, I headed for the kitchen.

I had plenty reading to do that afternoon, including the newly arrived journal, though I dozed off a few times, thanks to a full stomach. Eventually I surfaced from reading to have dinner, then relaxed for a couple of hours with an old movie before going to bed.

Sometime later, I woke to the sound of a ringing phone.

C H A P T E R · 8

"ANDY, ARE YOU THERE? Did you hear me? I said I think someone tried to kill me!"

That cleared the fog out of my brain. "Good lord, Rob, are you all right?" I grabbed my glasses off the bedside table and peered at the clock—2:04 A.M.

A snort came over the wire. "Is this Andy Carpenter, or a refugee from the Twilight Zone?"

"I'm sorry, Rob, I was sound asleep, and it's taking me a while to focus. What happened?"

"When I got home after class this afternoon, I was exhausted. I unplugged the phone and took a mild sleeping pill and went to bed," he explained. "About an hour ago, I woke up. I was kind of fuzzy, but I had to have some water. When I came downstairs, I heard a noise in the living room, so I went in. There was enough moonlight coming through the window to see somebody fiddling with the videotapes beneath the TV set.

"I guess I made some sound at that point," Rob said. "I was so out of it, I probably giggled, because I vaguely remember thinking that surely no one had broken in to steal Charlie's 'Mary Tyler Moore Show' tapes. Whoever it was didn't see the joke, because he came at me with the largest and longest flashlight I've ever seen. I yelled and ducked, and he came down on my left shoulder like a ton of bricks. I went woozy for a minute or two, and by that time, the guy was gone—out the patio door. I was in no condition to hold him back, even if I had wanted to."

"Good lord, Rob, he could have killed you!"

"My point precisely!" He laughed tiredly. "Anyway, when I could concentrate again, I got up and looked around. Whoever it was really snooped around. Books and knickknacks were out of place, that kind of thing. I have no idea what he was looking for. Surely if it was a simple burglary, he would have taken the VCR and gone away, right?"

"Probably. The whole thing sounds odd. Have you called the police yet?"

"Oh, yes, right after that." Rob laughed again, amusement in his voice this time. "The boys in blue were here in half an hour, and they weren't very quiet when they banged on the front door. I can't believe you slept through all the commotion."

"For one thing," I replied, "I really zonked out, and besides, my bedroom is in the back, so I didn't see or hear anything."

"Lucky you!" Rob snorted. "Well, at first, the police took me seriously, but when I told them they might need to contact the Rice campus police, and why, they suddenly got suspicious." His voice turned querulous. "They saw no connection between this and a murder case at Rice. I'm sure they think I made all this up to divert suspicion from myself. Even when they found the lock forced on the patio door, one of them, acting like he was whispering but intending me to hear, said that it was easy enough to force a lock like that, even for a guy with a limp wrist."

This was worse than I expected. If the police believed he had faked a break-in, that made Rob's position even more difficult. Or was it simply the homophobia of some members of HPD? Would Herrera act the same way?

"How can we convince the cops the break-in was legitimate?" I asked.

"I don't know," he responded wearily, "and I'm too tired to think about it right now."

"I know. Do you want to come over here for the rest of the night?" I wasn't sure he should be alone, despite my reservations about having him living even temporarily under the same roof.

"No, I'll be okay. I've got an ice pack on my shoulder, and the police said they'd drive by every once in a while to keep an eye on things. I'm not sure I believe them, but it's a moot point, anyway. No one's going to try to get back in here tonight." He paused, then continued with a different note in his voice. "Could I take you up on that offer tomorrow night, though? I don't think I can stand to stay here for a while."

I responded immediately to the uncertainty in his voice, ignoring my misgivings after my impulsive offer. "Of course you can. Larry's going to be gone for at least a couple more weeks, and I know he wouldn't mind you having his room."

"Thank you," Rob said quietly. "This is getting too weird, too fast, and I need all the support and help I can get."

"See you tomorrow." I said good-bye and hung up, switched off the lamp, and tried to get comfortable in bed.

My mind hummed with all sorts of chaotic thoughts, and I knew I'd never get to sleep again. Most of the afternoon I had done my best to keep Rob and the big scene between us out of my mind, but now the whole thing came flooding back. The anxious note in his voice just now, the note of dependence, frightened me. Earlier, I had been swept away by emotion and Maggie's determination to make things right between Rob and me, but in the darkness of my bedroom, at two-thirty in the morning, all the potential problems assailed me.

I had acted impulsively in the hay barn ten years earlier, led by my heart and my hormones, and he had reacted with devastating cruelty. He had hurt me badly, and after that day we avoided each other. Later I realized that I had something, at least, to be grateful for—Rob hadn't told anyone about it. Nor did he do anything to out me in our small community. I'd been so stunned by what happened that I withdrew even further, trying to suppress my feelings and the truth about myself, though that didn't last long.

Rob's words to Maggie and me, the day before, had struck a definite chord. I knew exactly what he meant. We both had come to terms with our sexuality, and it hadn't been easy. Coming out to my family had cost me dearly, because my father hardly spoke to me, and my mother called only when he wasn't around. One brother talked to me, the other was uncomfortable around me. Suddenly I wondered about Rob's family and whether they had reacted any differently from mine. Had he even told them?

The whole situation was nuts. I didn't know what Rob wanted from me. Did he simply want to be friends? Was he looking for some way to assuage his guilt? He said that I was—once upon a time—the person he loved most in the world. Every time I thought about that, my stomach hurt. Despite what he had done, and the way it affected me, I still had strong feelings for him. And the basic physical attraction was there, as it had always been. Could I put aside ten years of anger and well-nourished resentment to get to know him as he was now? Could I let my memories go? And what would be the outcome?

That was as big a mystery as the identity of the person who killed Charlie. The attack on Rob frightened me, since it forced me to consider that Charlie's murder might not be the only one, if the killer wasn't caught soon. Was his killer the person who broke in next door? If so, what was he searching for? Did Charlie have some sort of record of his alleged blackmail schemes? Or was this simply a coincidence?

Earlier in the day, I'd been skeptical of Charlie's possible blackmailing activities, but after I looked over that issue of the *Medieval Quarterly*, I decided that Julian Whitelock might have had a motive to murder him.

I read his article carefully, and I was convinced that it was simply a rewrite of a seminar paper Charlie had written the year before. The writing style had definitely been Whitelock's, but the arguments and evidence he used were lifted bodily from Charlie's work. Whitelock had mentioned Charlie in a footnote, but that was little thanks for outright intellectual theft. No wonder Charlie had had a paper accepted at a prestigious conference where Whitelock had served as program chairman. Surely that was the least the old shit could have done. The wonder was that Charlie hadn't tried to kill *him*.

I had been tempted to downplay Whitelock's motive for murdering Charlie, despite the evidence of the plagiarized seminar paper. But the attack on Rob put things in a different light. I didn't think someone was simply burglarizing the place, although Charlie had enough electronic equipment to make it worthwhile.

My head ached from all the speculation, so I made a conscious effort to turn my mind off and get some sleep. I began conjugating verbs in Latin. This did the trick, as usual. By the time I reached the subjunctive of *morior,* I was pleasantly hazy.

When the alarm sounded at six-thirty, I was being chased by a robed figure demanding the whereabouts of Bracton's notebook. "Bracton *who?*" I kept asking, but to no avail. The pursuit was relentless, as well as senseless.

The steady beep-beep, beep-beep of my alarm finally roused me to semiconsciousness, and I stretched out a wobbly arm to shut it off. I smiled over the dream as I threw off the covers and sat up. One of the deadly dull books on medieval English law I had been reading had stuck with me more than I thought.

Fifteen minutes later, showered, dressed in underwear and T-shirt, and nearly coherent enough to confront the world outside my bedroom door, I went downstairs to microwave my breakfast. When it was ready, I carried breakfast and the newspaper upstairs and got comfy in bed. I turned on the TV and tuned in to "Bewitched," which had just started.

During commercial breaks, I skimmed the newspaper. The university murder rated only a small article near the end of the main section; front-page coverage had been given, instead, to a grisly double homicide in the Memorial area, one of Houston's most affluent neighborhoods. According to the newspaper, the university victim had apparently died after a blow to the back of the head with the traditional blunt instrument, in this case, left nameless. The article suddenly recalled the whole scene to mind, and I put my third sausage biscuit away uneaten. I took a long pull at my Diet Coke to steady my stomach.

What the paper didn't state, of course, was the time of death, perhaps waiting for the autopsy. Who knew how long it would take to get an autopsy done in a city like Houston? Here homicides and violent death seemed like daily occurrences. More details might be released to the press, but since the murder seemed so ordinary, despite its setting, it had apparently aroused little interest. Charlie's killing couldn't compare with the mutilation murders of wealthy socialites.

Scanning the article again and ignoring the antics of Samantha and Darrin, I noted how little information about the murder the newspaper actually offered. I groaned; I would certainly be accosted by everyone I knew on campus, even though my name wasn't mentioned. I'd have to thank Lieutenant Herrera. I was simply identified as "a fellow student." Obviously the campus news office was doing its best to keep a lid on any adverse publicity for the university. And if that meant protecting the identity of a witness, that was all to the good for me.

I put away the newspaper and decided to concentrate on my morning TV schedule. Once I had watched the third episode of "Bewitched" (a rare one, which I remembered seeing only twice before), I reluctantly decided to get something done. Something constructive, like finishing that book on medieval English law that had contributed to my dreams.

Before I could move, the doorbell rang. I had barely made it to the head of the stairs, after quickly pulling on some jeans, when the doorbell pealed again. Somebody was in an all-fired hurry. And at just after nine o'clock in the morning, too.

"Rob," I said when I opened the door. "What's wrong?"

Rob, a wild, frantic look in his eyes, thrust past me and charged into the living room, waving a piece of paper. I caught up with him and grabbed his arm to slow his agitated pacing back and forth.

"Rob, what's wrong?" I repeated. "What's that you've got?"

"It's a letter from Charlie!" he said. "And I think it's going to get me in a lot of trouble."

CHAPTER · 9

"I DON'T UNDERSTAND, ROB," I said. "Where did you get a letter from Charlie? Was it in the mail?"

"No," he replied. "I found it in his desk."

"Well, calm down and tell me about it." I tried to soothe him but didn't have much luck.

"I was looking through Charlie's desk, trying to find an address book or something with his parents' address and phone number in it, and couldn't, so I started looking through the files and found a folder labeled 'Will.' I thought I should turn it over to Charlie's lawyer, if he had one." Rob paused and took a deep breath, making an effort to calm himself further.

"In that folder I found an envelope that said 'For Rob.' I debated a while, but I figured if it had my name on it, I could open it, right?" He looked to me for assurance, and I nodded.

"So I opened it, and this is what I found." He thrust the paper at me, and I took it.

"Dear Rob," I read aloud, "if you're reading this, it means that I'm dead and gone." I looked up, not appreciating Charlie's slightly macabre sense of humor, and Rob nodded wearily. "But don't worry about me. I've taken care of you, and if you're careful, you'll never have to worry about money again. Just open the large manila envelope in this folder, and follow the instructions enclosed inside. With all my love, Charlie."

"Wow," I said. "So what did you do with the will?" I tried not to think about the implications on that piece of paper.

"I didn't do anything," he said grimly, "because it wasn't there! The folder was empty, except for the letter. Then I looked all through Charlie's desk, but there was no manila envelope."

"Good lord! Do you think the person who broke in last night took it?"

"It's possible," Rob replied. "One of the desk drawers wasn't quite shut when I started looking, but I didn't think much about it at the time. Charlie may have done something with it, instead. Who knows?"

"Did Lieutenant Herrera look through the desk yesterday?" Maybe that was the simplest explanation.

He shook his head. "No, but I thought he would at some point. Now it's too late."

"What could someone want with Charlie's will?" I asked.

"To get me in trouble!" Rob said, his head in his hands. "This is it. If Charlie left me a lot of money, then Herrera will be convinced now that I killed him for it. What am I going to do, Andy?"

In the face of his panic, I forced myself to focus. "Look," I said, putting a hand on his arm to get his attention. "Just because Charlie might have left you some money doesn't mean you're automatically suspect. The police have to prove that you knew Charlie was going to leave it. *Did* you?"

Rob was calming down, listening and considering what I'd said. "No, I didn't, but if a copy of the will was just sitting there in Charlie's desk, the police will find it hard to believe that I *didn't* know about it." He took another deep breath. "How many graduate students have wills, for heaven's sake? Why should I think Charlie had a will, or that he would have left *me* anything?"

"You're right, Rob," I replied. The idea of a will did seem a bit weird, but if I came from a wealthy family, maybe I'd think differently. With the exception of my cousin Ernestine, no one in my family had much of anything to leave, beyond a few pigs and the odd chicken or two.

"Since Herrera didn't go through Charlie's desk yesterday," I said, "why don't we hide this letter here, in my place? That's one piece of evidence linking you to the will that we can produce only if we have to, and we can keep it safer over here."

He leaned away from me on the couch, watching me closely as he spoke. "Are you sure you want to do that? What if Herrera finds out? You could be an accomplice."

I shrugged. I wasn't sure I wanted to get in any deeper, but seeing his distress, I didn't have the heart not to help him. "Why should Herrera even think I'd have such a thing? It won't be a problem, I promise you. And by the time he finds about any will, he'll have arrested the murderer, and it'll all be moot, anyway."

"Okay, if you're sure."

I forced myself to face him directly. "It's okay, Rob. Now, let me put this away somewhere." I brandished the piece of paper before trudging upstairs. I stuffed it into a box in the rear of my closet. I couldn't imagine the police, or anyone else for that matter, digging through the junk in my closet to find it.

Downstairs once more, I motioned for Rob to follow me into the kitchen, where I offered him something to drink.

"How about some coffee?" he asked. "I can't do Diet Coke until around lunchtime." He indicated the can in my hand.

"Sure," I said. I didn't drink the stuff, and I figured he was better off making his own. My roommate was a coffee drinker, so I pointed him to the coffeemaker and the coffee.

While Rob waited for his coffee, I sipped my Diet Coke and thought about Charlie's will. Obviously, Rob's friendship had meant more to Charlie than Rob had realized. Who knew, though, why Charlie would have left him something in his will? And the Good Lord only knew how much it would be. Could be in the millions, if Charlie meant what he said in that letter. Had it been merely Charlie's way of thumbing his nose at his family? Or had he genuinely appreciated Rob's friendship? Maybe Charlie really had been in love with Rob.

The groaning and grinding of the coffeemaker brought me into the present.

"Thanks, Andy," Rob said as he poured himself a cup.

"It's only coffee," I said, deliberately misunderstanding.

"That's not what I meant, and you know it." He sat down across the table from me. He took several sips of his coffee, and I waited. "Yesterday and today, I've asked a lot of you, presuming on an old friendship. If I could go back and do some things over again, believe me, I would, for your sake, if not for mine. But we *can't* go backwards, and I *can't* erase the past. Maybe we can go forward, though?"

I turned to look out the window, not wanting to acknowledge the question in his eyes. "We'll see, Rob. Let's just get through this mess, and then we'll see. We should concentrate for now on who killed Charlie, and why."

"You're right." Rob, suddenly brisk, drained his coffee cup and set it down on the table. "Now that I'm calmer, I'll go home and get some work done, gather my stuff together for later. I guess the police aren't going to come breaking down my door for a few hours yet. What are you going to do?"

Without giving much thought, I answered, "I'm going to campus to get some books I need. I'll be home again in a couple of hours, then I'll help you bring your stuff over." I hesitated. "Are you going to be okay?"

He smiled, holding my gaze for what seemed a long time. "Yeah, I'll be fine."

With that, Rob departed, and I headed for my car, trying to get my breathing back to normal. I couldn't believe he still had this effect on me.

I wasn't sure what I would accomplish on campus, but I couldn't face reading that book on medieval English law. There were other books I had to work on, but they were in my carrel in the library. I was taking two readings courses for the semester, in addition to my once-weekly seminar, so most of the time my nose was buried in a book. (Otherwise known as Heaven, to the masochistic species known as Graduate Student.)

Something about a book teased at my memory. I shrugged it off. Whatever it was, it would come to me. For now, I could concentrate on other things. At the very least, I might hear something interesting on campus, and I could chat for a while with my advisor, Ruth McClain.

Twenty minutes later, I knocked on Ruth's office door, on the fifth floor of the library. After hearing "Come in," I opened the door but stopped abruptly and began to make apologies, for she already had a visitor.

"No, please, it's quite all right," the visitor said as she stood. "Ruth and I have finished our business, and I'm afraid I was just wasting her time chitchatting."

Ruth's visitor was Margaret Wilford, whom I had seen with Selena and Azalea the night of Dr. Farrar's lecture. She wore a charcoal gray business suit and carried an expensive-looking leather briefcase. Her blonde hair, which she wore in a fashionable short cut that highlighted a strong, attractive face, gleamed in the fluorescent light of the office.

Ruth stood up also. "Margaret, I'm glad we've had a chance to talk before the big day. I'll see you then." She shook hands with Margaret, who smiled at me in a vaguely friendly fashion, though I could see her attention was focused elsewhere.

Once Margaret had gone, Ruth motioned for me to take the recently vacated seat and made herself comfortable in her chair.

At forty-two, Ruth McClain, thin, attractive, and passionate about her subject, made the study of the Middle Ages a joy. Her blue eyes lit up and her voice conveyed her enthusiasm whenever the conversation veered toward anything in which she was interested—and her interests were wide-ranging. In the five years she had been a member of the history department, she had won two teaching awards, and her classes were always full.

Ruth and I had quickly established an unusual rapport. I felt I had known her for years. She was comfortable enough with me to indulge in a little discreet gossip from time to time, and I appreciated her obvious concern for my well-being and my progress in my studies. She was the kind of mentor I had hoped for when I entered graduate school, and I was extraordinarily lucky to be working with her.

"Is Margaret Wilford one of your students?" I asked, because I really didn't know that much about the woman.

"Yes, she took a couple of my seminars several years ago," Ruth answered. "Margaret is defending her dissertation next week. She's one of the dwindling number of Julian's students." She paused uncomfortably at the segue. "How are you?" she asked. "From what I hear, you had a pretty horrid shock yesterday." Then she shook her head. "I shouldn't force this on you right now."

"No, it's okay." I smiled. "I don't mind talking about it."

"Then I must admit to a certain curiosity." She smiled back gently. "I wasn't that fond of Charlie, but it's difficult to imagine a reason for killing him."

"That's what I've been trying to figure out. I saw him that night, you know. I came over to the library after Dr. Farrar's lecture, and then I went upstairs with Maggie McLendon to check my mailbox. Charlie and Rob Hayward were in the lounge, and Charlie was acting completely in character, of course, so my last words with him weren't exactly friendly."

"Few people ever exchanged friendly words with him, myself included," Ruth contributed wryly. "He wasn't a man who engendered neutral reactions. I've never met a person who seemed to enjoy being malicious as much as he did." She shook her head. "It's a pity, his talent wasted like this. He had the intuitive gifts and the flashes of inspiration that it takes to make a first-rate historian."

"We sound like we're writing a eulogy."

"Not a very comforting one, I'm afraid, to anyone who truly liked the man," she said, the shadow of sadness drifting across her face.

That was one of the reasons I liked Ruth. Even when she didn't particularly like someone, she nevertheless had the charity to feel compassion.

She continued. "As much as most everyone disliked him, I *still* can't imagine why anyone would murder him."

This was an issue I had to skirt carefully; although I trusted Ruth, I couldn't share with her speculations on Charlie's possible blackmailing activities just yet. But because I needed all the information I could get, I steered the conversation in a different direction.

"In this case," I said carefully, "the police may be more concerned for a while with opportunity, rather than motive. At least, that's the way it often happens in the police procedurals." Since Ruth was as devoted a mystery reader as I was, I had no doubt she understood the reference. "I think the murder occurred at some point before the library closed at midnight. There aren't many people around here late at night, and whoever did it could move around with little worry about being noticed."

She agreed. "That night was certainly a good choice, if this was planned. With the reception for Ms. Bladen"—a reference librarian who had retired after forty years of service—"and Elspeth's lecture, most of the history faculty and graduate students were on campus. And, as distasteful as the idea is, the murderer must be someone we all know. The coincidence would be too great for it to be a complete stranger. I guess I've read too many mysteries to think otherwise."

"That's what I think, too," I answered. "Everyone up here on the fifth floor knows everyone else's habits pretty well, and Charlie often stayed late in the library. The killer didn't have to take much of a chance on finding him here."

Ruth shivered. "I might have been here myself." Her office wasn't far from the graduate lounge. "I work here several nights a week, often until eleven or eleven-thirty. I may revise my habits for a while until the murderer is caught." She frowned. "Julian and Elspeth are here late as often as I am, but Elspeth would probably never notice anything."

"Have you talked to Dr. Whitelock lately?" I asked casually.

"Oh, yes," she answered, grimacing. "In our faculty meeting this morning, you should have heard Julian's tirade against campus security for allowing such a thing to happen. He seemed genuinely upset. I doubt he was actually *fond* of Charlie, but Charlie was the most talented student he's had in a while, and that must have counted for something. There was something odd, though, about the relationship between Charlie and Julian," Ruth continued in a reflective tone. "Lately, Julian seemed almost afraid of him for some reason. If this were a Patricia Wentworth scenario, I'd say that Charlie was blackmailing him."

My stomach did a quick dance. What could Ruth know?

"Of course, it's sheer fancy on my part," she continued before I could respond. "Charlie may have had a malicious wit and a razor-sharp tongue, but that doesn't mean he had criminal tendencies." She shrugged. "The last few days, Julian has seemed . . . well, I suppose *apprehensive* is the best word. I'd have expected him to be crowing over his new article in the *Medieval Quarterly*, but he hasn't said a word about it to me."

For the first time, she noticed that I was finding little to say; she couldn't know the effort I was making to remain aloof, especially after she mentioned Whitelock's article. "You're not chiming in on cue, you know, to agree that I'm letting my imagination run riot. Do you know something I don't?"

"Well," I replied in a considering tone, drawing the word out into almost three syllables. How could I sidestep this one? "Blackmail always makes a good motive for murder . . . in fiction. I'm not saying Charlie *was* blackmailing anyone, or Dr. Whitelock in particular. But . . . who knows? It's just as possible as anything else, I would think." I shrugged and lifted my hands in a vaguely interrogative gesture. I hoped that, by ignoring her remark about the article, she would forget it, at least for now.

Ruth stared at me coolly from across the desk, blue eyes narrowed in speculation. I gazed back, trying to look innocent. After two years of working with me, however, she knew better.

"I'm willing to bet you know *something*, but you can't or won't tell." She smiled, lest I think she was annoyed. "I know more about how your mind works than you realize, Andy. Someone should point out to you, though, that playing detective can be dangerous in a situation like this. Whoever killed Charlie won't take kindly to interference from you."

"Warning duly noted," I replied, but not flippantly. I appreciated her concern. I had realized the possible dangers only too well when Rob woke me with his story of the attack on him. This was no game, but I couldn't just sit calmly by and see him charged with a murder he didn't commit, simply because it would be an easy and—to the police—obvious solution. I couldn't explain this to Ruth at the moment, although I felt she would sympathize with my motives.

She stood up. "That's all the homily for today—not quite the *Sermo Lupi ad Anglos,* but suffice it must. We both have work waiting. Papers to grade for me, plenty of reading for you."

"I'll be careful," I promised, avoiding the subject of reading. Who knew, the way things were going, when I'd get back to my books?

Saying good-bye to Ruth, I stepped out into the hall and immediately—and literally—ran into two of my friends rounding the corner.

CHAPTER · 10

I DISENGAGED MYSELF from Bruce Tindall, the male half of the duo, and straightened my glasses. "Sorry," I mumbled. "I never look where I'm going."

"No problem," he replied easily. "No damage done."

His companion, Bella Gordon, laughed. "It's okay, Andy, he comes with a guarantee. All damaged parts easily replaced. My father will send you the bill."

They both smiled broadly. I just looked at them, tired of the joke. Bella frequently referred to Bruce as some form of property or as an inanimate object. Most of the time, that's the way she treated him, too. I wondered how she would treat a bodyguard she didn't like.

She offered me a spider's grin. "I've just *got* to hear *every*thing you know about what's been going on up here." She took me by the arm, giving me little chance to argue, and steered me into an empty seminar room, not far from Ruth's office. I cast a quick glance at Bruce, but, inured by now to his charge's enthusiasm for scuttlebutt, he gave me a smile that offered little sympathy.

Bella settled me, none too gently, into a chair at the head of the long seminar table, seating herself on my right and motioning for Bruce to sit on the left. Were they afraid I'd try to escape? Bruce did as he was directed, while I tried to organize my thoughts. I had to be careful what I told her, because whatever I said was bound to be repeated for the benefit of anyone willing to listen. Bella never failed to find an audience.

"Tell me about finding the body," she commanded. "Again," she said, anticipating my protest.

It hadn't taken long for Charlie to become "the body," I reflected, but at least Bella wasn't hypocritical. She and Charlie had never liked each other when Charlie was alive; *de mortuis nil nisi bonum* was evidently not part of Bella's vocabulary.

"There's not a lot to tell, Bella," I said, though without conviction. "I was on campus early, as usual, to retrieve a couple of books I'd left in the grad lounge the night before. When I walked in, I found Charlie lying on the couch. At first I just thought he was asleep, but then I realized something was wrong. I could see that he'd been struck on the back of the head and that he was dead. Then Consuelo came in, she called the campus police, and that was it, more or less."

If my bland recital of the bare minimum of facts disappointed her, she didn't show it. When Bella retold the story, though, I'd be willing to bet it would be suitably embellished.

"Who do you think did it?" she asked abruptly. "Was it Rob?"

"Why on earth do you think *Rob* would do such a thing?" I asked indignantly.

"Relax, Andy. I don't know *who* did it, but knowing the nature of the relationship between the two of them, and knowing what a jerk Charlie was, I wouldn't be surprised if Rob had some reason to bash his boyfriend over the head."

I took a firm hand with my temper. "Rob did not *bash* Charlie over the head, for any reason. And I don't know what you mean by 'relationship,'" I added frostily. "If you think they were lovers, you're mistaken. They were friends and roommates, nothing more. And as annoying as Charlie was, he didn't do anything to Rob to make him commit murder."

Bella snorted and tossed her head, like a temperamental horse. "Well, if you think they weren't lovers, that just shows how naive you Mississippi boys can be. Didn't you ever see the way Charlie looked at Rob? He had hungry eyes. But if you insist that they weren't in a relationship, I guess I'll take your word for it." She paused. "And why are you getting so hot under the collar, anyway? Were you jealous of Charlie? I've noticed the way you're always looking at Rob."

"Don't be ridiculous!" I snapped. "You're imagining things, as usual! I'm not interested in Rob." My denial sounded weak, even to me. Maybe Bella was right and Rob had lied to Maggie and me about his relationship with Charlie. Charlie was the only person who could have contradicted Rob, and he was dead. And if Charlie left Rob something in his will, that surely meant Charlie had strong feelings for him. What was it Charlie's letter had said? That Rob would never have to worry about money again? Sounded like love to me.

Then I thought of something else. Was Rob trying to make peace with me simply to disarm me? Did he want to divert suspicion from himself? Was he lying about his relationship with Charlie? This left me more shaken than I wanted to admit.

I tuned back in to Bella. "Charlie must have annoyed *someone* an awful lot. Who knows, Whitelock may have finally gotten enough of Charlie's misunderstood genius routine and done it himself. It sure irked *me* most of the time."

Bruce spoke, startling both me and Bella; we had forgotten he was there, he had been so quiet. "Then that gives you about as good a motive as Dr. White-lock, doesn't it, Bella? If sheer annoyance with the little twerp were the motive, hell, I could have done it myself." He shrugged.

The "twerp" had taken special delight in making maliciously jocular remarks about the relationship between Bruce and his charge, most often within Bruce's hearing. Fortunately for Charlie, Bruce's even temper and tolerant good nature had kept him from responding to the taunts. If he had, no doubt Charlie would have emerged the loser; Bruce could easily have broken any bone in Charlie's body. So could Bella, I thought suddenly. She was in excellent physical condition; she worked out with Bruce, who made sure she knew how to defend herself. I shifted uncomfortably in my chair.

"I think annoyance is an inadequate motive for murder in this case, or else you both might be in trouble," I responded spitefully. "Charlie certainly gave you cause—not to mention practically everyone in the history department, for that matter."

Perplexed, Bella shook her head. "I know. I've never seen anyone who put so many people's backs up deliberately."

I wanted to laugh. Talk about the pot calling the kettle black.

"And the worst thing," she added, "Charlie got away with it."

Bruce laughed. "Everyone was afraid of what he'd say next—Bella, even his professors. No one else was quite that fast with his tongue, or enjoyed being that malicious. And you have to admit, he *was* pretty funny sometimes."

Recalling Charlie's remarks about Azalea, I had to agree, although I felt uncomfortable in doing so. She was fully capable of defending herself; some of Charlie's other targets, like Elspeth Farrar, had not been.

"He was really bright," Bella said. "I give him that, even though I was jealous. Seemed like every time I turned around, he was winning some sort of award. This year, I heard he was a shoo-in for the Dunbar Award. I was hoping for a chance at it, so I could go to North Carolina to do research in the Southern Historical Collection."

She rolled her eyes in annoyance; her father, who, before seeking political office, had been one of the Southwest's most successful criminal lawyers, could certainly afford to fund his daughter's research trips. But since Bella had defied him by seeking a Ph.D. in history, rather than a law degree, Frank Gordon was unsympathetic to her needs as a history graduate student. "But Logan," she continued, "who's on the awards committee, you know, hinted to me a couple of days ago that Charlie was going to win."

Anthony Logan, professor of Southern history and an amiable gossip, was Bella's advisor and, often, the source of the interminable flow of information about the goings-on of the history department. She was probably right, since Logan was seldom wrong. He made it his business to know something about everyone in the department.

I focused abruptly on something Bella was saying. "Of course, Charlie really didn't need the money, since his parents are so wealthy. He could have taken off for Paris and the *Bibliothèque Nationale* anytime he wanted. He didn't have to wait for university travel money."

"Well, Bella," Bruce responded, "now that Charlie's definitely out of the running, you may just win the award yourself." He grinned wickedly at me. "How's that for a motive? Beautiful graduate student kills obnoxious fellow student in dispute over travel money."

I wasn't amused; I hadn't liked Charlie, but making speculative jokes about his death seemed inappropriate, even under the guise of being open about one's feelings. Bruce sensed my disapproval and had the grace to look somewhat abashed, but Bella was oblivious as ever.

"That award doesn't offer enough money to kill for," she replied. "It's entirely possible that I might win now, but I'm not so sure I want to, given the circumstances. Thank goodness they don't make you keep that horrible little trophy. I can't stand the thing."

"Bella," I asked quietly, "how did you know Charlie came from a wealthy family?" I put aside my mental picture of "that horrible little trophy" and the role it had played in Charlie's death.

She peered suspiciously at me, as if my question was some sort of trap. "Bruce and I ran into him and his mother one time in the Galleria last year. Believe me, the clothes his mother was wearing, the family is loaded." With Bella's experience as a model, she knew clothes and what they cost. I believed her.

That settled, I decided I'd had enough. "Well, guys," I said as I stood up, "that's about all from Crime Central right now. I've got books to read."

Bella didn't look happy; she would have enjoyed gossiping about the murder for hours, but I was ready to get away from the two of them.

Before she could make more than a token protest, I was out the door. Just a few steps into the hallway, I pulled up short. Heads bent together, backs in my direction, Selena and Margaret were whispering. Pretty heatedly, too, from the way Selena's head bobbed up and down.

The two women were blocking my way in the narrow hallway. If I didn't get past them and on to the door leading to the stairs, I was afraid Bella and Bruce would come charging out after me again.

"Excuse me," I said, and Margaret's head whipped around in my direction.

Her face flamed scarlet, but Selena smiled coolly and waved me through with a "Hi, Andy."

I could feel their eyes on me as I walked down the hall. I hadn't gone far before the whispering resumed. Probably just dissertation nerves, I thought.

Down on the fourth floor, I headed for my carrel, picked up a couple more of the books on my reading list, and took them to the circulation desk to check them out.

My transaction completed, I headed gratefully for the parking lot, sweating and wiping my brow as I went. The inside of my car was at least a hundred degrees, and it had just cooled off by the time I finished the short drive home.

I had barely gotten out of my car before Rob's front door swung open, and he came running across the yard to greet me. He was carrying a videotape.

As I put my key in the front door, he exclaimed, "You're not going to believe what's on this tape!"

C H A P T E R · 1 1

ROB WAS HARD ON MY HEELS as I unlocked my front door and went inside. I was intensely curious, of course, but I didn't want to talk on the doorstep. In the living room, I dropped my books on a table and plopped down on the couch, motioning for him to sit beside me.

"You won't *believe* what's on this tape," Rob repeated as he settled on the couch.

I took the tape from him and read the hand-printed label. "So it's not *Conan the Barbarian*?"

"No," he laughed. "It's surely not."

"Why would you even think twice about this?" I brandished the tape, and he took it back from me.

"I was cleaning up," he explained with exaggerated patience. "My late-night visitor left things a bit messy. He had been pawing through the videotapes, and I was too tired to pick them up last night. Or this morning, rather. So, while you were gone, as I started reshelving the tapes, I noticed a couple with odd titles. Like the *Conan* one." He looked expectantly at me.

"I guess Charlie wasn't a Schwarzenegger fan?"

Rob nodded. "Got it in one. He hated the guy, so I didn't think there was any way he'd have one of his movies on tape. Another was labeled *Predator*. I thought there was something strange about them, and, boy, was I ever right!"

"So show me what's on the tape," I responded, getting up, ready to head upstairs to my TV and VCR.

He shook his head. "I don't think you want to see this, trust me. It's pretty hard-core stuff."

I sat on the couch again. Now was not the time to discuss my ability to view pornography without being permanently warped. "We-e-ell," I said in slight exasperation, "what is on the tape?"

"*Tacky* is not the word for it, let me tell you," he responded with a grimace. "First of all, this tape is definitely amateur work, and in this case, the amateur had to be Charlie. I told you he had an expensive video camera, didn't I?"

At my nod, Rob continued. "I'm pretty sure he must have recorded these . . . these activities, but when and where I don't know."

"What activities are you talking about, Rob?" I asked impatiently.

I wasn't completely surprised when he answered baldly, "Kinky sex, involving Whitelock and some woman. Or women. I'm not sure. There are lots of scenes with whips and other devices, and the woman is dressed in leather, wearing a mask. Whitelock is naked as the day he was born. He's not wearing a mask, so you know right away who he is. I did a lot of fast-forwarding." He paused to scrunch up his mouth in distaste. "We're talking serious S and M here. Gracious, what a sight! Whitelock naked is enough to put you off sex for a lifetime! I couldn't even make myself fast-forward through the second tape. I just looked at the beginning long enough to determine that it was more of the same. I had enough with the first one."

"You don't have any idea who the woman was?"

"No," Rob said. "Unless she happens to wander by wearing one of the leather outfits from the tape! I told you, she wore a mask of some sort."

"Maybe there are some distinguishing marks, or something else that could be used for identification."

"Probably, if you want to go through the tape looking for them!" Rob made a funny face. "To think of Whitelock. . . ." He shivered with revulsion. "And the kinds of things they're doing. I'm not sure I can even look at him in class again." He flourished the videotape. "This kind of thing goes on all the time in certain parts of the gay community, and I've got one friend who's really into it, but I've never known anyone—anyone straight, that is—who went in for it." He shook his head.

I laughed. "I didn't know you were such a prude. Those kinds of *activities*"— I mocked his tone—"are probably a lot more common than you think, in both the gay and straight worlds."

Flushing, Rob riposted, "I guess I don't have your wide experience, then. The sight of people beating each other while they're having sex doesn't do much for me, I'm afraid."

"You don't know anything about my *experience*. But just because you don't approve of their sexual practices doesn't mean you can get on some moral high horse. It's none of your business. As long as they're consenting adults, they can do what they want with each other."

Rob glared at me, breathing hard. I returned his stare, refusing to back down.

Then, to my surprise, he laughed. "People in glass houses shouldn't throw stones, I guess. I don't want anyone telling me what I can do in my bedroom, either. Point taken."

I shrugged. "Good. So, what do we do now?" I asked. "I suppose we should call the police and turn it over to them. The longer we hold on to this tape, the more trouble we could be in."

Rob stood up and began to pace to and fro. After a minute or so, he turned toward me, scratching his nose.

"That's my first inclination, too," he admitted. "I want to shove the responsibility onto someone else. I dragged you into this because I was scared they'd arrest me, and now that I've actually got evidence that could implicate someone else, I'm having second thoughts." He laughed hollowly. "This tape is such a gross violation of privacy, and I don't want to carry it any farther. I wish I'd never looked at it."

I leaned back on the couch. "The best thing we could do is throw the tapes in the garbage and forget them. If I believed they had absolutely nothing to do with Charlie's murder, I'd do that and not think twice about it. But I have a hard time believing there's no connection between Charlie's having this stuff on videotape and his murder." I thought for a moment. "Besides, you could've been severely injured, or even killed, last night, possibly because of the tapes, if that's what the burglar was after. That, frankly, scares the hell out of me."

"Agreed." Rob returned to the couch and stood solemnly looking down at me. "I think the tapes make Whitelock look like Suspect Number One. That reminds me, did you have a chance to read his article in the *Medieval Quarterly* yet?"

"Yes, and I think it was probably plagiarized from a seminar paper of Charlie's that I read. Whitelock uses exactly the same evidence and arguments. And speaking of that paper, I know I have a copy of it in my files upstairs. I'll go get it right now."

Rob nodded, and I jumped up and ran up the stairs. It took only a couple of minutes of rummaging through my desk to find the paper. I skimmed it quickly as I walked downstairs.

"I was right. Some of the phrasing is even the same. I'm positive he plagiarized Charlie's work." I paused to measure Rob's response; receiving none, I continued, "Does that confirm what you suspected?"

He gave me an odd look. "Actually, Andy, it was more than suspicion on my part. I didn't tell you everything yesterday. Charlie . . . confided in me the afternoon of the day he . . . died." Rob was having a difficult time maintaining his composure, thinking about Charlie's last day, but he took a deep breath to steady himself before continuing.

"I'd never seen him that upset." Rob shook his head slowly, remembering. "Charlie had just found his copy of the *Medieval Quarterly* in his mailbox, and he glanced at the contents page and found Whitelock's name on the lead article. After he looked over the article, he came straight to me. He could hardly talk, he was so angry. He shoved the journal at me and pointed at Whitelock's article, but I didn't understand what was going on. I hadn't read his paper, so I had a hard time believing that Whitelock had stolen his work."

"Charlie actually accused Whitelock of plagiarism?"

Rob nodded. "When he could finally talk without cussing, he told me Whitelock's article was essentially a rewrite of one of his old seminar papers. Then he went on to say that was probably why Whitelock had gotten him on the program of the S.H.F., with another paper that Charlie didn't think was quite as good. How come you had a copy of Charlie's paper?"

"During the first week of classes, I was talking to him about what Whitelock expected from us in his seminar, and he offered to let me read one of his papers that he said Whitelock had liked." I paused, reflecting. "I think he couldn't resist showing off a good paper. And, if Whitelock was going to steal, I guess he'd steal the good one."

"Why bother, otherwise?" Rob laughed bitterly. "To be honest, though, I thought Charlie had to be exaggerating. I couldn't imagine Whitelock doing such a thing and expecting to get away with it."

"That's a good point," I responded. "All Charlie had to do was dig out a copy of his paper and cause a big enough stink to embarrass Whitelock, if not prove that he was guilty of plagiarism."

Rob shrugged. "That's what I would have done. And Charlie was angry enough when he first told me about it that I thought he was ready to do something rash. But then he started calming down. I asked him what he was going to do, and he smiled at me. It was a pretty repulsive smile, though."

"What did Charlie do after he talked to you?" I asked. "Did he confront Whitelock?"

"He did, right after lunch that day. The next time we had a chance to talk about it was later that night in the grad lounge, after the lecture. He told me about his first confrontation with Whitelock, but he didn't say anything about what went on when they talked after seminar that afternoon. You walked right into the middle of our conversation."

I thought hard until I recalled what I'd overheard. "You were saying something about someone making a threat." I closed my eyes. "'. . . really threatened you if you didn't stop?'" I quoted triumphantly.

"Good memory," Rob replied, impressed. "When you walked in, Charlie had just finished relating the big confrontation scene, and I said something like 'You mean he really threatened you if you didn't stop?' After you left, Charlie and I kept talking. He had gone to Whitelock's office early Tuesday afternoon, before the seminar. Charlie showed him the article and accused him, flat out, of plagiarism. According to Charlie, he blanched a little, but then he laughed in Charlie's face.

"Charlie kept trying to argue the point with him, but all Whitelock would ever say was that, while Charlie's work may have suggested certain trains of thought, he hadn't taken anything substantive from it. He insisted that the footnote that mentioned Charlie was sufficient, and he didn't see why Charlie was so upset."

Whitelock certainly had the nerve to brazen it out. The man's upbringing had given him an aristocratic bearing and supercilious mannerisms. I could see him remaining coolly superior while Charlie just got more and more steamed.

Rob kept talking. "Whitelock had the nerve to threaten *not* to approve Charlie's dissertation *and* have him kicked out of school if Charlie persisted in such wild accusations."

"Geez," I said, "no wonder Charlie was upset. I'd've been ready to start ripping the hair off his head at that point."

"Me, too," Rob responded, "but Charlie had something else in mind. He realized that Whitelock was going to try to outbluff him, so he tried threatening him another way. I know he added some things to the paper he was working on recently, to contradict Whitelock and make him look like a fool. That was in between the time he talked to Whitelock and the time of our seminar." He frowned. "After Charlie told me that much, he got real vague, but he hinted that he knew things about Whitelock that Whitelock didn't want getting around to people in the history department or the university administration. I tried to get him to explain what he was talking about, but he wouldn't. I finally gave up and left him there in the grad lounge a little after ten. When I looked back, before I went out the door, he was reaching for the phone. I don't know who he was going to call."

Wearily, Rob rubbed his eyes. "I stayed up pretty late that night reading, well past midnight, and I never heard Charlie come home. And I thought yesterday morning, when I got up and didn't see any sign of him in the apartment, that he had hidden in the library overnight. Sometimes he did, since he thought campus security was such a joke. I never imagined . . . well, you know."

I laid my hand lightly on his arm. "If Whitelock killed him over this, he'll be found out and punished for what he did."

Rob raised his head to look at me. "I hope so," he replied softly. "Heaven knows Charlie could be a colossal prick, but he didn't deserve this."

"No, he didn't," I said quietly. "I wonder, though, what led Whitelock to steal the paper in the first place. He's tenured, and it would take an earthquake or a major scandal to get rid of him. His position is about as secure as it can be. After all, he's *the* big name in this country in Frankish history. Why would he want to steal Charlie's work?"

"Charlie said Whitelock hasn't published anything but book reviews for nearly ten years now—no books or articles. He thought Whitelock was desperate to demonstrate to the rest of the history department that he was still capable of doing publishable work. Maybe he needed to boost his ego." Rob rubbed his shoulder absentmindedly. "Also, it wouldn't hurt when it came time to talk about salary increases. Charlie found out somehow that Whitelock hasn't had anything more than the lowest possible raise for five or six years. I guess he went through Whitelock's drawers that time he was house-sitting for him. I wouldn't have put it past him, frankly. I told you he had an insatiable curiosity about other people. I doubt Whitelock's privacy meant very much to Charlie, given the evidence of those videotapes." He expelled a heavy sigh. "I'm getting a little sidetracked. I suppose the simplest answer to your question would be money and respect."

I was quick to agree. In the rarified atmosphere of the academic world, where the monetary stakes were small, reputation counted for a lot. Someone as egocentric as Julian Whitelock might not balk at a little intellectual theft to bolster a stale or expiring reputation.

Rob shook the copy of Charlie's paper, which he had taken from my hand. "Now, with this, I can nail Whitelock's ass to the wall, and he can't squirm away from it."

"Are you ready to call the police?" I asked, moving toward the phone.

"No!" He looked earnestly at me. "I think we should give Whitelock a chance to explain first, as much as I'd like to dump all this on the police right away." He waved his right hand in the air. "Call it some atavistic notion of 'fair play,' but I don't think I can turn over the tapes without talking to him first, even if . . . even if he did kill Charlie."

"We'll probably get into a lot of trouble for interfering, but I agree with you."

"Good." Rob stood up, looking at his watch. "It's about ten minutes till one. Whitelock ought to be in his office this afternoon." He moved toward the door.

"Wait!" I said. "You'd better call Azalea first to make an appointment. You know how Whitelock is."

Rob's nostrils flared in annoyance. "You're right. If I just burst in on him, he'll get huffy and not talk to me, unless I insist and make a scene." He picked up the phone and punched in the number of the history department office. After a few seconds, he said, "Hello, Azalea, this is Rob Hayward. I was wondering, does Dr. Whitelock have any free time this afternoon? I need to talk to him. It's important." He waited a moment, glanced at his watch, then responded, "Thank you. One-thirty is fine." He hung up.

"Do you want me to go with you for moral support?" I offered. "He might find it more difficult to deny if there are two of us."

Rob hesitated, obviously tempted. "No," he said. "If we're wrong, and this has nothing to do with the murder, I don't want him to have any reason to be vindictive toward *you*. No reason to drop both of us into the shit, if we can avoid it."

Reluctantly, I had to concede that this was true, and since Rob remained adamant, I decided to stay at home.

"I'll be back as quick as I can," he promised. He glanced at his watch again. "Got to hurry." As he reached the front door, the doorbell rang. Rob, startled, swung open the door. "Lord, Maggie, I forgot," he apologized as she stepped inside.

"Forgot what?" I asked, coming up beside him and smiling a greeting to her.

Rob turned to me, shaking his head. "I talked to Maggie earlier, and she said she wanted to help us. I asked her to come over this afternoon. You'll fill her in while I'm gone, won't you?" Without waiting for a response, he was out the door.

I waved Maggie inside. "I guess I will, then."

She settled in the room's one comfortable chair, a worn leather armchair in which I did most of my reading. Crossing her jean-clad legs, she eyed me warmly and said, "Before you launch into your explanation, I just wanted to tell you how happy I am to see you and Rob still talking today. I know this can't be easy for you, but I admire you for putting old feelings aside and standing by him."

"Despite what Rob may have done in the past, I can't believe he's capable of killing Charlie," I told her, suppressing my own doubts from earlier in the day. I still couldn't decide whether to force the issue with Rob over his relationship with Charlie. Could they have been lovers, if not recently, at some point in the past?

I also didn't want to analyze all my motives for wanting to know the answer to that question. I refused to think that jealousy had any part in it. That would be too twisted, even for my sometimes tortured psyche.

"Good," Maggie said, then returned to more pressing matters. "Rob told me quite a bit this morning on the phone. What's this about videotapes?"

Grimacing, I made myself comfortable on the couch and began my recital. Throughout, Maggie listened with a look of intense concentration, her green eyes gleaming.

As I wrapped up all that Rob and I knew or suspected, the phone rang, startling us. I got up to answer it, glancing at my watch. Maggie and I had been talking for about an hour; it was a couple minutes shy of two o'clock.

Rob's agitated voice rushed into my ear as I picked up the receiver. "Andy, it's me. I'll be there in a few minutes to explain, but I've already called Lieutenant Herrera and asked him to meet me at your place. We don't have to look any further for the murderer." He hung up abruptly, leaving me staring blankly at the receiver in my hand.

C H A P T E R · 1 2

MAGGIE JUMPED UP from her chair when I turned toward her. "What is it?" she cried. "Is Rob okay?"

No, I wanted to say as I hung up the phone. *I think he's gone completely round the bend.* Instead, I nodded. "I guess. He said we don't have to look any further for the murderer. He also said he's asked Lieutenant Herrera to meet him here."

She sank down into her chair, one hand twisting the hem of her floppy football jersey into a knot at her side. "What on earth does he mean? Surely you don't think Julian Whitelock actually *confessed* to him?"

I had to laugh as I resumed my own seat. "Do you really think Whitelock, suddenly stricken with remorse, would just confess to Rob? Even if he is the murderer?"

When Maggie looked at me, I felt the icicles forming down my back. Then she relented. "You're right, of course. Whitelock wouldn't give in to even Attila the Hun that easily."

"Whitelock probably made him angry, and now Rob's convinced he's the killer and is ready to turn the tapes over to the police." I hoped that was all it was and that Rob hadn't done something rash. His temper had gotten him into hot water on more than one occasion. I didn't want to dwell on that at the moment, though.

Barely ten minutes later, after Maggie and I had picked it over to the point that we were going to argue, the front door opened and Rob rushed in. He must have caught every light green to get there so fast.

Before he could say a word, Maggie patted a place on the couch beside her and said, "Sit down and tell us what happened."

"Geez, that smarmy bastard!" he said. "I came close to smashing his face with that ridiculous ashtray he's got on his desk."

Rob's teeth clenched as he described the scene. I gave silent thanks that he had refrained from his impulse. The ashtray he was talking about was made of clear glass and was big enough for a duck to take a bath in.

"Calm down a little, Rob," Maggie said. "It's a wonder the top of your head doesn't come off. I can practically see steam coming out of your ears."

"All thanks to *him*." Rob spat the words out.

The doorbell rang, and he went still and pale. I got up and opened the door.

"Good afternoon, Mr. Carpenter," Herrera said, stepping into the short hall-way. As I nodded in welcome, my throat suddenly raw, he continued, "Is Rob Hayward here?"

"Yes, Lieutenant. We're all right in here." I led the way into the living room.

Herrera pulled up short upon seeing Maggie. She stood and thrust out her hand, introducing herself. He seemed reluctant to turn her hand loose, but then he recalled himself to the business at hand. He was so obviously annoyed with Rob, he just plunged ahead.

"Do you mind explaining, Mr. Hayward, what that phone call was about? And why you couldn't talk to me on campus instead of here?" He looked over the room for somewhere to sit. Locating the rickety folding chair we kept around for extra company, he opened it up and sat down. The rest of us resumed our seats.

Herrera's face seemed to darken by the second, as we all waited for Rob to reply. Maggie was watching the lieutenant with great fascination, but then her gaze shifted to Rob. She was about to say something, which I didn't think would be a good idea, when Rob finally spoke.

"I apologize for calling you like that, Lieutenant, but I believe we've uncovered some significant evidence that you should know about. And the evidence is here, not on campus." Rob's voice betrayed his nervousness.

Herrera smiled at him, and Maggie and I shared an uneasy glance. How should we interpret that smile? Something about his air of barely controlled patience was disturbing.

"That's okay, Mr. Hayward," the lieutenant said. "If what you have to say is as important to the case as you told me, then I don't mind." But *get on with it,* the tone of his voice seemed to be saying.

Rob reached over to retrieve the videotape and my copy of Charlie's paper from the table beside the couch, where he had left them earlier.

"These," he said, offering them to Herrera, "are proof that Julian White-lock, Charlie's major professor, had the motive to kill him."

"What are these supposed to mean?" Herrera asked in puzzled irritation.

Rob scrunched back into the couch and looked at the lieutenant defiantly. "That videotape, and at least one other that I found, show Julian Whitelock having kinky sex with a woman. Or women—I couldn't tell how many. Charlie had the tapes. He wrote that paper for a class, and Whitelock had it published under his own name in an academic journal."

The lieutenant's response, logical as it might have been, was what I had dreaded. "Just where did the videotapes come from, and how did you know what was on them?"

Rob seemed to shrink a little more into the couch, and I probably did the same in my chair. "Well," he said, his voice rising, "the videotapes were Charlie's. I *didn't* know what was on them, but after looking at the labels, I realized there was something strange about them."

"What was that?" Herrera prompted.

"Charlie was a movie buff, but he didn't like much made past 1960. He loved the old screwball comedies—you know, Cary Grant, Katharine Hepburn, Irene Dunne movies, that kind of thing." Rob leaned forward, gaining a little more confidence as he talked. "There were two tapes in his collection labeled with the names of movies I knew he'd never have: *Conan the Barbarian* and *Predator*. He hated Arnold Schwarzenegger movies. Someone who didn't know Charlie as well as I did, though, wouldn't see anything strange about them."

Eyes narrowed in thought, Herrera nodded. "Maybe," he said. "But what made you take such a close look at these tapes? Did you expect to find something like this?"

Rob breathed deeply, and he didn't sink farther into the couch, the way I expected. "I was kind of out of it last night, when my place was broken into. Did the Houston police report that to you?"

Herrera nodded curtly.

"I discovered this morning, while I was trying to clean up, that the intruder had gone through the tapes, among other things. And while I was replacing them on the shelves, I noticed the two. The more I thought about it, the more I realized something was fishy about them. Then I popped one into the VCR."

"Okay," Herrera said, the clipped tone making me want to squirm. "I'd like to take a quick look at this tape. Do you mind?"

Rob stood up quickly. "No, of course not, but why don't you come over to my place and use that VCR? The rest of Charlie's tapes are there." He headed for the door, Herrera on his heels.

Maggie and I sat there, neither of us eager to talk, for once.

In ten minutes, Rob and the lieutenant returned. If anything, Herrera's face appeared even darker with emotion than before. But what emotion was it? Anger? Or something more complicated? Was he going to relinquish Rob as his chief suspect? "These tapes are going to require some investigation, Mr. Hayward."

"They're all yours, Lieutenant," Rob said, relieved that Herrera was going to take the tapes seriously.

"Is there anything else you'd like to tell me?" Herrera asked sardonically.

From the look on his face, I knew Rob was tempted to make some smart remark to get a rise from the lieutenant, but he just shook his head and held his tongue.

Herrera bade us good-afternoon, lingering slightly when he looked at Maggie, and then he was gone. I closed the front door and returned to find Maggie and Rob, glum and silent, sitting on the couch.

"Come on, you two," I said, trying to sound jocular. "Lighten up. It could have been worse."

"Thank God *that's* over," Rob replied, shooting me a sour look.

"Amen," I said, dropping into my chair.

"I still want to know," Maggie announced, "what Whitelock said to you."

"Oh, no," I groaned, and the other two turned startled faces toward me. "Rob, you forgot to tell Herrera that you confronted Whitelock today."

"No, I didn't, Andy. I told him just now, while we were over at my place. He wasn't thrilled with what I had done, I can tell you. That's why he asked if I had anything else to tell him."

"Whew. That's something, at least." Having those tapes out of our hands was a great relief. I got comfortable in my chair and waved at Maggie. "Proceed."

She gave me one of her looks before turning to Rob. "What did Whitelock say this afternoon?" she repeated.

"Not much." Rob snorted, angry again. "He had the nerve to deny everything . . . until I mentioned that I just *happened* to have evidence of his various indiscretions. He squirmed a little then, but that man is cool. He gave me the same spiel he must have given Charlie and tried to brush me off like I was a pesky fly. He didn't even deign to inquire what kind of evidence I had. And I figure I might as well drop his seminar tomorrow, because I have a snowball's chance of making a decent grade now."

Turned sideways on the couch next to Rob, Maggie sagged, her mouth hanging open. "The man must have ice water in his veins. How could he just sit there like that when you practically accused him of murder?"

Rob shrugged. "Maybe that's the way it works when you can trace your family tree back to one of Charlemagne's slutty daughters."

We all laughed. Whitelock liked to tell people that he was interested in Frankish history because his lineage could be traced to Charlemagne's court. He took for granted the fact that most of his listeners didn't know enough about Frankish history to know the stories about Charlemagne's daughters.

"He didn't want to give an inch," Rob continued, "but he let me know right quick that I'd better not try to blackmail him with this 'preposterous taradiddle,' or he'd see that I was asked to leave the graduate program. Obviously I had been 'unhinged' by the death of my 'paramour' and needed help." Rob's voice gave emphasis to the words which only Whitelock would have used in this situation. "Obviously he thought Charlie and I were lovers, simply because we were roommates and he knew Charlie was gay."

"What did you do then?" Maggie asked, her voice tight.

Rob laughed, much to my surprise. "Frankly, I was so floored by the sheer gall of the man, I just left. I did remark, as I went out the door, that the police might think differently. He didn't make any effort to stop me."

Maggie's smile expressed the grim satisfaction that we all felt at the thought of an encounter between Herrera and Whitelock. That unctuous, old-South gentility wouldn't go over too well with the lieutenant, who had enough steel in his backbone, I suspected, to withstand whatever aristocratic nonsense Whitelock tried to pull.

"Those tapes," I said slowly, trying to express an incompletely formed thought.

"What, Andy?" Maggie asked when I didn't go on. "What are you thinking?"

I took a minute before replying, trying to force my thoughts into some sort of order. "Well, say Charlie had already let slip to Whitelock something about the tapes. Then maybe Whitelock talked to the woman, or women; and she, or they, would probably have as strong a motive as Whitelock. He could be on the phone right now, warning them, or he could have called them after his argument with Charlie, and one of *them* actually killed Charlie."

"You're right, Andy," Rob replied quietly. "Knowing Charlie, he probably did threaten Whitelock. And I'll bet Whitelock did, or is doing now, just what you said."

Maggie grinned. "That's good news for us, then. It means, as soon as the police identify whoever's on tape, they'll have plenty of suspects to deal with and they'll leave Rob alone."

I shrugged. "Maybe you're right. Surely, the more that Herrera digs into this case, he'll see that there are other people who had real motives to kill Charlie."

Rob nodded, his forehead creased in concentration. "I hope you're right, Andy. I don't like feeling I'm in a corner."

"From what I've seen so far," Maggie observed, "I think it's going to turn out okay. Herrera seems to be acting in a professional manner. He seemed to take these tapes seriously, and I'm sure, once he investigates them further, like Andy says, he'll turn up someone with a stronger motive than you could possibly have had."

I hoped she was right, but I didn't think Rob could afford to count on that. We had to be prepared for what might come next. We spent a few minutes speculating idly on the identity of the woman involved with Whitelock, but it was difficult to think of someone—except Azalea—we all disliked enough to imagine in that kind of scenario.

Then, seeing that Rob was tired—after all, he'd had a pretty eventful couple of days—Maggie and I tacitly agreed to change the subject. We were all hungry, so we piled into Maggie's car and drove downtown to a Chinese restaurant that had an all-you-can-eat buffet for a price that wouldn't stretch a grad student's budget too unmercifully. We arrived ahead of the dinner crowd and spent a good two hours gorging ourselves and talking about everything except the murder.

Later that night, I helped Rob get settled into Larry's bedroom.

"Thanks for letting me stay here, Andy," he said. "I feel safer here, I have to tell you."

"Good," I answered. "Just try to relax and get some sleep. I think maybe the worst is behind you now."

"I hope so!" He moved closer to where I was standing in the doorway. "I can't believe all the trouble I may be getting us both into, but you're being a good friend to me, and I appreciate it."

At that moment, I knew that if I gave any sign of encouragement, Rob would be in my arms. I could sense the need and the desire in him, and—if I was completely honest—I felt it, too. He had never looked more attractive to me, but I still didn't quite trust either one of us. I forced myself to turn away.

"You're welcome, Rob," I said, my voice strained. "See you in the morning." I went downstairs without looking back. I heard his door close softly, and I breathed more easily.

Concentrating on my book on medieval English land law was actually a relief, after the past two days of emotional turmoil. I read about fifty pages of dense prose and took a few notes, then decided it was time for bed. As I stripped off my clothes and went to sleep, I tried not to think of Rob, so close.

After a miserable night, I woke up grumpy. I stumbled out of the shower, dragged on some clean underwear, and went downstairs to find Rob singing softly to himself and cooking breakfast.

Oh, shit! I thought. In my usual morning haze, I had forgotten he was staying with me. I started retreating from the kitchen before he could see me.

Too late! Rob turned around and a huge grin split his face. "You *have* changed since the last time I saw you in your skivvies." He walked over to where I stood frozen in the doorway, and had the nerve to reach out and brush the thick hair on my chest with his hand. "I definitely approve. Tall, blond, and furry."

"Thanks," I said sourly. "I'll be back in a minute." Then I ran upstairs, blushing at Rob's wolf whistle.

Downstairs again, dressed this time, I told Rob, "If you say anything perky or cheerful, I'll throw something at you."

"Don't worry, sunshine," he laughed. "I think I like you better the way you were before, though, for what it's worth." For all his good humor, his eyes had dark shadows under them, just like mine.

Good! I thought viciously, pouring myself a large glass of Diet Coke.

As we finished breakfast, which I had to admit was delicious, the phone rang. Wondering who could be calling me at seven-fifteen in the morning, I grabbed the receiver from the wall by the fridge. I gave up on getting upstairs in time for "Bewitched."

"Hello," I growled. "Oh, hi, Mama. How are you?" I leaned against the wall, turning slightly away from Rob.

"I'm doing fine, honey," she assured me, her voice determinedly cheerful. "How are you? Are you doing well in school?"

"So far, I'm doing just fine." I paused. "Mama, how's Daddy?" I closed my eyes and could see her sitting in the kitchen, her favorite place for talking on the phone, already late for work, but seizing the opportunity to call when she could.

"He's doing just fine, too, Andy," she said. "He's already out in the fields this morning. They've got the last of the cotton to see to, and you know how he is this time of year."

"Yes, Mama, I know," I replied. "Has he said anything about me, well, you know, coming home for Christmas?"

She caught her breath with a little sob. "Oh, honey, I don't know. I mentioned it to him, but I just don't know. Cary and I have been talking to him, trying to get him to see some sense, but you know how stubborn he is. And Joey too. I just don't know. I want to see you so bad, honey. Maybe you can come and stay with Ernestine, like you did last time?"

I hated to blight the note of hope in her voice. "I guess I probably can, Mama." Ernestine Carpenter—Ernie, to her nearest and dearest—was my father's cousin and probably my best friend in all the world. She was the one member of my family who never let me down. She didn't even bat an eyelash when I came out to her. I was twenty at the time, and her only response was "I wondered if you knew." Then she grinned and hugged me, and I felt like I was going to be okay after all. That was before I told my parents, of course. And that's another story entirely.

As much as I loved Ernie, and she loved me, I still couldn't help wanting to spend Christmas in the house where I had grown up. But I guess that was not to be. At least, not this Christmas. Families can be sheer bloody hell sometimes.

My mother and I chatted for a few more minutes, on less controversial matters, and she told me the latest news about my two younger brothers, Cary and Joey. I told her about some of my classes, but I didn't mention the murder. And I didn't say anything about Rob. After we hung up, I pulled off my glasses and rubbed my eyes, which were throbbing.

Rob had gone into the other room while I talked to my mother, but now he was back. "Andy, are you okay?"

I shrugged. "Wonderful. As usual. News from home always lights up my face this way."

"I'm sorry. Your dad?"

I nodded and asked, "Have you come out to your parents yet?"

He laughed bitterly. "Are you kidding? I think my mother knows, and she might be able to handle it if I talked to her about it; but if I told my father, he'd make your dad look like Mother Teresa."

"Maybe," I said. "But my dad's bad enough, as it is."

Rob squeezed my arm. "In time, maybe, he'll understand."

I couldn't bear to think about my family anymore. I moved away. "Thanks for breakfast. That was much better than my cheap frozen sausage biscuits."

"You're welcome." If Rob was stung by my abrupt retreat, he didn't show it. I helped him clean the table and stack the dishes in the sink, which took all of two minutes.

"Now," I said, "the important question. Shall we ride in together, or take separate cars?" Too bad I couldn't just hide upstairs all day and watch reruns of old TV shows. But there were things we had to do—and people to face—on campus.

"Together, if you don't mind," he said.

"Sure. I'll drive."

We arrived at the library not long after it opened. As we stepped off the elevator on the fifth floor, we could hear a woman screaming, somewhere toward the end of the hall.

We ran in the direction of the screams.

C H A P T E R · 1 3

ROB AND I RAN neck and neck down the corridor, our shoes squeaking on the old, waxed linoleum. I had a sinking feeling about the source and location of the screams, now diminishing in decibel level. I pulled up short in front of Julian Whitelock's office, where his door stood wide open. Consuelo, the cleaning woman, was huddled against the shelves just inside. Her screams stopped when she saw me. I didn't like the look she gave me. I silently agreed—we had to stop meeting this way.

Consuelo pointed, and Rob pushed into the room with me. A body lay in grotesque fashion on the floor, the head resting crookedly on the bottom shelf of a bookcase in the back of the room. I nerved myself to step forward to examine the body, while Rob persuaded Consuelo out of the room.

Whitelock's office was one of the most spacious on the fifth floor, about half again as big as most of the others. Usually tidy, with not so much as a paper clip out of place, the room now looked like someone had had a temper tantrum, for books and papers lay scattered around the floor.

I got close enough to the body to place my fingers on the wrist of one outstretched arm. I felt no pulse, and the skin was cold and lifeless. Whitelock was dead, felled, it seemed, in the same fashion as Charlie Harper. The white hair, always so perfect in life, was matted and sticky with blood.

I held my breath and stood up. My stomach had begun to lurch. I wanted to get out.

As I moved cautiously backwards, a shaft of morning sunlight glanced upon something a couple of feet from the body. I peered down at the massive, square, glass ashtray that usually resided on top of Whitelock's desk. I had never handled the thing, but it probably weighed five or six pounds. The surface around the shallow basin for ashes was beaded, as if it had been made of thousands of little drops of glass. Blood had settled in the minute depressions amidst the beads on one corner of the ashtray.

The sunlight glinted off the glass again, and I observed something else. The corner opposite from where the blood had collected had been chipped, probably right where the person who used it as a weapon had held it. From what I could see, without picking up the whole thing for a closer look, a little blood was on that edge too.

Could it be the murderer's blood? Had he injured himself when he struck Whitelock down? If he had, that would provide the police with a clue. The surface of the ashtray was too uneven to yield any usable fingerprints, or so it seemed to my layman's mind.

I was recalled abruptly from my reverie by an urgent hiss from the door.

"Will you get out of there, you fool?" Rob whispered, his nostrils flaring in agitation. "The campus police are on their way, and they don't want you messing around in there!"

I wasted no time in complying. I had become so caught up in my speculations that I forgot where I was.

"Where's Consuelo?" I asked as I came through the door.

"In the office, stretched out on the couch." Rob smiled grimly. "Just about where I'd like to be myself."

"Why? Are you feeling sick?" I gave him the once-over. He did look pale, but then, so did I, probably.

"We just lost our best suspect in Charlie's murder, that's why!" he informed me, obviously irritated that I had overlooked the obvious. "And the police are going to think I'm the number-one suspect in this murder, too!"

I didn't have any chance to contradict him, to remind him that he surely had a good alibi, because the campus police arrived then. They were the same two men, I noticed, who had responded to the call when I discovered Charlie's body. They were looking at me with ill-concealed interest. Clearly, they hadn't forgotten me. This was not the time to appreciate being memorable.

I didn't give them any chance to start making observations about my knack for finding corpses. I grabbed Rob by the arm and started dragging him away. "If you need us," I informed them politely, "we'll be in the department office waiting for Lieutenant Herrera."

I heard some muttered comments but no clear command to stop, so I kept pulling Rob along with me. I tried to ignore what my memory dredged up from my conversation with Officer Williams a couple of days earlier. If the campus police weren't worried about keeping us isolated, then I wasn't going to take it upon myself to remind them of their duty.

About the time we got near the office door, Bella Gordon, her arms full of blue books, rounded the corner.

"Morning, guys," she said cheerily. "What are you two doing up here this early?"

Rob and I exchanged looks, and we each took Bella by an elbow and guided her into the office with us. Consuelo had disappeared, but all the lights were on.

Bella stopped suddenly, jerking Rob and me to a stop. "What's going on?" she demanded. "Who died?"

"Why do you think anyone died?" I countered, taken slightly aback.

She rolled her eyes. "Why else would you be trying out these strong-arm tactics on me? What's going on?" Then she actually stamped her foot.

"Somebody murdered Julian Whitelock," I told her.

The armload of blue books Bella had been carrying dropped to the floor, and she took an involuntary step backwards. She looked down at the pile on the floor, then up at me and Rob. "Geez!" was all she said as she plopped down into a nearby chair.

"Are you okay?" Rob asked, stooping to gather up the books.

I was a little concerned myself, because I had never seen Bella fazed by anything or anyone. Had she been closer to Whitelock than any of us knew? She graded for his freshman history class, hence the blue books. But normally Bella had no more good to say about him than she did about many of the other professors. Her tongue was only slightly less caustic than Charlie's had been.

"Of course I'm all right," Bella snapped, coming back to life. "Give me those!" She held out her hands to Rob. "Good grief, don't you think you'd startle *anybody* with news like that?"

While Rob muttered "sorry," I watched her.

Bella continued, arranging the blue books in a neat stack in her lap. "The old bastard and I had a knock-down, drag-out yesterday afternoon over these exams. I didn't get them finished, like he wanted, and he was royally peeved. He was already mad about something else, I could tell."

I looked at Rob and found him looking at me, our minds in tune.

"But I wasn't going to let him get away with that!" The satisfaction in Bella's voice meant she had probably given as good as she had received in that argument. "I told the old twit I'd have them here by eight o'clock this morning, and he had to like it or finish them himself."

Even Whitelock had probably known when to retreat.

"What time was that?" I asked when Bella ran out of steam.

"Oh, I'm not sure." She waved a hand vaguely. "Maybe around three o'clock.

That's when I was supposed to turn them in, all graded. I showed up a few minutes early, I guess. So, around three." She favored me with a shrewd glance. "Already trying to figure out the time of death?"

I shrugged. No need to let her know how interested I was in that information. Bella had seen Whitelock after Rob had visited him, so that should put Rob in the clear on this murder, since he had been with me the rest of the time. But I would have felt more comfortable if I did have some idea of the time of death.

"What the hell is going on here? Who let you into the office?" Azalea Westover, outraged virtue ringing through in her voice, stood in the door. All three of us turned to watch as she marched in. "Well?" She thrust her face at me. "Answer me! How did you get in here?"

"Consuelo let us in," I explained. "This is a rather unusual situation."

"What do you mean?" she demanded, her eyes narrowed in distrust. She didn't like any encroachments on her territory—especially from nonentities like graduate students.

Why did I always have to make these announcements? Wasn't finding the bodies enough? "There's been another murder," I told her, not caring about the impact of what I had to say. "Someone killed Dr. Whitelock in his office."

Shocked into stillness for a moment, Azalea then whirled to face Rob. "You son of a bitch!" she screamed. "You killed him!" Then she slapped him before any of us realized what she was doing.

The harsh *thwack* of her hand against Rob's face stirred me to action. I grabbed her arm, afraid she might try to do it again. She struggled against me, while Bella jumped up, again dumping the exams to the floor. Rob stood there, his eyes widened in shock, one hand clasped against his reddening cheek. He let Bella lead him away as I pushed Azalea none too gently toward her desk.

"I think you'd better get a grip on yourself," I told her, my teeth grinding in anger. I felt like winding some of her hair in my hand and yanking it out by the roots. There was no excuse for what she had done. No doubt, she was shocked by the murder, but her reaction seemed over-the-top.

Azalea shot me a glance, bitter with loathing. "Take your hands off me," she warned.

"Don't threaten me," I snapped, looming over her.

She shrank back in her chair.

"You'd better hope Rob doesn't file some sort of assault charge against you."

"He wouldn't dare," she said, the venom still in her voice.

Then she smirked at me, and I lost it.

"Listen to me, you bucktoothed witch," I stormed. "I don't know why the hell you think you're so high-and-mighty. Just because none of the professors in this department have the balls to stand up to you and tell you what a damned, interfering, manipulative bitch you are doesn't mean that the rest of us have to sit back and take it. If Rob decides to file some sort of charge with the university for assault, I'll back him to the hilt, and I don't give a damn about what little games you try to play to get out of it. I'd be delighted to see them fire your smarmy little ass, and they ought to. You had no excuse whatsoever to strike Rob, and I hope you're ready to face the consequences."

I was so focused on Azalea that I hadn't realized other people had come into the room and Rob and Bella were gone.

"Andy, what's going on here?"

I turned to see Maggie, with Selena Bradbury behind her, standing in the doorway of the office. From the shocked expressions on their faces, I knew they had heard most of what I had just said to Azalea.

Maggie came in. "I saw Bella and Rob in the kitchen when we passed by, and it looked like she was putting something on his face."

I glared down at Azalea. She glared right back before shoving me aside to stomp out of the room. Selena gave me a nasty look, then followed Azalea. *Good riddance to both of them*, I thought. I'd had enough of Azalea.

"What is going on here?" Maggie asked again, dropping her backpack on the worn couch. "Whatever possessed you to light into Miss High-and-Mighty like that? Don't you know you've made just about the worst enemy you could make?"

Once more into the breach, I thought, suppressing the desire to laugh. I felt so good after letting Azalea have it that I didn't care what she tried to do in reprisal. All the stress I had been under for the past two days had suddenly boiled over, and it couldn't have been directed at a more deserving person. I motioned for Maggie to sit, and I joined her on the couch. While I was in the middle of my explanation, more campus police arrived. I saw Herrera go by and knew I'd be spending more time with him, before long.

Bella and Rob returned, adding their remarks to my account of the scene with Azalea. Maggie's eyes blazed as she looked at Rob's cheek. Then she told Bella and Rob what she had heard of my tirade, and Rob grinned at me.

"The Terminator strikes again," he laughed. "I'm not the only one with a temper."

His eyes dared me to say anything back. I looked away from him.

"Good work, Andy," Bella said. "I've been meaning to tell her off for the last two years, but you beat me to the punch." She chuckled evilly. "Don't worry, guys, if she tries to turn spiteful on us, I know where the woman lives, and Bruce owes me a favor or two."

Maggie and Rob stared at her. Bella was probably just kidding, but you never knew with her.

"Where *is* Bruce, anyway?" I asked. "Why isn't he with you this morning?" As far as the rest of us could tell, Bella didn't make any step, except into the bathroom, that Bruce didn't make with her. And for all I knew, he might even go to the bathroom with her. Our dear mayor was slightly paranoid on the subject of his daughter's safety.

"Oh," Bella replied casually, "I thought I could manage to turn in some papers without being kidnapped or attacked, so I talked him into staying behind. He had something he needed to do, anyway." Whatever it was, Bella evidently found it amusing, because she grinned.

Azalea and Selena chose that moment to return. Azalea ignored us, evidently having decided not to dignify my outburst with any kind of direct response, but Selena offered an uncertain smile, which, for her, was a strong emotional statement. She started to say something, but a man in uniform stepped into the office and inquired for me.

"Come with me," he ordered and turned without even waiting to see whether I would follow.

Waving good-bye to the others, I went to the same seminar room where I'd had a chat with Herrera after finding Charlie's body. The air in the room was just as stale and sultry as it had been the first time. Herrera motioned at a chair, and I sat down. He didn't look pleased with me, and I couldn't really blame the man, given my luck lately.

"What did you do yesterday after I left your house?" was his first question.

I gave him a quick outline, being careful to stress the fact that Rob and Maggie had been with me until fairly late. Thank God that Maggie had been with us. I didn't know whether Herrera would put much stock in any alibi that Rob and I gave each other. *Maybe if I tell him we spent the night together, screwing our brains out,* I thought viciously, *he'll leave both of us alone.* I struggled to keep my face neutral.

Herrera prompted me to tell him about discovering the body, and I did so, finishing up with an account of the scene in the department office. I knew if I didn't, Bella and Azalea certainly would give him their versions of the incident, and I wanted him to have my version, although I was sure Bella's sympathies lay with Rob, after that attack. But you never could be sure *what* Bella would say or do.

"In light of what's happened this morning," Herrera told me when I finished, "I'd like to get your fingerprints today. That is, if you still have no objection."

Once again, I assured him I'd be delighted to cooperate. He instructed me where to report, then let me go. The others would now each take a turn. I hoped Rob wasn't too rattled. If he hesitated over anything, Herrera would pin him down. But, I thought, vastly relieved, he'd been with me and Maggie, so now he had to be in the clear. Whitelock's murder would be linked to Charlie's, and if Rob had an alibi for the second murder, surely Herrera would realize that he hadn't committed the first one.

Lost in thought, I rounded the corner and just about bowled over one of my favorite professors. "Dr. Logan, I'm so sorry! I wasn't watching where I was going. Are you all right?"

Fortunately for both of us, I hadn't knocked the poor man off his feet. He clutched at the steadying hand I offered and frowned into my face.

"I'm quite all right, Andy," he informed me, "though I've had a slight shock. I just heard that the Whitelock Curse struck again. And finally, it hit in exactly the right place!"

CHAPTER · 14

I STOOD THERE for a moment, staring like a goggle-eyed fish. I was so surprised by what Dr. Logan had said that I couldn't come up with anything to say in response.

Taking pity on me, he tucked his hand in my arm and towed me along in the direction of his office. We must have made an amusing sight. He was about a foot shorter than I and proportioned like a garden gnome.

He patted my hand as we moved along. "You poor boy. I'm sure if I had seen what you saw this morning, I'd be prostrate. Let me fix you a cup of tea."

This was much more like the Anthony Logan I knew, and as we approached his office, my mind began to work again. I scented a story or two in his remarks about Whitelock, and now would be an excellent time to find out what scandals he might be able to divulge.

A member of the history department for thirty-five years, Logan was like the proverbial spinster in the English village mystery. He enjoyed nothing more than having a good natter and sharing tidbits with those he liked. He and I had gotten on very well together in the year I had known him, and I knew he would be more than willing to give me anything juicy he knew about the recently deceased, whom he had disliked heartily.

With my curiosity sufficiently aroused, I followed him into his office and sat in a chair as he fussed around with his kettle. Fond of his tea, Logan kept a hot plate in his office, and he almost always had plenty of hot water and cups for any graduate students who happened to wander by. The department's distinguished Southern historian, he was an internationally recognized expert on the colonial South, and he himself was descended from one of the oldest families in Virginia. I had often thought it fitting that this charming and friendly Southern gentleman should be a student of the South, for he seemed to me to embody the best qualities of the region he loved and studied. Hospitable and helpful,

Logan was a great favorite with students, graduate and undergraduate alike. Though he and Whitelock didn't care for each other, they had always managed to get along, at least in public. Then again, I couldn't imagine Logan not getting along with anyone, but Southern manners could mask all sorts of hostility. That made me simply all the more impatient to find out what he could tell me.

I came out of my reverie as Logan handed me a cup of hot, sweet tea, with a smidgen of milk, the way I liked it.

"There, Andy," he said, settling in behind his desk, with his own steaming cup. "That should make you feel better."

"Thank you, sir. It was quite terrible this morning, but I'm doing okay, I think."

He nodded. "You're a sensible young man, and I know you're not going to shed any crocodile tears over Julian's death. You haven't known him long enough, for one thing; and besides, he wasn't the kind of man to engender benevolent feelings in anyone. You shouldn't waste any time grieving over a man who never cared in the least what other people felt."

I was more shocked by the professor's candor than by finding Whitelock's corpse. I took a moment, as I sipped at my tea, to study Logan as unobtrusively as possible. What I saw did not reassure me.

Logan was about sixty-two, and he looked every bit of that and more. Normally he was cheerful, bustling around with energy and bonhomie, but now he seemed drawn in upon himself. The sparkle in his eyes and the bloom in his cheeks had been replaced by a gray weariness.

I decided to volunteer a remark, in the hopes that I could get him going again. "You're right, sir. I never cared much for Dr. Whitelock. I regret that he died this way, but I'm certainly not going to grieve for him."

Logan smiled at me, and the smile made me uneasy.

"That's quite an epitaph for Julian," he said. "I don't know that *anyone* is going to grieve for him. He seemed to go out of his way to alienate people. Even his own family stopped bothering with him, years ago." He shook his head. "Julian treated most of those around him dishonorably, and he died in the same way. If I were a superstitious man, I really would believe in the Whitelock Curse, as I referred to it earlier. The lives of the people around him could be blighted quite easily. His relationships with his students were always fraught with emotions—mostly with his female students, I must say."

I didn't say anything, just took another sip of my tea and nodded. Logan needed no prompting, and I didn't want to interrupt his train of thought. He seemed troubled, and I supposed talking about Whitelock was his way of dealing with it.

"When Julian first came here, I had been a member of the faculty for five or six years. He was quite the dashing young professor then, and he set more than a few hearts—and hormones—fluttering." Logan paused to take a drink of tea. "Julian was very handsome, and female students by the dozen had crushes on him. His freshman history classes were always packed with young women. He fell into a trap, though, which many young professors can't resist. He let himself get involved with one of his students, a senior history major whose family took a dim view of the relationship."

The tone of Logan's voice darkened as he continued the story. Obviously he still felt strongly about what had happened, though it probably had occurred at least twenty years earlier. "The girl was twenty-one, so there was nothing the family could do legally, but the father promised her a year abroad if she'd give up Julian. I think, by that time, Julian was rather willing to be given up, though it certainly didn't help his pride when the girl decided that Europe was more attractive. She left him strictly alone until she went overseas."

There was a certain amount of satisfaction in Logan's tone, as if he had been delighted to see Whitelock come out the loser in that particular incident.

"That didn't stop Julian, though," Logan went on. "He's always had a thing for students, although he was careful to make certain that they were of age. I used to imagine that he asked to see their birth certificates first." He looked directly at me, and I couldn't suppress a somewhat embarrassed smile of complicity. "But Julian did manage to keep his nose clean, so to speak, after that. As he grew older, he grew wiser. He began to find the charms of older women more enticing, though he still couldn't quite manage to separate his work from his private life." Logan's gaze slid away from mine.

What was *that* supposed to mean? Was he hinting that Whitelock had messed around with someone in the department? Once more thinking of Azalea's reaction to Whitelock's death, I nearly choked on the tea I had just sipped. I had speculated that Azalea might have been the woman in Whitelock's sex tapes, but I hadn't seriously believed this was what Logan was hinting at.

Evidently, Logan had decided to say no more on the subject, because he went quickly on to something else. "Julian has been something of a jinx on his male students as well. Two of them have died violent deaths." He shook his head sadly. "I don't know what he had to do with either of the deaths, if anything, but the coincidences are startling, to say the least."

I ventured a remark. "I know about Charlie, sir, only too well, but what other student of Dr. Whitelock's died violently?"

Logan blinked at me. "That was poor Philip Dunbar. He was one of the best graduate students we've ever had in this program, and he would have made a fine historian, poor lad, had he lived to fulfill his promise."

The name "Dunbar" made me flash on the truth. The Dunbar Award, that macabre little statue in the graduate lounge.

Logan noticed my reaction. "I see you've made the connection with the award."

I nodded. "Yes, sir, but I'm afraid I don't really know the story."

He refilled his teacup, then continued. "About five years ago, Julian had an exceptional student named Philip Dunbar. He was a handsome and gifted young man, and he passed his qualifying exams with the highest honors. He spent several months in Paris and provincial French archives, doing research for his dissertation. He and Julian had apparently agreed, very loosely, on a topic. Julian was rather afraid of him, I think, so he didn't supervise Philip closely. Julian knew Philip needed him only for a signature on his dissertation." Logan sighed sadly. "In this case, the student had outpaced the master, and Julian was smart enough, as were the rest of us, to realize that.

"Well, Philip had completed his dissertation. I believe he had even typed it himself. This was before all of you students had word processors at home. Philip was on his way to have copies of the dissertation made for his readers when he was killed in an accident on the freeway. The car exploded and destroyed everything."

Logan fell silent, and I felt great sadness for the violent end to such promise. The story, coming on top of everything that had happened in the past two days, touched me in a way that even the deaths of Charlie and Dr. Whitelock had not.

"So someone established an award in his name," I said finally. "The money that's given each year to a graduate student for travel expenses for dissertation research." Once again, my mind unwillingly conjured up an image of that grisly little statue.

Logan must have seen the sick look on my face, but he couldn't know just what bothered me so much. I made an effort to control my emotions, and he continued.

"Yes, that's right. Philip's family gave the money to begin with, and people associated with the university more than tripled the original sum, so it grew to quite a valuable prize." He sighed. "But at such cost. We wanted to look at Philip's dissertation, since it was supposedly complete, with a view to awarding his degree posthumously and even trying to get it published, if possible. Julian was in charge, of course, since Philip had been his student. But look how we might, we couldn't find any other copy of it. Julian swore at the time that he hadn't seen any of it, other than a brief proposal. It seems so bizarre now, but Philip had either destroyed any copies he had, or else he had them with him in the car when he died. No rough drafts of the manuscript were found, only some of his note cards." Logan shook his head and looked at me, an unreadable expression in his eyes. "Even Philip's close friends, Selena Bradbury and Margaret Wilford, couldn't explain it."

The sadness of the story touched me deeply; but, although poignant, and certainly curious, in light of what had happened to Charlie Harper and Julian Whitelock, it seemed to have little to do with the murders, as far as I could tell. The only link was that statue. I found it hard to believe that all traces of Dunbar's dissertation had vanished. What if someone had found a copy? But surely it would have surfaced by now. Though the story didn't seem relevant, I supposed that Logan wanted me to know, for some reason. Maybe he just needed to talk to someone, but I had the idea there might be more to it than that.

Logan seemed to have run out of things to say, and I decided I had better be on my way and get the fingerprint business taken care of. I didn't relish the thought, but I wanted to do my duty as a good—and innocent—citizen.

"Thank you for the tea, sir." I stood up. "I feel better now. I think I needed it more than I had realized. And our discussion has been quite . . . well . . . enlightening."

Logan shot me a sharp look, but he stood up to usher me out of the office. "You're quite welcome, Andy. You should never underestimate the effects of shock." He paused, and I registered once again the tiredness in his face. "We're all terribly upset right now." He shook his head. "Such a tangled web. Well, with regard to our conversation this morning, I'm certain you'll be discreet." He looked expectantly at me, and I dutifully nodded before I left.

As the door closed behind me, I glanced around the hall. Logan's office was at the same end of the hallway as Whitelock's, and Dr. Farrar's office was between the two. I wondered if she had observed anything. Had she heard Rob's argument with Whitelock? And maybe she had heard anyone else who had talked with the man. If he had contacted his videotape partner, as we suspected he must have, he might have talked to one or more in person. Surely the police would be checking phone records. But of course, I didn't have access to phone records. Maybe, just maybe, Dr. Farrar might have noticed whoever came in and out of Whitelock's office the day before.

I decided to wait until later to ask her about it. For once, her office was dark. Besides, Herrera wouldn't be happy if he discovered I talked to her before he did.

I glanced at my watch. It was already eleven o'clock, and I was getting pre-lunch munchies. I often reacted to stress this way. Since one of my few physical gifts was a metabolism that made binge munching of little consequence, I decided to look for Maggie and Rob and persuade them to join me. I didn't have any set time to share my fingerprints with the campus police.

I walked through the halls of the fifth floor, looking and listening, but didn't catch any glimpse of them. A peek in the door of the department office earned me a dagger-sharp glare from Azalea. I grinned at her in defiance, then withdrew.

Maybe the police had finished with them and they were both on the fourth floor. I took the stairs near the grad lounge. I was right. Maggie and Rob, along with Bella and Bruce, were huddled around Maggie's carrel.

"Are you kidding?" I heard Bella hiss as I approached. "She and Whitelock were screwing each other's brains out!"

CHAPTER · 15

"SURELY NOT," Maggie protested, as I walked up. The others barely acknowledged my presence, they were so intent on what Bella had to say.

"They were," Bella asserted, looking to Bruce for confirmation.

He nodded. "We saw them not long ago. We were down in Galveston with the mayor one weekend, and we saw the two of them together at a restaurant."

"Maybe he was just taking her out for a meal," Rob offered, "to thank her for doing something extra for him." Even he didn't believe his own explanation.

Bella sniffed. "Professors who want to say thanks to secretaries take them to the Faculty Club for lunch or send them a big bouquet. They don't go all the way to Galveston on a weekend." Her scorn was sharper than necessary.

I decided I had waited long enough to find out who "she" was. "Who are you talking about, Bella?"

"Azalea Westover and Julian Whitelock, of course." She seemed surprised that I had to ask.

I glanced at Maggie, then at Rob, the three of us trying carefully to seem nonchalant. None of us wanted Bella to know how important this information could be.

"That's why she overreacted this morning when she slapped you, Rob," Bella concluded with smug satisfaction. "She thought you'd killed her lover."

That explanation made sense, and if Azalea had thought she and Whitelock were going to be the victims of blackmail at Rob's hands, her reaction signaled the depth of her unease. Perhaps it was time to have a talk with the police and give Herrera a hint where to look.

"I have to say, though," Maggie interjected, "that they seem like an awfully odd couple."

"Chacun à son goût," Bella observed, with an accent that sounded more

Urdu than French, but we all got the point. "Besides," she went on, her voice dripping with venom, "you *don't* think that dear ol' Julian contented himself with just li'l ol' Azalea, now do you?"

I had the impression that a theatrical gasp would be just what Bella wanted. Maggie obliged, with a quick wink in my direction. Bella liked to think that Maggie was slow on the uptake, and Maggie was usually willing to play along, for reasons of her own.

"Really, Bella," she whispered. "What*ever* do you mean?"

"Selena Bradbury," Bella replied, nodding her head. "I'll bet you she's logged a few hours in Julian's bed."

"Oh, come on!" Maggie said, frowning. "Did you ever see the two of them together anywhere?"

"Well, no," Bella was forced to admit, the reluctance obvious in her voice. She thought for a moment, then brightened. "But they'd act kind of strange around each other. You know, like people who are more intimate than they want anyone to know. I caught them a couple of times in ol' Julian's office, and the air was distinctly heavy between them."

Maybe Bella wasn't exaggerating, for once, and Whitelock *had* been having an affair with Selena, as well as with Azalea. I had difficulty imagining the Ice Queen in bed with anyone, let alone with someone who liked his sex kinky. Then again, I mused, maybe that was exactly what Selena liked. I could easily see her as a control freak.

A new voice broke into the discussion. "Don't you guys have something better to do than disturb the real scholars around here?" Dan Erickson had come quietly from his carrel and stood grinning. "What's all this frantic whispering about, anyway?"

"Gossip, what else?" Maggie replied, her voice cool. She and Dan had dated a few times, but then they stopped. Maggie hadn't told me why, but she had been polite and reserved with him ever since. Dan pretended not to notice anything off-putting in her manner and always treated her with friendly courtesy. Their paths didn't cross that much anymore, because Dan, in the final stages of his dissertation, spent most of his time writing, either at home or in his carrel— when he wasn't working. I wondered again about his job at a gay and lesbian bookstore. Curious, to say the least.

Bella failed to notice the coolness between the couple. Bent on spreading the dirt, she quickly filled Dan in on what we had been talking about.

"How tacky." He gave Bella a sardonic look.

Maggie, unable to help herself, grinned at Dan, then quickly extinguished the grin when he grinned back.

Taking for granted that Dan meant Whitelock, Bella said, "The man had all the self-control of Jell-O in the desert. He just couldn't keep his pants zipped. You should have seen the way he leered at some of the freshman girls in his class!"

Bella could cheerfully have sat all afternoon chattering away, but Maggie had had enough. "Well, guys," she said, "I hate to shoo you away when we're having such fun trashing somebody's reputation, but I've got to go over my paper for this afternoon."

"Oh, no," Rob cried, "I forgot you were reading your paper at the Medieval Club today!"

I had forgotten as well, but we all had sufficient cause. Anyway, with the murders of two members of the group, composed of medievalists from the various disciplines around campus, the ranks of attendees might be a little thin. Then again, maybe not—academics were no less ghoulish than the rest of the population, and where better to gather the latest dirt?

Bella stood up reluctantly. There was nothing she disliked more than a *short* session minding someone else's business. "I guess you're right," she said. "Besides, I'm ready for lunch. All the excitement this morning has made me hungry."

With another goal now in mind, she disappeared rapidly, Bruce on her heels. Next to gossip, Bella adored food more than anything else. Fortunately for her dynamite figure, she had a metabolism even more active than mine.

Maggie, Rob, Dan, and I stared after the other two, trying not to laugh. *Thank God for Bella*, I thought affectionately. Nobody else could invest the situation with quite that note of vulgar normalcy. Life must go on, and Bella would enjoy every minute of it.

"Anybody for lunch?" Dan asked.

"Might as well," Maggie replied, as Rob and I nodded.

The four of us spent a companionable hour at the cafeteria in the student center, discussing anything but the murders. Dan talked a lot about his favorite subject—the post-doc at Harvard for which he had applied. He never needed much encouragement; he couldn't see why we weren't as fascinated as he was by the topic. We also managed, eventually, to talk about Maggie's paper, which examined the role of Matilda, the queen of Henry I of England, as her husband's regent in his frequent absences from England.

Rob was skeptical about the subject of Maggie's research. "You're going to have a lot of convincing to do," he told her. "Everything I've read paints a very consistent picture of her. She gave a lot to the Church, and that was her main claim to fame. Other than belonging to the old West Saxon royal family, that is."

"I know that's the conventional view," she answered patiently—for her. "But you have to realize that the standard portrait of Matilda has been painted mostly by men, some of them incredibly misogynistic, like R. H. C. Davis. He was downright waspish in the way he talked about her. But," Maggie said with a feline smile, "if you actually look at the sources themselves—say, the chronicle of Abingdon abbey, or documents in the *Regesta Regum Anglonormanorum*—you find something different."

Turned slightly away from Maggie, Rob winked and said, "If you say so. Though I'm going to take more than a bit of convincing."

I should have warned her that Rob could be a terrible tease when he liked someone. Obviously he was feeling more and more comfortable with her, or he wouldn't string her along in such a way.

Maggie seemed to catch on, though. "I'm not worried," she said, sure of her research. "Just you wait and see!"

After lunch, Maggie and Dan returned to the library, while Rob and I made the trek to the campus police office. Lieutenant Herrera needed Rob's fingerprints as well, so we went off together to do our duty. We assured Maggie that we would do our best to be finished in time for her paper.

Half an hour later, our fingerprints taken, Rob and I were leaving, when Lieutenant Herrera stuck his head in the room and asked us to come into his office. He waved us into two chairs in front of his paper-strewn desk, and we sat down. For a long moment, he didn't speak. I was tempted to say something—anything—to break the unnerving silence, but I kept quiet, as did Rob.

"You two have been pretty busy," Herrera finally said, his tone sarcastic. "Stumbling over dead bodies, finding mysterious videotapes, and so on."

Rob and I stared mutely at him. What did he expect us to say?

"When someone is as involved in a case as you two seem to be, that makes me suspicious. Why do you keep turning up every time there's trouble?" he mused.

"Bad luck?" I said, the words slipping out in spite of my best intentions.

Herrera stared at me. "I would have thought so, because I couldn't figure a good motive for either of you to kill Charlie Harper or Professor Whitelock." He reached into his desk and drew out a thick set of papers, stapled in one corner. "Take a look at this," he ordered. "Don't worry, it's a photocopy, not the original."

Hesitantly, I took the document from his hands. Rob and I had just put our heads together to examine them, when suddenly I felt Rob's body go taut. So did mine.

Herrera had just handed us a copy of Charlie's will.

CHAPTER · 16

STUNNED, Rob and I stared at each other, not saying anything. If Charlie's will contained what his letter to Rob had hinted at, then the shit had hit the fan.

"Where did you get this?" I finally managed to ask Herrera, my voice thin and strained.

"Anonymously," he replied. "It popped up in my interoffice mail this morning. Aren't you going to read it?" He gestured at the papers I was still clutching. "Or do you already know what the will says?"

Rob and I shook our heads.

"No, I don't know," Rob said, his voice firm and controlled. "I've never seen it before." He pulled the papers out of my hand and shoved them back on the desk. "How the hell should I know what's in Charlie's will?"

Herrera laughed. "According to our anonymous benefactor, Harper's will was in his desk, where anyone could have found it. And obviously someone did, or it wouldn't have been sent it to me."

"Doesn't that make you suspicious, Lieutenant?" I asked indignantly. "It looks like someone is trying to point the blame away from himself or herself and at Rob instead."

"Why do you assume the will points a finger at Mr. Hayward?" Herrera riposted smoothly.

I sat there, my mouth gaping open.

Rob stepped in, his voice steely. "Andy makes a logical assumption. You wouldn't be interrogating us if that will didn't contain something to to do with us."

Herrera nodded. "According to this will, Harper left the bulk of his estate to you, Mr. Hayward. You're the chief beneficiary of several million dollars in trusts and real estate holdings."

Rob went very still in his chair, and I struggled for a deep breath.

"That is," Herrera continued, "if you're not convicted of murder."

"I didn't kill Charlie," Rob said flatly, "and I didn't kill Julian Whitelock. I knew nothing about this will, I swear to you. I didn't have any reason to murder anyone."

In a conversational tone, Herrera went on, "I see the case like this: You, Mr. Hayward, lived with Harper for a while, all comfy and happy. But next door to you was an old friend, another gay man. Something happened, and you rekindled your relationship, and the two of you, knowing that Harper was going to leave all his money to you, decided to get him out of the way. In order to divert suspicion from yourselves, you came up with these videotapes and other false leads to encourage me to look elsewhere. But all the time, you two plotted the whole thing."

Stunned, Rob and I just sat there, staring at him. Herrera was nuts, I thought. He surely couldn't think Rob and I were so devious and twisted.

But as my breathing returned to normal and my thoughts settled down, I could see that the situation made a mad sort of sense. Given the evidence at hand, Herrera, by twisting everything around slightly, made Rob and me look attractive as the murderers.

"If someone were to take that interpretation seriously," I said—and my tone of voice made that doubtful, "he would also have to prove that either Rob or I knew the contents of Charlie's will. Since we didn't know what the will contained, we certainly would have had no motive to kill him."

Herrera nodded. "As you say, I'd have to prove that you knew about the will. That might be tough. Just as tough as you proving that you *didn't* know about it."

He had me there.

"Well, gentlemen," Herrera stood up. "Thanks for dropping by. I'll be in touch when I have further questions for you. And, by the way, don't leave town." He smiled wolfishly as he offered this last bit of instruction.

Rob and I stumbled out of his office. As we walked across campus toward the library, I asked him the questions running through my mind: What kind of game was Herrera playing? Why, if he was convinced of his own little scenario, would he stop the interrogation and just let us leave? And why did he question us together, rather than separately? Was he simply trying to upset us?

"Maybe he doesn't really believe all that about the will," Rob said, as we approached the front doors of the library. "Maybe he's trying to warn us that someone wants to implicate us in the murder."

"Maybe," I said doubtfully.

Rob stopped in the shelter of the library's cloistered walkway and looked at me intently. "You and I had better try to save our own asses. Whatever he's after, we have to do what we can to figure this thing out. I don't want to be arrested, and neither do you."

I nodded emphatically. "I'm with you on that."

He smiled. "Good. But now, of course, I've got work to do before we go hear Maggie's paper. I hope I'll be able to concentrate."

I followed him inside, and we parted ways on the fourth floor. It was only two o'clock. That little interlude with Herrera had seemed to last forever, but we'd been in his office less than thirty minutes. The Medieval Club gathering wasn't until four, but, too restless to work in my carrel, I trotted up to the fifth floor to see what was going on.

Lindy and Thelma were busy typing in the department office, but Azalea wasn't in, and I wasn't unhappy about that. Facing her from now on was going to be difficult, and not just because of what had happened between us a few hours earlier. I wasn't sorry about blasting her, but I had to figure out a way to get through the days until the murder investigation was complete. In the meantime, she had been tainted forever in my mind by my suspicions.

As I stood irresolutely just inside the doorway of the office, Selena came in with Wilda Franken, one of the junior professors in the department. In her vivid clothing, Wilda—as she insisted everyone call her, abhorring academic titles as pretentious—presented quite a contrast to Selena, though both had blonde hair and a compact, athletic figure. Maggie swore that Wilda got her fashion tips from music videos on MTV, and I couldn't argue with that. The colors she wore made my head ache.

Her clothing made Wilda stand out in person, and the courses she taught made her stand out in the college catalog. Every year the history department fielded countless questions about the courses with titles like "The Politics of Menstruation in Preindustrial Societies" and "The Symbology of Female Castration in the Western Historical Tradition." The department's resident Marxist and radical feminist historian, Wilda thrived on being the center of attention, usually controversial. But her courses were popular with the undergraduates, and her scholarship was generally considered impeccable by her peers—the three or four people in the scholarly world, that is, who actually understood what she was talking about. And cared.

Wilda and I had had one tense encounter, my first week on campus, when I mistakenly opened the door to the library for her. I had to endure a ten-minute lecture on the insult I had offered her. When she finally ran out of breath, I told her—with remarkable calm, I thought—that only an idiot would mistake common courtesy for chauvinistic behavior and that I would have opened the door whether she had been male, female, eunuch, or gerbil, simply because I had reached it ahead of her. If she had reached it ahead of me, I continued, then I fully expected her to hold it open for me. Even Miss Manners would approve my calm response in the face of such provocation.

Since then, Wilda had always been friendly to me—maybe I was the only man who had ever said anything to her after one of her little lectures. Even so, I didn't take any pains to seek the woman out. With her, feminism was more a weapon than anything else. She didn't mind "exploiting" Lindy and Thelma; if only she could hear the way the two of them talked about her last-minute demands for typing and copying tests with never a thank-you!

At the moment, Wilda looked more upset than I had ever seen her, and Selena had a hand on her arm in a gesture of comfort. They were oblivious to Lindy, Thelma, and me, and I suppressed the urgings of my finer nature and stayed to listen.

"I'm sorry you had to hear it this way," Selena told her. "I had no idea you knew Julian so well."

Wilda wiped a stray tear from her cheek. "Well, only recently were we able to get past those unfortunate incidents that clouded our early relationship. Lately I discovered that Julian wasn't quite the unregenerate sexist I thought, and I was enjoying the revelation."

Belatedly, the two realized they weren't alone, and Selena hurried Wilda out of the room. Thelma and Lindy grinned, and I flashed a smile and disappeared before they could say anything.

I decided to check out the periodicals room, so I headed downstairs to the first floor. While mindlessly thumbing through a recent issue of the *English Historical Review,* I thought about Wilda and the scene I had just witnessed. Surely she couldn't be one of Julian's women? I had easily subscribed to the idea that there was more than one woman on those tapes. Until Herrera decided to tell us about them—if he paid any attention to the tapes at all—there was no way to know for sure. After our little session with him, I was growing more nervous about the direction of the lieutenant's investigation.

I whiled away the time, thumbing through journals and speculating, with little result, on the two murders. The number of suspects seemed to be growing, and it was looking more hopeless all the time that we could actually solve the killings. But we had to, now that Charlie's will had surfaced.

At ten minutes before four, I trotted upstairs to the room on the second floor where the Medieval Club held its gatherings. Rob and I sat together at the front to give Maggie encouragement, but once she got started, she needed little.

Her paper spoke for itself, with a clearly reasoned, succinctly stated presentation of evidence and conclusions. She took a number of questions when she finished, and we didn't get out until after five-thirty. Rob was too preoccupied to tease Maggie with questions, and she glanced his way more than once, expecting him to say something.

Ruth McClain had waited to say a few words to her before leaving. Then Dan Erickson congratulated Maggie, and she thanked him with more warmth than usual. Flushed with success, she was happy with everyone right then. Dan made a remark about getting back to work, but he stopped to talk to Bella and Bruce, who were among those still milling around outside the meeting room.

"May Rob and I treat you to dinner?" I asked Maggie. "You've earned it with that paper."

She grinned. "Sounds good to me. Let's go. And then maybe you can explain why you didn't challenge me on anything!"

Rob smiled. "How about I was just too dazzled by your evidence and your presentation?"

Maggie caught something in his tone. "I'd like to think so, but there's more to it than that, I suspect."

"We'll fill you in later," I promised her.

Waving to the others, the three of us went down the stairs to the main door of the library. Outside, the air was heavy, as usual. The humidity curled into every opening it could find in my clothes, and it wasn't long before my shirt clung damply to my body. The late evening sunlight bathed the campus in a mellow light, and the architecture looked its loveliest. For a moment, I imagined that I was walking around Oxford or Cambridge. I returned to the present with regret.

Maggie wanted to go home and change out of the clothes she had worn to present her paper, and we agreed to meet an hour later at her favorite Italian restaurant in the Village. Rob and I didn't have to change, so we wasted time at a record store about a block from the restaurant, looking at all the CDs we couldn't afford, until time to meet Maggie. Resolutely we avoided the subject of Charlie's will while we ate. When all this was settled, Rob would be able to afford all the CDs he wanted.

We had a great time that night. Rob and I were both still keyed up over the interview with Herrera, and even Maggie, with her relentlessly logical mind, couldn't come up with a convincing or reassuring explanation for it. As a consequence, we got a little too merry over our wine, and I decided, around nine o'clock, I should have some coffee if I was going to drive home. Maggie insisted she was fine, and we let her drive off by herself.

Rob was a little squiffy, though, and didn't say much on the short ride home. He was singing something under his breath as we walked to the front door. Once inside, he headed for the couch in the living room and flopped down. He patted the space beside him, but I shook my head. I was sober enough not to let the two of us get entangled in a situation we both might later regret. Besides, I was in a hurry from all that coffee.

I didn't pay much attention as I went upstairs and through my bedroom to the bathroom. When I came out, though, I realized something wasn't right. I couldn't figure out what was wrong. Then it hit me. I had a TV set and VCR, Christmas presents from my cousin Ernestine, in my bedroom. I kept my tapes—I didn't have that many—on a small shelf beside the television. I noticed there were several gaps where tapes should have been. Usually the shelf was full, with no room for any additional tapes.

Someone had been in my bedroom and stolen several of my videotapes.

CHAPTER · 17

IN DISBELIEF, I moved over to the shelf and bent down to examine it. From my hasty inventory, I figured that four tapes were missing. Two of them, thank goodness, were spares that I used to tape occasional programs from TV, so there wasn't much I'd miss. The other two, however, contained old screwball comedies I'd taped off cable, and who knew when they'd run again. That irritated me almost as much as the fact that someone had broken into my home.

My blood pressure rising, I went downstairs to tell Rob. He was snoring contentedly on the couch, and I hated to wake him up. But if someone had broken in, the perpetrator might have tried next door as well, although Rob and Charlie had a burglar alarm. Larry and I didn't, because we literally had very little worth stealing, except for my TV and VCR. Since we both kept such irregular hours and were often home, we hadn't felt it necessary.

I prodded Rob, and he stirred. One eye popped open, then focused, and gradually he came awake. "What's wrong?" He sat up, alarmed by the grim look on my face.

"Someone broke in while we were gone today and took four videotapes from my collection upstairs."

Rob rubbed a hand wearily across his face. "Damn! I'm sorry, Andy. I wonder why they broke in over here?"

I shrugged. "Just covering both bases, I guess. Whoever it was had no way of knowing that you'd already turned the tapes over to the police."

Rob swore again.

"What's wrong?" I asked.

He looked at me, embarrassed. "You know, I think I forgot to set my alarm the last time I was over there." He got to his feet, not very eager to go check.

"I guess we'd better find out, though, before we call the cops," I responded, following him to the door. "Then we can come back and figure out how they got in here."

Rob unlocked his front door and flipped on the hallway light. Checking the keypad inside the door of the living room, he groaned. "I can't believe I forgot to set it. You'd think I would've learned my lesson after the other night when someone tried to brain me."

I didn't say anything, just followed him through the apartment, checking behind him as we went. I stifled a few pangs of envy as we progressed, because Charlie had furnished the place in the way that only someone with a comfortable bank account could do. There was nothing flashy or ostentatious, but the furniture had that simple look that meant good quality and, more than likely, a healthy price tag as well.

Rob skimmed over the videotapes in Charlie's collection. "Looks like a few are missing besides the ones I gave the police." He laughed. "Whoever got them is going to have a revolting little surprise."

We made a rapid survey through the rest of the place, then returned downstairs. As far as Rob could determine, nothing else was missing. The intruder hadn't even bothered any of Charlie's expensive electronic equipment.

"Our visitor," I announced grimly, "wasn't too worried about making this look like a burglary. I would've thought he or she'd at least take something expensive, or trash the place, so maybe we wouldn't realize the tapes were missing."

"You're right," Rob replied. "That is odd."

"Maybe whoever stole the videotapes thinks we won't go to the police, because they also think that you were planning to try blackmail. Or maybe Herrera will think we've staged this to divert suspicion away from ourselves."

"Well," Rob said grimly, "someone's going to find out just how wrong he or she is. And Herrera can think whatever he likes. We'll figure this out, one way or the other, in spite of him." He reached for the phone and called 911.

While waiting for the police, Rob and I returned to my half of the duplex and discovered that the intruder had sneaked into my place through the sliding glass door, which led from the kitchen onto the patio out back. The intruder had entered Rob's place the same way. Fifteen minutes later, two uniformed cops showed up to investigate.

The officers, a man and a woman, listened with little interest to our recital of the facts, but their ears perked up when Rob reminded them that this was related to a homicide case being investigated at Rice. Other than making a few pointed remarks about security and promising to share information with the campus police, the two HPD cops did nothing. There probably wasn't much they actually could have done, but Rob and I were relieved when they finally left.

By that time, it was ten-thirty, and we were both too tired to talk anymore, so we headed off to bed. I still hadn't told Rob about the strange scene I had observed in the history department office with Wilda. I was curious to see whether he'd interpret her behavior and remarks in the same way. But as I brushed my teeth, I decided that could wait until morning. We had worried enough for one day.

That night I was so tired, not even dreams of Bracton's notebook disturbed my sleep. When I woke up about eight o'clock the next morning, I felt refreshed and ready to tackle almost anything.

By the time I made it downstairs, remembering to dress completely first, Rob was in the kitchen, making breakfast. A guy could get spoiled by such attention, I thought, especially since Rob was a much better cook than I. If I didn't watch it, though, I could slip into this too easily, and that might be dangerous in the long run.

But the old saying about the way to a man's heart being through his stomach had some validity after all. Rob's fluffy bacon-and-cheese omelets and crunchy, buttery toast put me in a good mood.

"Where did you learn to cook this well?" I asked, munching contentedly on my fourth piece of toast.

He regarded me with a smile over his coffee cup. "It's really not that hard, Andy, I promise you." He took a sip of coffee. "As for where I learned, I didn't have much choice. Once I was out on my own, I couldn't afford to eat out all the time, and I got tired of frozen dinners real fast."

I rubbed my stomach. "I guess I haven't gotten to that stage yet. I can scramble eggs and cook a pretty good hamburger, and, well, I do make good instant mashed potatoes, but that's about the limit of my culinary skills."

"There are a few things I could teach you—simple, easy recipes—and they're not that expensive either," Rob assured me.

"We'll see," I said. This was feeling too easy, too cozy, all too soon. I'd be glad when the whole situation was resolved and Rob could go back next door. He was too disturbing a presence to have around.

To get away from domestic issues, I told him about Wilda and Selena in the history department office.

His mouth full of omelet, Rob goggled at me. He swallowed before he said, "So you think the Cyndi Lauper of the historical profession may have been one of Julian's women?"

I crunched on the toast before I answered. "I know it sounds preposterous, especially when you think about how politically different they were. But that remark she made about 'enjoying the revelation' sure sounded weird to me." I shrugged. "Maybe they weren't beating each other with whips, but do you honestly believe Julian Whitelock had thrown away fifty-odd years as a confirmed male chauvinist pig just because Wilda's rhetoric was so powerful?"

Rob laughed. "No, and I certainly wouldn't put it past him to con her with some sort of reformed sexist routine, just to see if he could get her into bed. People like her can be so willfully stupid about some things. He would've had her electric skirt up over her head before she knew what was going on."

I laughed too. "And, despite the weird clothes and jewelry she wears, she *is* attractive—just his type, I'll bet."

Rob made a face at me. "I'll take your word for it."

I laughed again. "She's not my type either."

"I hope not," he replied, giving me a sly look.

My heart beat a little faster. Damn it, after all this time, he shouldn't be so attractive to me. Over the years, I had tried everything I could think of to erase his image from my memory, and nothing had ever worked. And here he was, sitting across the breakfast table from me, my fantasy made flesh. My head kept telling me "No," while my heart—or was it my hormones?—kept shouting a defiant "Yes!"

I had to get away from him. "Just for that," I said, standing up and dropping my napkin on the table, "I won't tell you how much I enjoyed breakfast."

"Right," he said with a knowing grin. He, too, stood up and began clearing away the dishes, but I stopped him.

"You cooked," I said, "so the least I can do is clean up. Why don't you go get the newspaper, and I'll join you in the living room when the kitchen is clean."

"Sure," Rob said, frowning a little.

I sighed as I piled everything into the dishwasher. What was I going to do? He was patient, like a faithful dog with an ill-tempered master. I thought I was managing pretty well, being friendly and supportive, standing by him in a difficult time. I thought he appreciated that, but I got almost constant messages that he wanted something more overt.

But maybe it was my imagination working overtime. Maybe I was projecting my mixed-up feelings and had both of us confused. Once I had let go of the anger I'd held inside for so long, I felt strangely bereft. The bitter feelings had insulated me, for a long time, from having to care deeply about anyone else, even Jake, with whom I had spent three years a while back. Now that the anger against Rob was gone, I wasn't quite sure what I felt for him.

Lust, certainly. He was as physically attractive to me as he ever had been. But I wasn't interested in a casual affair, just for the sake of sex. I had to admit to curiosity about what it would be like to be with Rob, to make love to him, to fulfill that long-ago, abortive attempt. And maybe that's all he wanted.

I slammed shut the door of the dishwasher. I didn't know what I wanted, and I didn't know what Rob wanted. And I didn't really want to ask him right now. I didn't want to make a fool of myself all over again.

In the living room, he was sprawled out on the couch, reading the newspaper. I plopped down in my chair and picked up a section of the paper from the floor.

"What should be on the agenda for today?" I asked as I glanced through the comics.

Rob lowered the paper to his chest and twisted his head to look sideways at me. "I don't know what we can do, except just sit here and go over everything ad nauseam. My head hurts just thinking about yesterday and trying to come up with something to get Herrera off our tails for good." He sighed deeply. "Or we could be productive and get on with our reading. I don't think the history department is going to consider playing Frank and Joe Hardy a sufficient excuse for not getting our work done. I know I've got piles and piles to sort through before my next session with Ruth McClain. What about you?"

"Same here," I assured him. "Not that I'm in the mood for it, though. I guess I could catch up on a few other things, like letters. I need to write to cousin Ernestine, but I've been putting it off because my typewriter is acting up. Maybe one of these days I can afford a computer."

"You can use Charlie's," Rob offered, then realized what he'd said. He continued, his voice flat, "Mine, I guess I should say now. It's not that difficult. I can show you enough of the word-processing program to get you through a couple of letters."

"Okay," I said, a little reluctantly. I wasn't afraid of using the computer, I just felt weird using Charlie's computer.

"The computer!" he yelled. "How could I have been so stupid?" He was rocking back and forth on the couch, shaking his head.

"What are you talking about?" I asked.

Rob got up. "I can't believe how stupid I've been."

He headed outside, and I was right behind him. He unlocked his front door and turned off the alarm.

"What on earth is going on?" I asked as I followed him upstairs.

He went into Charlie's bedroom, sat down at the computer, and flipped it on. "Andy," he said, as we waited for it to boot up, "you won't believe this, but I forgot all about something." Sensing my impatience, he hurried on. "Charlie used to spend a lot of time at the computer, even when he didn't have any papers due. He had some games he liked to play. Plus, he never said for sure, but I think he was keeping a journal."

"And there could be something in his journal which would give us a clue as to who Julian Whitelock was involved with." I finished his train of thought.

"Exactly," Rob replied. Then he started playing with the keyboard.

I had a little experience with computers and word processing, thanks to the university's computer center, where students could use hardware and software for free, but Rob was obviously more experienced with this thing than I was.

"There!" he said, pointing to the screen.

In the midst of a list of files on the computer's hard disk was PRIVE, followed by DIR in brackets.

"What's that supposed to mean?" I asked.

"It's a subdirectory," Rob replied, playing with the keyboard once more. "That means there are files grouped together under that directory, and when we bring up a directory of the subdirectory, we may see what we want."

The directory of the PRIVE—French for *private?*—subdirectory revealed lists of numbers which looked, after I thought about it for moment, like dates. There were about twenty-five files. If the numbers did indicate dates, I calculated that the files stretched back about six weeks before Charlie's death.

Rob turned on the printer, then printed the list of files from the screen. As I watched, he opened up the word processing application. Next he retrieved the text of one of the files, the first one on the list.

When the text of the document appeared on the screen, Rob and I said, "Damn!" at the same time. There was a meaningless jumble of letters on the screen.

"If Charlie wrote this, he must have done it in code," I said.

"You're probably right." Rob called up a second file, which looked just like the first. "Charlie loved word games and puzzles, so he probably had a blast doing this." He indicated the screen. "And it makes me all the more certain that this is what we're looking for."

At that moment we were both startled by a loud "Yoo-hoo!" coming from downstairs. "Anybody home over here?" the voice called out.

"Bella!" Rob and I said the name together. What was she doing here at nine o'clock on a Saturday morning?

CHAPTER · 18

WHEN I CAME DOWN into the hall, Bella and Bruce were standing inside Rob's front door, looking expectantly up at me.

"Morning, Andy!" Bella said cheerily. "What are you up to?"

Wanting to know what the hell you're doing here so early on a Saturday morning, I should have said. Instead I said, "Oh, Rob was just going to show me how to use his word processor so I could write some overdue letters."

Both of them laughed, as Rob came down the stairs behind me.

"Sorry to interrupt all the excitement!" Bella found this all terribly amusing, I could see. "Come on, now, Andy, surely you and Rob could have thought of *something* more interesting to do upstairs than write letters!"

"It's not for lack of trying on my part," Rob said, laughing.

I blushed furiously, which made me angry with myself, but when I got Rob alone again, I'd tell *him* how the cow ate the cabbage, as my cousin Ernestine would say.

"If y'all came by for a *visit*," I said through clenched teeth, "why don't we go over to my place? I think there may be some Diet Cokes in the fridge."

"Sure," Bella said, suspiciously amenable, and she and Bruce followed me out while Rob set the alarm and locked the door.

I got the two of them settled on the couch with Diet Cokes. I didn't offer Rob anything. "What brings you over here on such a beautiful day? You look like you're headed for the beach at Galveston."

Both were dressed in tank tops and shorts, but while Bruce's were the Target variety, Bella's togs screamed Neiman Marcus. Her days spent modeling had given her expensive taste in clothes.

"Who wants to go to Galveston?" she asked scornfully. "There are too many people on the beach for me to enjoy myself anymore." She sat back and crossed her shapely bronze legs. "Besides, our pool is more than adequate for tanning purposes."

She probably didn't mean that the way it sounded, but with Bella, one never knew.

Bruce looked uncomfortable, as always, when Bella's lack of tact made itself felt. "It's just a lot more convenient," he said apologetically, "even if it isn't very scenic. Trying to get down the Gulf Freeway on a day like today would be well-nigh impossible."

I smiled at his turn of phrase. Sometimes he sounded like one of the nineteenth-century novels he was fond of reading while Bella worked in the library.

What are Bella and Bruce doing here? I asked myself yet again. I knew Bella's bump of curiosity was an Everest to my molehill, but this Saturday morning visit was a bit much.

"Mind if I use your bathroom?" Bruce interrupted my thoughts.

"No, of course not," I said. "It's upstairs and through the bedroom."

"Right," he said and moved toward the stairs.

The previous owner of the duplex, in his infinite wisdom, had done away with the downstairs half bath and turned it into a big storage closet, so our infrequent guests had to trot upstairs, like Larry and I did.

But then, I remembered with sudden clarity, Bruce and Bella knew that. They'd been here before. I looked over at Bella, demurely sipping her Diet Coke, and suddenly realized that they must have planned this. I was willing to bet that Bruce was now upstairs looking at my videotapes.

The question, of course, was why? Why were Bruce and Bella interested in the videotapes? Bella's only connection with Whitelock was through serving as grader in his survey course. Or was it? I watched her as she and Rob chatted about restaurants in Galveston.

At least we could exonerate them from having broken into both apartments before, as far as I could see. If Bruce was boldly upstairs at the moment, going through my tapes, that meant he, or they, hadn't sneaked into my place the day before. But it didn't get him off the hook for the earlier break-in at Rob's.

Bruce came back into the room a couple of minutes later. He picked up his Diet Coke and smiled his thanks smoothly in my direction.

Bella, believe it or not, had run out of favorite Galveston eateries to recommend, and no one offered a new topic of conversation. The silence lengthened as Bella and Bruce slowly consumed their drinks.

I was determined not to be the one to speak first, and I silently willed Rob to remain quiet also. I wanted to know why Bella and Bruce had come. They had never dropped by casually before, either alone or together. Was it simply Bella's curiosity, or was there a more sinister purpose? I was still certain Bruce had been looking through my videotapes, although he appeared innocent as he gazed at me.

Finally Bella couldn't stand the silence any longer. "Well, Andy," she began, "have you heard anything more about Whitelock's murder? The items in the paper and on the evening news have been so brief, they don't really tell you anything." She looked expectantly at me as she set her drink on a coaster.

I repressed a smile as I answered. "Why should I know more than what you've read in the papers or seen on TV, Bella? Do you think the campus police have taken me or Rob into their confidence?" I settled back into my chair.

She looked uncomfortable, a distinct phenomenon as far as I was concerned, since the woman's sangfroid was well-nigh—to use Bruce's phrase—unshakable. I watched her struggle to frame a diplomatic reply.

She wasn't the mayor's daughter for nothing. "Well," Bella rejoined, "I remember your saying how much you love reading murder mysteries, so I thought you'd probably be following this one. Besides, that detective seemed pretty interested in both you and Rob yesterday." She shrugged. "If it had been me, I certainly would have asked *him* a few questions."

I had to laugh. "I wish you luck asking Lieutenant Herrera questions. Believe me, he tells you only what he wants you to know." I smiled primly. "Not that I've been asking him questions, mind you. As much as I enjoy reading *fictional* murder mysteries, I can't say I like being mixed up in the real thing."

Bruce started to say something—probably apologetic, I thought—but Bella cut him off. "Don't get your knickers in a knot," she admonished. "I was just curious. I wasn't accusing you of anything." She frowned crossly.

Rob tried to relieve the tension. "Both Andy and I—for different reasons—can't help but be right in the middle of this whole thing, Bella, so it's only natural the police spend a lot of time talking to us." He laughed, but there was no amusement in the sound. "Hell, I'm their favorite suspect—of course they talk to me."

Bruce leaned forward to look intently at Rob. "Are you still a suspect? I mean, with the second murder, surely they can't think you had any reason to kill Whitelock?" He looked uncomfortable as he continued. "Everyone heard about your argument with him, but if everyone who had argued with that guy was a murder suspect, the police would have to investigate practically the whole campus." He shot a thumb in Bella's direction. "Even Bella argued with him that afternoon."

That contribution earned him a sour look from Bella.

Rob laughed, in genuine amusement this time. "Thanks for the vote of confidence, but the campus police certainly haven't told me that I'm no longer a suspect. We don't know yet whether they think there are two murderers or one. If there's only one, then I think I'm in the clear, because it seems possible Whitelock was killed when I was here with Andy and Maggie." He neglected to mention that Herrera had been here during part of that time.

Bella grinned smugly. "So you *do* know a little bit more than we do," she said smoothly. She rubbed the tip of one elegantly manicured fingernail around the rim of her Diet Coke can. "The papers and the newscasts haven't said a word about the time of death, as far as I can remember." She looked at me.

I returned the stare evenly and replied, "We don't know the time of death ourselves, Bella, but Maggie, Rob, and I were together most of that afternoon and evening. And that certainly should cover the times when Whitelock was probably murdered." I smiled grimly at her. "So, you see, we *don't* know any more than you do."

Frustrated, Bella's mind went off on another tack. She shook her head. "You know, Whitelock could be a royal bastard when he wanted, but that doesn't explain why someone murdered him—or Charlie either."

"I imagine," Bruce said, "that the police are searching for some sort of connection between Charlie and Whitelock—beyond the obvious one, of course." He looked at me in puzzlement. "But how does it all add up to murder?"

I shrugged, although by now, I was virtually certain both Bella and her tame hunk could probably answer that question if they didn't have to maintain facades of innocence. Although I was now suspicious of them both, I just couldn't picture Bella having an affair with Whitelock. Of course, if she had, and her bodyguard had found out about it, he could have killed both Charlie and Whitelock in anger, the former for his blackmail threats and the latter simply because of his affair with the woman I was convinced Bruce loved. If he didn't love her, surely he could have found another job by now. As stingy as the mayor was, Bruce couldn't be earning that cushy a living. Only love, I was willing to bet, made Bruce put up with her.

Bella still played with the rim of her can, running her finger round and round. With her eyes centered on her moving finger, she commented, "There is one *good* motive, I guess, in Whitelock's case."

Content that she had our close attention, she continued, after a quick glance in my direction. "You know—what we talked about yesterday. The guy simply couldn't keep his pants zipped whenever he saw a woman he wanted. You wouldn't believe some of the outrageous comments he would make in class to pretty undergraduates."

She looked at each of us in turn, as if expecting one of us to contradict her or to utter some form of protest. When no response came, she smiled wickedly and continued, "But I think he had the sense to confine his attentions to consenting adults, most of the time."

Rob shook his head. "So he was having an affair—or was it more than just Azalea, like you were telling us yesterday? From the way you talk, it sounds as if you were keeping a scorecard." There was a challenge in his tone, one Bella couldn't resist. Baiting Bella was generally a sure bet.

"Not really," she retorted, "but I couldn't help overhearing things when I was in his office. He wasn't always discreet. I suppose he thought of me the same way some people think of servants—I was simply beneath his notice most of the time." She grinned, reminding me of a cat about to pounce on a sluggish mouse. "It wasn't only secretaries or graduate students he fooled around with," Bella stated smugly.

She was bursting to tell what she knew, but neither Rob nor I would give her the satisfaction of asking. Bruce looked as if a dog had peed on his foot.

Seeing that no one was going to ask what she meant, Bella sulkily continued, "One member of the history department managed to overcome her political differences with him lately." She giggled.

Wilda! I was suddenly excited, but I didn't want Bella to realize the depth of my interest. "Oh, really," I said, "and who might that be?"

"Give me a break, Andy!" she said scornfully. "You can't be *that* dense. Darling Dr. Wilda Franken, of course."

"How do *you* know?" Rob asked, putting emphasis on the word *you*. That was always the best tactic with Bella.

"Like I said, I overheard a few things in his office. Besides, Bruce and I saw them coming out of a restaurant here in Montrose one night during the summer." She laughed. "They were holding hands—it was *so sweet*. They didn't see us."

"How do you work an alleged affair with Wilda into a motive for Whitelock's murder?" I inquired.

Bella laughed. "Well, you know how those Marxist feminists are, once you get them all riled up. The minute Wilda figured out ol' Julian was cheating on her, she would've been ready to whack him over the head. That woman's got a temper like you wouldn't believe."

If anyone should know, it was Bella, who had taken several of Wilda's courses. I imagined that Bella, as dearly as she loved the art of professor-baiting, had had an occasional argument with the volatile Wilda.

I refrained from pointing out that a hot temper and a broken heart over

Whitelock's infidelities were not motives for killing Charlie. The two murders had to be linked, and Bella was either ignoring the connection entirely, or she thought I was dumb enough to let her pull the wool over my horn-rims. Besides trying to get at those videotapes, she and Bruce might have come here to spread the compost around a little and get it out of her backyard. Otherwise, why was she being so chatty all of a sudden?

"So both Wilda and Azalea were involved with Whitelock?" Rob asked. "Plus I think you mentioned Selena. Anybody else?"

Bella smirked. "I wouldn't put it past that Margaret Wilford. I don't know much, but there's something peculiar about her that I haven't quite figured out." She frowned in irritation. "But she certainly seemed like ol' Julian's type."

"Oh, and what type was that?" I asked, prepared for some off-the-wall answer.

"Blondes with short hair and good figures," she replied, surprised that I hadn't unraveled it for myself.

Amazed, I looked at Rob. Damned if Bella wasn't right. Every woman in the case—Azalea, Wilda, Margaret, Selena, and even Bella herself—was a blonde.

"Somebody'll get it all sorted out soon, I bet." Bella stood up. "I guess we'd better be going, Andy. There's a party tonight for my dad, and it's a command performance." She patted Rob's arm rather vaguely as she moved past him in the general direction of the front door. Now that she'd done what she had come to do, she seemed ready to move on.

"Thank you for the drink," Bruce said; Bella echoed him as an afterthought.

I closed the front door gratefully behind them.

Rob had followed me, and he laughed as I gave the deadbolt a dramatic twist. "I know just how you feel."

I shook my head. "What do you think she was after?" I moved away from the door and toward the living room.

"I'm not sure," he responded, "but I wouldn't be surprised if Bruce had a look at your videotapes while he was up in your room."

"We're both getting suspicious in our old age," I told him. "That's exactly what I thought too. Hold on while I go up and take a look."

I was back in two minutes. "It's hard to tell, but it looks like he might have pulled a few out to look at. He didn't take any, though."

I reiterated aloud my earlier thoughts, that at least we could exonerate them from having broken into my place the day before. Rob didn't think the intruder in his place had been either Bruce or Bella, though he hadn't been in a condition to notice much.

"Then maybe they didn't get what they were here for," Rob said. "By now everyone concerned should have had a look at those tapes and concluded that what they're looking for isn't there." He tilted his head to one side. "Of course, there's really no way for anyone to tell, since the blackmail tapes look just like any other tape."

"Yes," I said, "so we're probably not any better off. Anyone who knows about the tapes will think you or I still have them somewhere." Thinking about that did nothing to cheer me up. I didn't want anyone else sneaking into my house.

"There is one thing, though," he offered.

"What's that?"

"It confirms that Whitelock was involved with more than one woman. Unless it was Bruce who broke in here each time, trying to get a look at the tapes, and I don't think it was."

"You're right," I said. "Whitelock must have called whoever he thought was on those tapes with him, so potentially everyone involved in those little games of his knows about the tapes and thinks you have them."

Rob nodded. "Cheery thought, ain't it?"

"I guess we'll have to spread the word somehow that the police have those tapes," I said. "That's the only way we'll be safe."

He laughed. "Just give Bella a call, and that's all we'll have to do. It'll be all over campus within an hour."

"Right." I grinned.

"I don't know about you," Rob said, nodding in the direction of the door, "but I want to get back to the computer."

"Good idea. Those files may be the clue we're looking for."

"Okay," he said, opening the door. "Why don't you wait here, and I'll go over and print them out for us to work on. Call Maggie, too." The door shut behind him.

Three heads would be better than two, and, besides, Maggie would be annoyed if we left her out. I dialed her number, and she answered on the third ring. I explained what Rob and I were going to do.

"Be there in ten minutes," she said and dropped the phone into its cradle. The sharp click echoed in my ear, and I hung up.

Maggie lived with her father near the university, which meant she wasn't very far away. By the time she arrived, Rob had returned with a small stack of paper.

I fetched pencils and paper for each of us, and we all set to work at the kitchen table. For more than an hour we bent over our task, emitting grunts and groans of frustrations as we tried to break Charlie's code. I kept trying various complicated combinations, but every one of them failed.

Maybe I was making this more difficult than it really was. I next tried several simple formulas, then hit upon one that seemed to work; but after I had done the first two words, which came out *hodie audivi,* I thought I was wrong yet again. I started to crumple up the paper and throw it away, but then I realized sheepishly why the words looked familiar.

I had broken Charlie's code.

C H A P T E R · 1 9

THE JUMBLE OF LETTERS which constituted the first entry in Charlie's journal danced before my eyes as I tried to control my excitement at breaking the code.

Ipejf bvejwj k ejdfsf vu dpowfojbu b ipsb tpmjub. Fshp jotusvyj, fu qfstdsjqtj rvbn dpohsfttjpofn, tjd vu opoovmmbt dfufsbt qfstdsjqtj. Gpstjubo dvn ufsnjobwj, k fsju pcpfejfoujps.

By experimenting, I had transcribed the first word, *ipejf,* as *hodie,* which I recognized belatedly as the Latin word for *today.* The second word, *bvejwj,* thus became the Latin *audivi,* or *I heard.* I continued transcribing and soon had several sentences in Latin.

Hodie audivi j dicere ut conveniat a hora solita. Ergo instruxi, et perscripsi quam congressionem, sic ut nonnullas ceteras perscripsi. Forsitan cum terminavi, j erit oboedientior.

Charlie's system was simple; he had merely shifted the alphabet forward by one letter. *A* became *B*, *B* became *C*, and so on, right through the alphabet, ending with *Z* becoming *A*.

He had been clever, using a simple code to disguise notes kept in Latin. Only someone familiar with Latin would likely figure it out.

I watched the other two, still frowning and scribbling away. "What's the matter, guys? Haven't figured it out yet?"

They looked up at me, and Maggie said, "I suppose that's your way of telling us that you cracked it?" She dropped her pencil and sighed.

Smugly, I nodded.

"Good work!" Rob said. "I was getting a headache."

"So give, already," Maggie demanded impatiently. "How does it work?"

"First of all," I replied, "what made it stranger than it had to be was that Charlie did the code from Latin instead of English." Charlie had been a whiz at foreign languages, fluent in French, German, Spanish, and Latin, with a decent knowledge of Italian as well.

I showed Maggie and Rob how the code worked, and they began transcribing their entries with renewed enthusiasm. I turned back to my page. Translating as I read, I decided to get my Latin dictionary to verify certain words.

"Where are you going, Andy?" Maggie asked as I got up.

"My Latin dictionary's upstairs, and I'm afraid I'm going to need it. Charlie was a little better at Latin than I am."

She laughed. "While you're at it, bring your German dictionary, too. This one's in German."

Rob groaned. "Do you have a French dictionary?"

Bemused, I shook my head. Latin, German, and French—the guy was a showoff, even in something so private as a journal. But maybe there had been enough of the child in Charlie—a child who enjoyed the "secret code" game— that could help me understand his writing a journal like this. "I guess I might as well dig up my old high school Spanish dictionary, just in case."

In a few minutes I returned with an armful of books. I paused in the doorway of the kitchen, arrested by a disturbing sight. Rob, unaware that I stood behind him, was carefully folding a piece of paper, while Maggie peered in the refrigerator, her back to him. As she investigated the contents of the fridge, Rob tucked the folded paper inside his shirt. Then Maggie turned around, Diet Coke in hand, and saw me.

"Here they are," I said, moving forward and brandishing the dictionaries. For the moment, I decided not to query Rob on his strange behavior. What he'd hidden in his shirt must have been part of Charlie's journal. Had he read something incriminating? Or maybe something very personal? I was curious to know the answer.

While Rob and Maggie worked on their pages, I picked up my first page and scanned the Latin, stopping a few times to check words and jot down notes. Then I was ready to read the whole passage.

Today I heard J say that he would meet A at the accustomed hour. I made my preparations accordingly, and I have recorded that meeting, as I have recorded several others. Perhaps when I have finished, J will be more amenable.

So much for that one; I was eager to decipher the others. I could consider their meaning after I finished. Wrapped up in the task, I forgot all about Rob and Maggie.

The next one on my page turned out to be in Spanish, which I considered my best foreign language. I didn't need the dictionary for it. After that came French and German, and I had to borrow the German dictionary from Maggie. Most of the entries, it turned out, were brief records of times when Charlie had happened to discover that Whitelock had made an assignation. Apparently the professor had grown somewhat careless in his student's presence, presuming—to his eventual dismay—trust where there was none. What was more likely, however, was that Whitelock had treated Charlie just as he had treated Bella, like part of the furniture. Except that furniture didn't videotape your sexual escapades and blackmail you with them.

Charlie had also noted several occasions, like the first, when he had recorded meetings, presumably the ones in Whitelock's house. The Latin verb was used out of context, but I didn't think Charlie meant a written record, as the verb indicated.

The initial *A*, which probably stood for Azalea, was mentioned frequently. Then I came upon an entry in Spanish which gave me even more to ponder after I transcribed and translated it.

> Finally I discovered the identity of J's second mistress. The tigress W, who has subverted her politics in favor of her genitalia, debuted on camera last night. Such unexpected depths to our feminist hypocrite!

Here was confirmation of our speculations—Wilda Franken *had* been having an affair with Whitelock! Charlie's references couldn't apply to anyone else.

Charlie could easily have threatened Wilda with exposure. The fear of becoming a laughingstock in a university that was a bastion of old-boyism might have been enough to make her lash out at both Charlie and Whitelock.

And what about Azalea? I could imagine how she would have reacted to threats from Charlie. Her position of responsibility and trust among the history professors was her driving force. Any threat to this position would arouse all of her instincts for self-preservation; she could have struck Charlie down in a moment of anger.

But what about Whitelock? As I had reasoned it, he might have panicked after Charlie's murder and threatened to expose the women involved with him, one of whom he must surely have suspected of murder. Feeling cornered, Azalea could have struck before Whitelock had time to make good his threats.

My head whirled. The field of suspects was already expanding, and we hadn't finished deciphering Charlie's notes yet. Maybe we could convince Herrera that these two made better suspects than Rob and I did! I picked up the pencil and set to work again, eager to see what other revelations Charlie's notes held.

The next entry, in Latin again, intrigued me further. My translation of it read:

> A and B have been spying on me lately. I wonder why? Is A having an affair with J also? Strange situation, if it's true, and why haven't I been able to record them? Maybe I'll record more often to catch them together. In the meantime, I want B to lay off. They're both making me a little uneasy.

A could mean Azalea, I thought, but who could *B* be? The only *B*'s I could think of were Bella and Bruce, and I just couldn't imagine a reason for either one of them to do Azalea a favor. Maybe Selena Bradbury, though. She and Azalea seemed to be pretty friendly. Or *B* could be our unknown factor—someone who was involved but who was unknown to us.

Maggie expelled a loud breath just then and dropped her pencil and paper on the table. Rob laid his down more quietly, but it looked like both of them were ready to take a break. So was I. My head had begun to throb.

"Time for a caffeine break?" I asked.

Rob nodded, and Maggie waved her nearly empty can at me.

I got up and looked inside the fridge. "We're in luck," I said, pulling the cans of Diet Coke out as I spoke. "I have exactly three left."

Maggie glanced at her watch. "I don't know about the two of you, but I'm about ready for some lunch."

"Me, too," Rob said, after a big swig of his Coke, "but I'm curious enough right now to put lunch off just a little longer."

"Okay either way by me," I said, watching Rob. He certainly was eager.

Maggie grinned, her earlier irritability gone. "I'm more curious than hungry, I guess, so let's finish what we've got."

Renewed by the fresh infusion of caffeine, we went back to work. Only three more entries were on my set of pages, and two were brief notes of Charlie's recorded "meetings," one between *J* and *A*, and another between *J* and *W*. The third made my tired eyes widen in surprise.

> Something must be rotten in the state of Texas concerning M's dissertation. I overheard her yelling at J in his office today, to the effect that he didn't dare not pass her. This bears investigation. Could she be one of his mistresses? J made an odd remark about PD, the saint whose virtues

so disgust me, and that shut her up. She came rushing out of the office and nearly caught me listening. I wonder if there are any records of PD's dissertation?

The *M* had to be Margaret Wilford. She was the only one of Whitelock's three remaining doctoral students whose initial was *M*. I puzzled over the *PD* for a moment, then recalled Dr. Logan's tragic story about another of Whitelock's students, Philip Dunbar, who had died under such sad circumstances.

I glanced again at the final entry. What could Dunbar's dissertation have to do with Margaret and a double murder? How was she involved, if at all? I reconsidered the details of the story Dr. Logan had told me, then sat bolt upright. Margaret, along with Selena, had been one of Dunbar's closest friends. Surely close friends would have known something about extra copies of his work.

But no copy had surfaced, oddly enough. I hadn't thought much about it at the time, but the lack of a copy seemed strange. Most graduate students at the dissertation stage were obsessive, to say the least, about not letting anything happen to their work. Surely Dunbar would have had another copy *somewhere.*

But not if Margaret had hidden it away, claiming it was lost, perhaps intending to use it, at a later date, as her own.

I turned this thought around and around, and the more I considered it, the more attractive—and plausible—the idea was. According to Dr. Logan, Philip Dunbar and Julian Whitelock had not had much contact once Dunbar had reached the dissertation stage. Whitelock had been afraid of his brilliant student, who apparently had seen little reason to have his erstwhile advisor oversee his work through its various stages. Beyond Whitelock's signature on the form that registered his topic with the university's graduate studies committee, Dunbar could have avoided contact with his professor until the dissertation was ready for examination.

As cantankerous as he could occasionally be, Whitelock wouldn't have refused to pass his student's dissertation, if the student was as brilliant as Dr. Farrar claimed. The other members of Dunbar's committee wouldn't have let Whitelock turn down a good dissertation if they felt it warranted their support. Besides, they probably would have welcomed the opportunity to score a few points off the old bastard. Whitelock hadn't been any better liked by his peers than he had been by most of his students.

It was possible that Whitelock hadn't seen the dissertation and didn't know much about it. Margaret could have hidden it away these four or five years, intending to claim it as her own work when a sufficient amount of time had passed.

I knew little about the woman. She had been a graduate student long enough to pull it off, if that was indeed what she intended to do. By asking some discreet questions, perhaps I could discover just what the members of the history department had known about Dunbar's dissertation.

"Guys, you're not going to believe some of this. It just gets curiouser and curiouser, as Alice would say."

Maggie and Rob looked up at me and frowned.

"All right, all right," I muttered. "I'll wait till you're finished."

I didn't have to wait long. In less than ten minutes, Maggie had spread out our scribblings so that we could all see them. She and Rob sat together at the table, and I stood behind them and read over their shoulders.

Eager to hear their reactions, I pointed first to the entry about *M* and the dissertation. "What do you think about this?" I waited while they read.

"Damn!" Rob said. "Plagiarizing someone else's work. Could that be what he was talking about? Who's *PD*, by the way?"

Briefly, I told them Dr. Logan's story about Philip Dunbar and his missing dissertation.

Maggie looked at Rob, then at me. "So you think Charlie found out that Margaret had a copy of the dissertation—if, indeed, she *did* have a copy?" she asked, the doubt strong in her voice. I nodded, and she continued. "So then Charlie would have threatened both of them, because if Margaret was going to try to pull this off, Whitelock must have known about it. Was she sleeping with him, too? Geez!"

"So she murdered Charlie," Rob summarized, "and then she killed Whitelock when he threatened to turn her in to the police. It sounds plausible to us, but do you think a jury would buy it? I mean, would they really accept scholarly theft as a motive for two cold-blooded murders?" He shook his head. "As opposed to inheriting a multimillion-dollar estate? I don't know."

"I'll admit it would probably sound a bit incredible to a lot of people, but a persuasive D.A. could make it stick," I argued. "And, besides, most people probably think university types are strange anyway, and they might believe a psycho academic could do anything."

Maggie laughed. "And despite what people think, 'psycho academic' isn't redundant."

"Okay, okay." Rob held up his hands in a gesture of surrender.

"Sorry." I grinned. I indicated the rest of the pages. "So what else did we find?"

Of the entries which Rob had deciphered, most were simple records of meetings between *J* and *A*. Azalea certainly seemed to be the companion of choice.

One other entry was more interesting.

> A and B sought me out for another conversation, in which A kept digging, trying to force me into giving myself away. This time, the remarks were more threatening in nature, but I mollified them, temporarily, with protestations of innocence. I gave A a rather silly clue to think about, and that should keep her mind busy for a while. I need to watch them more closely from now on.

"Who are A and B?" Rob asked. "Is Bella or Bruce working with Azalea, for some ungodly reason? That one really gets me."

"Who knows?" Maggie shook her head. I could tell by the distaste in her voice that, although Bella irritated her, Maggie didn't like to think she was connected with something this awful. "Maybe kinky sex just makes strange bedfellows, if you'll allow me the pun."

Rob and I groaned.

"Anyway," Maggie continued, ignoring us and leafing through pages, "I'm not sure the rest of this is much help. At least now we can add Azalea, Wilda, and Margaret to the suspect list."

"How much of this journal did you print out, Rob?" I asked, thinking there must be more than the few pages we had.

He watched me with narrowed eyes. "I printed everything in that subdirectory. It'll take me a while to see whether there's anything more on the hard drive and to go through all the floppies Charlie had."

A pretty neat evasion, I thought. *Maybe he should be in law school instead.*

Maggie made a face. She knew how to use a computer, but she wasn't terribly fond of anything mechanical. "Better you than me." She stood up. "I'm ready to eat. How about if I run down to the grocery store and buy some stuff for lunch? It's on me."

While Maggie was gone, Rob excused himself and went upstairs to his temporary bedroom. He didn't reappear until Maggie returned half an hour later. We enjoyed the graduate student equivalent of the yuppie power lunch: ham sandwiches, potato chips, and more Diet Cokes.

As I munched, I asked a question that had been puzzling me. "How did Charlie manage to make those videotapes?"

Rob set down his sandwich and swallowed carefully. "I don't know for sure," he replied, "but I've been thinking about that too. You know Charlie did some house-sitting for Whitelock?"

Maggie and I both nodded.

"Well," he went on, "I think Charlie must have had copies of Whitelock's house keys made, because I found some unfamiliar keys on his key ring when I had to borrow his car one time. I asked him about them, but he just shrugged it off, saying they were from his house in South Carolina. But they disappeared off the key ring not long after that."

Rob took a sip of Coke before continuing. "While he was house-sitting this summer, Charlie took me over for a look through Whitelock's house. You know, just a tour, nothing else." He glanced from me to Maggie. "There was a room upstairs, right next to Whitelock's bedroom, that was locked, and Charlie said he didn't have a key." Rob's nostrils flared in disgust. "I imagine that's where Whitelock had his playroom. Charlie must have found the key somehow, and I bet he probably found some way to set up a video camera in there. He spent almost two months in that house last fall during Whitelock's sabbatical in France. Who knows what he could have done in that time?"

"Did Whitelock have an alarm system?" Maggie asked.

"No," Rob replied.

"Then, if Charlie did keep a key," Maggie speculated, "he could have gotten in and out of the house when Whitelock was on campus. Pick up a tape, set up a fresh one. But how did he get it to record at the right times?"

"Voice-activated camera," Rob responded grimly. "That camera can do just about anything, except wash the dishes."

"There's another explanation, though," Maggie said, staring off into space. "Maybe Whitelock himself made the tapes. I wouldn't have put it past him."

I nodded, considering the idea. "That sounds plausible to me. I guess Charlie could have found the tapes, then either stole them or made copies."

Those two explanations were probably as close to the truth as we'd ever get. Only Charlie and Whitelock knew for sure, and they couldn't tell us. If the police had discovered any information, I'd be willing to bet they weren't going to share it.

In silence, we finished our lunch. Once we had cleared the table, Rob departed to use Charlie's computer for a while, and Maggie and I reluctantly agreed that we should try to get some legitimate work done. In other words, it was back to our reading lists for both of us.

Maggie paused as she was going out the door. "By the way, Andy, do you have the library's copy of Stenton's *Anglo-Saxon England*? It's checked out, according to the library computer, and of course, they're not allowed to tell me who has it. I put a hold on it, but who knows how long it'll be out."

I shook my head. "No, I don't have it. I'd like to get ahold of it myself, because it's on my list, too." As I spoke, I had a quick flash of something in my mind. What was there about that book? Something nibbled at the edge of my memory, then it was gone.

"What is it, Andy?" Maggie watched me with sudden concern.

I shook my ahead again. "There's something teasing my memory about that book, but for the life of me, I can't remember what it is." I shrugged. "I guess I'll think of it eventually. In the meantime, if you do find out who has it, remember I'd like to get it when you're done."

Maggie nodded, curiosity in her eyes, but evidently she decided there was no point in questioning me further. She bade me good-bye and walked down the sidewalk to her car.

With Maggie gone and Rob working at the computer next door, I settled into my chair and picked up my turgid treatise on medieval English law.

That lasted about five minutes. I simply didn't have the willpower to force myself to concentrate on writs of right and writs of novel disseisin. I thought about the paper Rob had hidden. That really bothered me. I needed a distraction, so I pulled one of my favorites by Elizabeth Peters from a nearby bookshelf and spent several hours cavorting with the Emersons in nineteenth-century Egypt.

Rob dragged in around six o'clock, looking worn out and thoroughly disgusted. "No luck, huh?" I asked. For a moment my conscience bothered me about having a good time reading a mystery novel while he had sweated over Charlie's computer, but I remembered that he was hiding something from me, and I stopped feeling guilty.

Wearily, Rob shook his head. "Whatever Charlie did with the rest of his so-called journal, I don't know. Those recent entries were the only ones I could find. Maybe that was all he had. Maybe he just started keeping it this semester. Who knows?" He leaned back into the couch and tried to relax his shoulders.

"Oh, well," I comforted him, "what we have is enough to keep the police busy for a while." *Except for what you're hiding from me.*

"You realize, don't you," Rob asked, "that we should've called Herrera already?"

What is it that you don't want me to know? I asked myself. *And why can't I just come right out and ask you? Because,* I answered, *I want to trust you, and I don't want to hear an answer that would let me down.*

Ruefully, I nodded. "I thought about that—fleetingly, I'll admit—but it's Saturday night, and he's probably enjoying some time off. Surely it can wait till tomorrow or Monday." I tried to put it out of my mind.

Since Rob had cooked for us twice already, I thought it was my turn. My specialty was hamburgers, and hamburger meat was relatively cheap, as were instant mashed potatoes. I had one last package of hamburger meat in the freezer, and I thawed it out in the microwave.

Rob didn't complain about my cooking, and after we ate, we went to our rooms. He hesitated a moment over his "Good-night, Andy," and I knew he wanted something more from me than just a return of his good-night wish. But I only muttered "Good-night, Rob."

I almost asked about the piece of paper, but, unwilling to face a confrontation, I turned and went into my room and shut the door firmly behind me. I rummaged through my videotapes and decided to watch *Bringing Up Baby* for the umpteenth time. Maybe Grant and Hepburn could take my mind off things.

I laughed, as I always did, at this wonderful movie, but the romantic aspect of it hit me more forcefully than usual. I really was hopeless in some ways, because I secretly expected life to be like one of my favorite movies. I wanted Cary Grant to come along and sweep me off my feet, with witty dialogue, wonderful clothes, and lots of money.

Is Cary Grant waiting for me in the room down the hall? I wondered. Hell, I didn't know, and I was too confused to figure it out.

I rewound the tape, put it back on the shelf, then stripped off my clothes and got in bed.

The next morning, when I woke up, the house was quiet. I had slept better than I expected, given the mood I was in when I tried to go to sleep. By the time I finished my shower, I heard Rob stirring about in his room. I went down to cook breakfast.

About the time I had breakfast ready, Rob appeared, holding the Sunday paper. Neither of us was a chatterbox, for which I was grateful. Facing him over the breakfast table every morning would be more than a bit disconcerting. As we settled down to eat, each of us took a favorite section of the newspaper. Rob laughed over the comics, and I leafed through the book section, looking for reviews of mysteries.

I put aside the book page, disappointed to find no mystery reviews, and picked a section at random as I finished my toast. I grimaced—it was the society section—but shrugged and decided to look through it anyway. I would read even the cereal box if that was the only thing available. At least the society pages beat the cereal box—just barely.

I turned the page, shaking my head over the extravagance of the clothes I saw in the pictures. Not for the first time, I wondered how much money was really raised for charities at some of those events. As my eyes swept over the few photographs on the next page, they lighted upon a familiar face, then widened as I read the caption beneath it.

"*That's* who he meant!" I said aloud as I slapped the paper down on the table.

CHAPTER · 20

ROB LOOKED UP, startled, when my hand connected sharply with the table.

"What on earth are you making so much noise about?" he asked grumpily.

I thrust the folded paper into his hands and, pointing erratically at the picture which had caught my interest, commanded, "Look at this!"

"It's Bella," he replied, as if to ask, *So what?*

"Read the caption," I replied.

"The lovely Miss Arabella Gordon," Rob read aloud, "daughter of the Honorable Frank Gordon, Mayor of Houston, attended the gala benefit dinner with her steady companion, the dashing Bruce Tindall."

Rob looked up, and together we stated, in tones of smug satisfaction, "A and B."

"Exactly!" I said. "It wasn't Azalea and Bella, or Azalea and Bruce, after all. I had forgotten that Bella's name is really Arabella. I bet that's what Charlie meant in his journal."

"After their little visit yesterday," Rob mused, "I figured they had to be involved somehow. But do you really think Bella was screwing around with Whitelock? Who'd want him, with a hunk like Bruce around?"

"Good point," I responded, grinning, "but that's supposing Bella's interested in Bruce and vice versa." I'd thought for some time that Bruce had to be in love with Bella, but I wondered what Rob thought.

He laughed. "Come on, Andy. Don't tell me you're *that* blind. Bruce adores her. He's got hungry eyes. When he thinks no one's paying any attention to him, he watches her—and I'm telling you, he's in love with her."

"I won't argue that point, because I happen to agree with you. But it still doesn't mean Bella seconds the emotion."

"I wouldn't be so sure about that," he said. "She's pretty insensitive about a lot of things, but they have a feeling of intimacy about them when they're together. They're definitely a couple, in more ways than one. She treats him like a pet rock half the time, but she's very possessive. Charlie needled her once, joking that he was going to seduce Bruce away from her, and she really overreacted." Rob's face mirrored the distaste that he had obviously felt, having witnessed the whole thing. "I didn't think it was very funny myself, but she got downright ugly. And believe me, the woman knows how to be ugly."

I could easily imagine it. With the brief time Bella had spent near the top of the modeling world, I didn't have any illusions about how "nice" she had been then, in such a cutthroat business.

Acknowledging my agreement, Rob went on. "Anyway, I think there are strong motives there. If Bella was fooling around with Whitelock, and Bruce found out about it—especially if Charlie told him and taunted him with it—don't you think Bruce is capable of knocking both of them over the head?"

"Yeah, I do. Bruce is a still-waters kind of guy. It probably takes a lot to get him angry, but once he does, I'll bet his temper gets away from him."

I was like that myself. I rarely got that angry, but when I did, I went a little crazy. But at least I hadn't been trained to kill, like Bruce the former Marine.

"Lord," Rob moaned, "how would we ever convince the police that the mayor's daughter could be involved in a kinky sex-murder scandal?"

I snorted derisively. "Are you kidding? The papers would love it, the way they trash His Honor every other week. With the election coming up next year, he'd be out of office for sure."

The light dawned for us both at the same time, and Rob and I looked at each other.

"My goodness," he said, his southern drawl more pronounced than usual. "I never thought of that."

Chilled, I considered the implications. Neither one of us, until that moment, had carried the train of thought that far, but it was the logical conclusion. "Bella makes snide remarks sometimes about her father and his political ambitions"— he apparently had his eyes on the governorship—"but she gets aggressive when anyone else says something. If Charlie threatened to expose Julian Whitelock, that could have meant big trouble for her, if her name came up."

Rob paused briefly for thought. "But, from what we read in those journal entries, it didn't sound as if Charlie had any real proof that Bella was involved with Whitelock. It sounded more like he was suspicious and intending to find out more. He was like a terrier—he loved to dig."

I looked at him grimly. "Well, I guess after he confronted Whitelock, some-one just didn't give him the chance to dig any further."

His hand shaking, Rob took another sip of coffee. "No, they didn't."

I figured it was time to change the subject. "Don't you think we ought to let Herrera know about the journal?"

He sighed. "Yeah, since I couldn't find anything else. I know there has to be more, but where it is, I don't know."

Like in your bedroom upstairs, maybe? I thought but didn't say—though I was tempted, just to see how he would react. I still wasn't ready to force the issue. Either he would trust me, or he wouldn't.

Instead, I voiced a different thought, feeling stupid that it hadn't occurred to me sooner. "Well, disks are small and not that difficult to conceal. Maybe the person who broke in on you took some."

"You're right," Rob muttered in disgust. "I hadn't even thought about that. And I've been so erratic lately about turning on the alarm system, anyone could've sneaked in while we were gone. And Charlie had so many disks, I'd never be able to tell what was missing, unless it was one of his program disks."

I thought of something Bella had said the morning we discovered Whitelock's body. I reminded Rob. "You remember, Bella said something about Bruce having something to do, and she kind of grinned."

"That means Bruce was probably here breaking in, while we were on campus discovering a dead body."

I nodded. "It would have been easy for Bruce to swipe some disks. But if he broke in then, why would they come back here so he could get a look at the tapes in my room? It doesn't make sense." I had another thought. "Why didn't he just erase the other files from the hard disk?"

Rob laughed. "He couldn't have, I imagine. Charlie had it worked so you really had to dig to get into that subdirectory to find those files, and he had some sort of protection program to keep somebody from erasing or reformatting the hard disk. You'd have to be an accomplished hacker to figure it all out. At least he trusted me with the information."

"I don't know how much computer experience Bruce has, but from what you've said, I doubt it's enough to be able to get to those files."

"No, I don't think he could have." Rob laughed again. "Maybe, if he'd stayed there long enough plugging away, but he wouldn't have wanted to spend that kind of time. I mean, the longer he stayed, the more chance somebody would come back and catch him."

"You're probably right." I groaned. "I think we'd better get it over with and call the police. The sooner we get rid of this stuff, the safer we'll both feel. I don't like the idea of anyone trying to break in next door again for another chance at the computer."

"I guess," Rob said, though he didn't sound too happy about the prospect of dealing with Herrera again. He stood up. "I'll call."

The person who answered the phone at the campus police office promised to relay the message. It was around ten-thirty, and we had no idea how long it would take before we heard something from Herrera.

The phone rang ten minutes later. Rob was in the living room, reading, while I washed the dishes. I dropped my dishcloth and picked up the receiver. "Hello."

Maggie's voice rushed into my ear. "Well, I had a visit from the campus police this morning." She sounded a little indignant. "On a Sunday," she added, as if I needed reminding.

"What for?" I asked.

"Herrera was here to check up on your and Rob's alibis for the time of White-lock's murder." Her voice gave evidence of her satisfaction as she continued. I would've loved to have been the proverbial fly on the wall, listening to that interview. I'd bet the lieutenant didn't quite know what to do with Maggie. "I think I convinced him that both of you are in the clear."

"Thank you," I told her sincerely. The knowledge that she was on Rob's side meant a lot. "Rob will be relieved to hear that."

"Good. Oh, Herrera's probably on the way over there now. His beeper went off while he was here, and when he called his office to check in, I heard him mention Rob's name."

"Yeah, Rob called to let him know about the journal entries." I explained what Rob and I had decided about the *A* and *B* in the journals. "I expect we'll have fun explaining why it's taken us so long to turn over more evidence."

Maggie laughed. "Come on, now, he's not that bad. All things considered, he was pretty nice to me, even though he was persistent about your alibis."

"Yeah, right. *You* may fall for that lilting Spanish voice, but not me."

She laughed again. "He's pretty gorgeous, I'll admit. If he sorts this out soon, maybe I'll give him a call."

"You're utterly shameless, you know," I teased.

Maggie snorted in response. "Sometimes you have to be. It's hard enough finding a decent guy."

"Amen to that, sister!" I said fervently.

"Some people," Maggie said, her voice dry, "are lucky enough to have one literally in the next room, however."

"Don't push it, okay?"

"Oh, Andy, just relax, and get over yourself." She laughed.

"Why don't you give us about an hour," I went on, as if the previous exchange hadn't happened, "then come on over. Herrera should be gone by then, and the three of us can talk over everything and see if we can figure out who done what to whom and with what sex toy."

"Okay," Maggie replied, still laughing. "But I think I'll leave the sex toys to you and Rob, if you don't mind. See you later."

Hanging up the phone, I figured I'd be in for another lecture when she arrived. She seemed determined to play yenta for Rob and me. Oh, frabjous day. I looked up to find Rob standing in the doorway.

"Who was that?" he asked.

I explained, and he was relieved to hear that Maggie had given such a staunch alibi for both of us. I neglected to convey, however, some parts of our conversation.

"If Herrera's on his way over," he said, "I'll go get the printouts and have them ready for him." He turned to leave, and the doorbell rang.

"You go on upstairs," I said, "and I'll answer the door."

Herrera was standing on the doorstep with another policeman, whom he failed to introduce.

"Morning," Herrera responded to my invitation to enter the house. "Now, what is all this about more evidence you've found?" Along with his companion, he followed me into the living room as he talked. His tone of voice indicated that he was tired and irritated, but there was a note, as well, that I couldn't quite place.

Rob came downstairs and explained to the lieutenant the circumstances of finding Charlie's journal. "I knew he'd been keeping one, but I didn't know what was in it. And I didn't think about it until yesterday morning. That's why I didn't say anything to you before," Rob added quickly, to forestall the criticism he thought was coming. "I really had forgotten about it."

"Okay." Herrera nodded. His face gave nothing away. "So now that you've looked it over, what does it tell us?"

Rob glanced at me, and I realized that he wanted me to take over. I explained the way Charlie's code worked and how Rob, Maggie, and I had deciphered the entries. Herrera expressed admiration for our efforts, though again I detected irritation in his voice. By now, he was probably thoroughly tired of all this "help" from bumbling amateurs.

Suddenly I had an unsettling thought. What if Herrera thought that Rob, Maggie, and I had conspired to create these journal entries to deflect suspicion from Rob? No, he'd have to be really Machiavellian to think that. But as I watched the lieutenant's face, I realized that he probably *was* that cunning. He was intelligent, and he had to consider all possibilities. And Charlie's will made everything more complicated.

Herrera also had to consider the possibility, I reminded myself, that Rob was innocent and that the journal entries were the real thing. He would treat them seriously until he could verify the source. If he was a good cop, that is— and Rob and I had to hope like hell that he was.

But how would he do that? The little demon of doubt inside my head refused to let the questions dry up. I tried to push my worries aside and look as innocent as I knew how.

Rob and I waited in silence, while Herrera, fatigue etched in his forehead and around his eyes, read through the sheets of paper. When he looked up, I asked, "Does it help any?"

"If they're the real thing, they might," Herrera said.

"What do you mean, 'real thing'?" Rob asked hotly.

"How can I be sure you two didn't cook this up all on your own?"

"You have *got* to be kidding!" Rob almost shouted in disgust.

"Look, Lieutenant," I said, trying to keep calm, "how could Rob and I have come up with something this complicated in the last day or so?"

Herrera shrugged. "You're the academic whizbangs, not me. As far as I'm concerned, you two could do something like this as easily as I can name all the faculty on campus who don't pay their parking tickets."

"Geez!" I stood up and almost shouted at him. "Do you mean you're not going to take this seriously?"

Herrera stood up and eyed me calmly. "I have to take it seriously. That's my job. No matter what reservations I have about authenticity, I have to look at all angles."

"Well, thank God for that!" I said, subsiding into my chair again.

Herrera gestured with the papers again. "Now, about the information in these alleged journal entries. What do they mean? Give me a quick summary."

At a nod from Rob, I explained that we thought "A," by itself, referred to Azalea Westover and "M" to Margaret Wilford. Then I discussed our ideas about "A and B," saying that, upon being reminded that Bella Gordon's real name was Arabella, we had concluded that "A and B" most likely referred to her and Bruce Tindall. I finished with the visit that Bella and Bruce had paid us the previous day, and how we suspected that he had gone snooping through my videotapes.

Surely, once Herrera investigated the connection between the journal entries and the activities on those tapes, he'd have to concede that Rob and I hadn't manufactured Charlie's journal. And the more he dug into the truth behind the tapes, he'd also have to see that other people had powerful motives for murder, motives that went beyond mere financial gain.

Herrera sat back on the couch, his shoulders drooping tiredly. "I don't know whether to thank you or tell you to go to the devil. I'm not looking forward to questioning the mayor's daughter." He stared at Rob and me. His fellow officer, who had been unobtrusively taking notes in the background, couldn't help staring himself.

"You're welcome," I said, trying to lighten up the situation. "I guess."

Herrera focused his attention on me for a moment. Then, to my relief, he grinned. He stood, and the other policeman followed suit. "Let's have a look at that computer," he told Rob. "We're going to have to take it in for evidence."

"Sure," Rob said. "Follow me."

The rest of us trooped after him in silence.

Upstairs in Charlie's bedroom next door, Rob, wearing a pair of latex gloves the lieutenant gave him, quickly disconnected the computer's components and helped Herrera's companion—whose name turned out to be Eddy Brown—box it up. Rob also collected all the floppy disks and stored them safely in a special tray Charlie had for them.

Officer Brown and I took the two boxes and the container of disks and headed down the stairs. Rob and Herrera, empty-handed, followed us to the car. Brown quickly made out a receipt for the computer equipment and disks, and Rob signed it. Herrera and Brown bade us good-bye and left.

Rob and I walked slowly up the sidewalk to his apartment, where he turned off the lights, set the alarm, and locked the door while I waited. Once we were again inside my half of the duplex, he headed immediately for the couch and plopped down. Leaning weakly against the back of the couch, he smiled. The lines were erased from his face for a moment, and he looked about fifteen and totally carefree.

"What a relief!" he said.

"What's a relief?" I asked. "The fact that the police are gone?"

"Partly. But now that they've got Charlie's computer and his journal, and those videotapes, surely they've got to see that someone else besides me had the motive to kill him." He frowned. "I might have had a reason, if I'd known about the will, but why would I have murdered Julian Whitelock? It just doesn't hang together. Maybe the police will figure that out now."

"I think you may be right," I said, "but don't get your hopes up too soon. Herrera isn't going to mark us off the list just yet."

Rob nodded. "I guess not. But at least we've given him more to think about."

"Yep, and I hope he runs with it. But it's not over. You and I know that we're both in the clear, but someone else—*someone we know*—is still guilty. And that someone has done his or her damnedest to implicate us."

"And that pisses me off," he said. "I'm not going to sit back and let the police come after me. Herrera can't ignore all this other evidence and try to make me the guilty one, just because of Charlie's will. We can't let up on snooping until this is all settled."

That I could certainly agree with.

The phone rang, and we both started uneasily. I got up to answer it.

"Let me speak to Rob Hayward," a voice said abruptly, almost before I finished saying "hello."

"I'm afraid you have the wrong number," I replied. Rob's presence at my place was still technically a secret, although at least Bella and Bruce knew about it. The caller was female, but she was certainly not Bella.

"Andy, I know Rob is staying with you, so please don't waste my time with subterfuges. Could I speak to him, *please?*" She practically spat out the final word.

"Might I ask," I replied icily, though by now I had recognized the voice, "who is calling?"

"Wilda Franken," she responded, exasperated with the delay.

I placed a hand over the receiver and turned to look at Rob curiously. "Wilda Franken wants to talk to you. Are you up to it?"

"Might as well." He got to his feet.

"What does she want?" I whispered, as Rob took the receiver from me.

CHAPTER · 21

ROB'S TENTATIVE "hello" was apparently all Wilda needed to launch full tilt into her tirade. Standing near him, I could hear the strident tones of her voice, but I couldn't make any sense of the words.

His face took on an appalled look. "Just a minute," he said, then covered the receiver with one hand. "She wants to talk to me about the tapes," he hissed. "What are we going to do?"

I should have known Wilda would take the direct approach. "Good—she doesn't know the police have them." I paused, thinking quickly. "Tell her to come on over."

Rob gave me a glance of mingled alarm and amazement before he put the phone back to his ear and posed my suggestion. He waited briefly, gave her the address, then replied, "See you then." He replaced the receiver in its cradle.

"Lord, Andy," he said, grimacing, "what are we going to say to her?" He dropped onto the couch beside me.

"I guess we'll think of something. Maybe Maggie'll have some ideas. She should be here soon." I had suddenly remembered that I'd invited her to come over so we could all discuss everything. Boy, did we have a lot to tell her now!

Right on cue, the doorbell rang.

"Your timing," I told Maggie as I waved her into the living room, "is impeccable, as always."

Rob patted the couch. "Come and settle down. It's battle stations all around."

"What on earth are you two talking about? Have you been drinking?" Maggie peered at us as she got comfortable on the couch beside Rob.

"No, but that doesn't sound like a bad idea, right about now," I laughed, settling into my chair. "We're about to be visited by our favorite Marxist."

"Good grief," Maggie sputtered, almost coming up off the couch in surprise. "Why the hell is *she* coming here?" There was no love lost between Maggie and Wilda.

"She wants," Rob replied flatly, "to talk about the videotapes."

"O-*kay*," Maggie said. She rolled her eyes. "At least she's being direct. I'm not sure the word *subtle* was ever in her dictionary."

Rob and I laughed.

"Be that as it may," I said, "I suppose we ought to think about how we're going to deal with her. She'll be here soon."

"And you were the one who wanted her to come!" Rob groused. "Think of something!"

"Do you want me to disappear upstairs?" Maggie asked. "Having too many people here might make her balk."

I shrugged. "Who knows? It might not be a bad idea if you hid in the kitchen. She already knows I'm here."

Rob agreed. "To play it safe, I guess you should hide. Both of you, for that matter. I'll talk to her by myself—there's no need for you two to be involved."

Maggie and I looked at each other, united by a common thought. Wilda had such a powerful personality, she could run right over Rob, who might not have the emotional energy left to deal with her.

I shook my head. "No, Rob, I think it's better that you and I do this together."

Maggie nodded, and I could see that Rob was relieved.

A few minutes later the doorbell rang, minatorily it seemed. Maggie grabbed her purse and fled into the kitchen. Rob opened the door to admit an impatient Wilda. He led her into the living room, where I waited.

"Good afternoon, Wilda," I said, standing up.

If the woman was disconcerted to find me included in her business with Rob, she gave little sign other than the curt acknowledgment of my greeting.

As I motioned for her to be seated, the sudden hostility I felt was like a fourth person in the room. As Rob and I sat down on the couch, Wilda chose my chair.

While I waited for her to initiate the conversation, I gazed at her, not bothering to conceal my curiosity. The hostility I sensed had eased my tension; now I felt calm and detached.

Wilda's hair, barely shoulder length, was spiked around her face, more from agitation than artifice, I suspected. Her outfit, a relatively tame skirt and blouse, in a blue reminiscent of Caribbean water, might have been her Sunday-go-to-meeting suit, if she'd ever had one.

As always, her earrings intrigued me. She had the most outlandish collection I'd ever seen, and some of them were so large and heavy, I marveled that she didn't step on her earlobes when she walked. She wore a whale, about five inches long, hanging off one ear, and a bird, approximately the same size, in the other. I had noticed this particular combination before but had no idea what kind of bird it was. I was certain it was a politically correct endangered species.

"I hadn't expected to talk to anyone other than you, Rob." Wilda's voice was low-pitched and rough around the edges.

He didn't flinch at the accusatory tone. "Andy knows as much about all this as I do."

"What do you want for them?" she asked abruptly, startling Rob, who didn't know how to respond. "I'm willing to negotiate."

"For *what*, Wilda?" I replied neutrally.

She gave me a look that would have impaled a butterfly on a mounting board. I could almost feel the prick of the pin, but that only strengthened my resolve.

"For what?" I repeated when she failed to answer.

Wilda's eyes narrowed. "The damn videotapes. And don't pretend you don't know what I'm talking about. You must have them, *here*, somewhere."

The faint stress she laid on the word "here" convinced me suddenly that Wilda had been the intruder in Rob's apartment. She was almost as tall as Rob and certainly as muscular. In his exhausted, drugged state that night after Charlie's murder had been discovered, Rob had observed nothing about his attacker; there was no reason that the person couldn't have been female.

Though now I was furious, I decided to set the woman's mind at rest on one point. "We have no intention of blackmailing you, Wilda."

Now that the issue had been broached, some of the tension went out of her body. "How can I be sure of that?" she asked warily.

"What could you *possibly* do for me that would make it worth my while?" I asked, and finally she flinched. The note of dismissal in my voice caught her on the raw.

Rob had been momentarily forgotten, for this had become a contest of some sort between Wilda and me. Rob seemed more than willing to let me fence with her. He stared at his hands nervously.

Wilda had no answer to my question.

"There's nothing I—or Rob—want from you," I continued calmly, "except information."

Again a razor-sharp look was directed my way, but this one found no target. "What kind of information?" she asked.

"How did you know about the videotapes, for example?"

For whatever reason, Wilda decided to cooperate. Perhaps she felt she had little left to lose. "Julian called me that afternoon—the same day Charlie Harper was apparently killed." Her eyes flicked toward Rob, and I was unsure whether they looked at him with pity or contempt. "Julian was terribly upset. He said Charlie had come into his office, carrying on about some article of Julian's that had recently been published."

"Did Dr. Whitelock tell you *why* Charlie was upset?" Rob asked bitterly, no longer content to be a mere observer.

Wilda smiled grimly. "He was upset because Julian had plagiarized his work, or so Julian said." She laughed, contempt dripping from the sound. "Julian wouldn't admit it to me, but I wouldn't be surprised if he *had* stolen someone else's work. He was desperate to publish something. He'd been demanding more of a raise than the university administration, or the history department for that matter, was willing to offer, and he needed ammunition."

Wilda had gotten pretty close to Whitelock, and pretty quickly, I decided. I nodded to encourage her. "What then?"

"Then Julian informed me that Charlie claimed to have videotapes of our . . . the time we spent together." She paused and looked musingly into space. "Julian said Charlie had done some house-sitting for him, and I suppose he must have had a set of keys made so he could sneak in and out whenever he wanted." Her tone had grown angry as she contemplated again what had been done to her.

Ordinarily, I would have sympathized with her anger over such a gross violation of her privacy, but distaste for the woman's recent activities tempered that sympathy. I didn't care what kind of sex games she liked to play, but I thought she was pretty stupid to become involved with someone like Julian Whitelock.

The man had played her for a fool, and I doubted she even realized it. Whitelock had quite openly detested the politics she espoused, and either Wilda was simply an opportunist, riding the leftist, academic bandwagon, or she just plain didn't have the common sense God gave a rock. I figured on the latter alternative as the kinder interpretation.

"Were you on campus the night Charlie died?" I asked.

"Yes, I attended the reception in the library, and I was there pretty late." Realizing the implication, she shifted uncomfortably.

Although I sensed that she might be less willing to answer further questions, I pressed ahead. "Did you have any more contact with Dr. Whitelock after that one conversation, the day Charlie died?"

She frowned. "I managed to calm him down that day, but he called me again the next afternoon, and he was nearly hysterical again. I knew Julian was seeing another woman—or women. It didn't take long to discover that his appetite was voracious. But I'm not sure who he was seeing."

But I'll bet you've got a pretty good idea, I thought shrewdly.

Right then, her skin looked as if the blue of her dress had bled into it. "Julian had apparently talked to his other . . . er . . . friends, but he didn't mention anyone by name. I think he must have called them, too, to warn them about the videotapes."

Just as I'd thought.

Wilda continued without prompting, her eyes staring unseeingly at my Monet print over the fake fireplace. "Julian was frightened—of someone or something. The first afternoon, he was merely upset. The next day, he was terrified." Her tone had grown bleak. "He wasn't making much sense, making strange comments about graduate students and the past returning to haunt him. He even said something about not being able to get his typing done any longer." She shook her head. "I didn't have much chance to calm him, because someone must have knocked on his office door. He just told me abruptly that he had to go, and he hung up." She blinked rapidly, perhaps to forestall the onset of tears. "That was the last time I talked to him."

The blinking was a calculated appeal for sympathy—Wilda's attempt to place herself in the category of the bereaved. This irritated me, and I spoke more sharply than I intended.

"You're not certain, then, just who it was that frightened him?"

She shook her head; the whale and the bird danced. "Can I at least see them?" she asked suddenly, urgently, leaning forward in her chair, her eyes making direct contact with mine.

This was the moment I'd been dreading. Beside me, Rob shifted uneasily, then cleared his throat to speak.

"I should tell you," he said, and the discomfiture he felt was obvious, "that I looked at part of one of the tapes, and I couldn't tell who the woman was." Rob's cheeks had turned a fiery red.

Wilda had no immediate response. Staring stonily at a spot between Rob and me, she finally replied, "Won't you at least let me verify that for myself?" There was a new note in her voice, a note of appeal.

Rob sighed, then spoke gently. "I'm afraid we can't show them to you. We've turned them over to the police."

The color drained from Wilda's face as she stared incredulously at him. "You didn't," she whispered, trying to deny what he had told her.

"We had no choice." Rob grimaced at the apologetic tone in his voice.

I could tell he felt guilty, nevertheless, in having encouraged her to talk, knowing all the while that the conversation would inevitably lead to this point. He glanced sideways at me and read the same reaction in me. My anger had begun to dissipate, and I had a little more patience with her. She'd had her comeuppance with a vengeance.

Wilda stood up and, with great dignity, labeled the two of us with a variety of adjectives and epithets at which I could only marvel. The woman was well acquainted with words that seldom found their way into a standard dictionary. My cheeks burning, I dared not look at Rob. When her breath—or perhaps her vocabulary—finally ran out, she announced that she would let herself out, turned quickly, and was gone.

Seconds later, Rob and I heard the door close, followed soon by the slam of a car door. An engine roared to life; the sound diminished as the car moved swiftly down the street.

"Whew!" I leaned into the sofa and turned to look at Rob. I felt rather displeased with myself, but I wasn't ready to diagnose why.

Maggie came in from the kitchen.

"Did you hear?" I asked, not quite meeting her eyes.

"Yes," she replied, her voice grim.

I detected little sympathy for Wilda in her expression, but I could tell, nevertheless, that she had found the whole episode distasteful.

Rob stood up from the sofa slowly, wearily, as if the physical effort pained him. In a voice that held no expression whatsoever, he announced, "I'm going over to my place for a while."

Troubled, Maggie and I watched him walk slowly into the hall. Both of us wanted to go after him, but Rob needed to be alone more than he needed either of us right then. Seconds later the front door closed quietly behind him.

Maggie joined me on the couch. For a few minutes we sat there, saying nothing.

"I refuse to feel completely guilty," Maggie finally said, her voice flat and uncompromising. "Lord knows, I don't want to sound like some Puritan moralist, but the woman got herself into this, and she's old enough to face the consequences." She frowned. "So why do I feel grubby?"

"Well," I drawled, as I did whenever I was uncomfortable, "with the advantage of hindsight, I suppose you could say we didn't think this one completely through. Even in my favorite mystery novels, though, the detective often feels like a voyeur. It's an occupational hazard, I guess."

Maggie snorted. "Thanks for the deep analysis, Miss Marple."

"You're welcome, M. Poirot," I snapped back.

Rob chose that instant to burst into the living room, waving several sheets of paper in one hand and a large book in the other.

"We've got another suspect!"

C H A P T E R · 2 2

ROB'S ANNOUNCEMENT surprised both of us. I groaned. We had more than enough suspects to sort through, and here he was, claiming to have found another. Awaiting a response, he fairly danced with excitement, his earlier mood forgotten. Maggie asked him what he meant.

Before replying, Rob squirmed in between us on the couch and thrust the loose pages into my hand. He gave Maggie the large book he had been carrying. "Look at these," he announced, "and tell me what you see."

"This looks to be," I responded, glancing over the pages I held, "some sort of alumni newsletter from"—I peered at the highly embossed letterhead, glinting in the light from a nearby lamp—"some prep school near Boston."

"Maggie?" Rob asked.

"This," she replied, opening the book, "is a yearbook, also from a school." She turned to Rob. "Dare I guess that they're from the same school?"

"Right," he answered, his head bobbing in emphasis. "Now take a look inside them. Maggie, look for the senior class."

I thumbed slowly through the ten pages or so of newsletter that I held, finding little of interest until I came to a section labeled "Alumni Achievements." I skimmed through—the guys seemed a pretty accomplished lot—until I came to a name I knew.

"Dan Erickson?" I asked, puzzled. The entry congratulated Dan on his recent presentation of a paper at the Southern Medieval Association Meeting in Baton Rouge.

"Dan Erickson," Maggie repeated, her finger pointing to a picture of a younger Dan in the yearbook she held.

"What does this mean, Rob?" I prompted, although I was beginning to suspect the answer.

"Now turn to the freshman class, Maggie," Rob instructed.

She followed instructions, and there, in the class portraits, she found another familiar face—Charlie Harper's. This was a younger, more vulnerable Charlie. He was beardless and looked nearly innocent in that picture, though the aspect of haughty superiority almost spoiled it.

Maggie leaned back, letting the heavy yearbook close in her lap. "So Dan and Charlie were in prep school together. Why does that make Dan a suspect?" Her tone had a strained inflection. She had gone out with Dan a couple of times, but nothing had come of it. I had sensed she was withholding something at the time, but I hadn't felt I could press her for details. I wondered how she felt now.

Rob's gaze bounced between Maggie and me. "Don't you think it's more than a little suspicious that neither Dan nor Charlie ever even mentioned that they had been in school together?"

I shrugged. "Maybe they didn't know each very well. They were three years apart, and maybe their paths didn't cross."

Rob shook his head. "You don't really believe that. The school wasn't *that* big. There's something peculiar about this. As much as Charlie liked to brag about this school, he never mentioned the fact that he and Dan went there together."

Maggie riffled the pages of the yearbook as she spoke. "You're probably right, Rob. The whole thing does seem weird, but the question is, what are we going to do about it? Is one of us just going to march up to Dan and accuse him, simply because he and Charlie never told us about this?"

"I don't know," Rob groaned in response. "I was so excited by what I'd discovered that I didn't think it through."

"How did you come across this, anyway?" I asked.

He pointed to the newsletter in my lap. "That came in the mail today. I had never seen one before, and I just picked it up, out of curiosity. I was thumbing through it and saw Dan's name. I thought I remembered that Charlie had some old yearbooks in the shelves in the living room. I checked the picture to be sure, even though the info in the newsletter made it pretty clear that *their* Dan Erickson was *our* Dan Erickson."

"The question remains," Maggie reminded us, "what are we going to do? Do we follow it up just to satisfy our nosiness?" Her tone indicated that she preferred not to do it.

I picked up the newsletter. "I think one of us—meaning me, I guess—should at least talk to Dan about it. Is that okay with you two?"

They both nodded their assent. I didn't relish the task, but I figured it might be less emotionally wearing on me than it would be on either of them.

Maggie got up from the couch, dropping the heavy yearbook where she had been sitting. "Well, guys, I've got to get home and get to work."

I walked her to the door. "Are you okay?" I asked as I opened the door for her. "Is it my turn to play Ann Landers?"

She turned to look at me. I knew something had disturbed her, but she smiled and touched my cheek, her hand lingering briefly. "I'll be okay. One of these days, you and I will have a long talk about it." She turned and walked down the sidewalk to where her car was parked.

I closed the door behind her, feeling slightly frustrated. I'd have to quell my rampant curiosity for the time being.

After dinner, Rob and I separated to work on our respective reading projects. Once again, I couldn't concentrate on medieval English law; questions about Charlie and his connection with Dan kept interrupting. At this rate, I'd never make it through what was supposedly one of the seminal monographs on the subject. Instead, I immersed myself, for at least the fourth time, in one of my favorites, Dorothy Cannell's classic *The Thin Woman*, where love and humor leavened the bad, and everything turned out right. When in doubt, reread a favorite mystery novel. That was my philosophy for reducing stress.

Tossing and turning in bed that night, though, with the world of Ellie and Ben left behind, I couldn't keep my mind from returning relentlessly to the questions that had plagued me before. Could Dan really be involved in Charlie's murder? Why would he kill Charlie and Whitelock? For the life of me, I couldn't think of any plausible motive. I couldn't see how he fitted into the elaborate web of blackmail and sexual antics that we thought we had uncovered. But I tried, until, at last, my mind turned completely to fuzz and I finally fell asleep.

Rob slept late the next morning, and I ate breakfast alone, after sleeping later than usual myself. I was relieved not to have to face him over the breakfast table. How was I going to find out what was on the paper he had hidden from Maggie and me? I didn't want to sneak into his bedroom to look for it, and I still shied away from the thought of asking him point-blank.

Usually, satisfying my urge to poke into other people's business didn't matter all that much, because the people involved had been dead for many centuries. Trying to solve these two murders was different, however, the downside being that I had to ask uncomfortable questions of myself and of people I cared about. Maybe that piece of paper Rob had hidden didn't really matter, I told myself, then resolutely put it out of my mind.

I took advantage of the quiet to make a phone call. I punched in the numbers and waited, praying that she would be there to answer.

"Hello!" her voice came clearly through the wire.

"Hi, Ernie, how are you?"

"Andy, my dear, I'm doing splendidly. Nothing else will do, you know that." She laughed in my ear. "How are you doing, Andy? I hope you're not out every night, attending wild parties and neglecting your work."

"No more than I did when I was an undergrad," I responded wryly. She knew what a stay-at-home dullard I was.

"How is Rob? Do you see much of him?" Trust Ernie to cut to the heart of the matter. She always seemed to know, no matter what.

I sighed deeply into the phone. "That's what I'm calling about."

"Tell me about it, my dear." I could see her settling into her chair in the kitchen, propping her feet up, and preparing to give me her full attention.

I sketched out the two murders and the circumstances of Rob's staying with me for the time being. In some detail, I told her about his apology to me, after all these years, and his confession.

"I'm glad he has come to terms with his sexuality," Ernie said. "And I'm glad that old business between you is finally out in the open. How do you feel about Rob now?"

"That's what's driving me nuts, Ernie! If anything, he's more attractive now than he was when I realized I had my first crush on him. I spent a lot of time trying to hate him and to work out my bitterness over the way he treated me, but I couldn't do it. He's always been there, lodged in my head—and my heart—and now that he's in my life again, I don't know what to do with him. How can I trust him after what he did to me?"

Ernie was the only person, until I confided in Maggie, who had known what happened between me and Rob.

"Honey," she said, "I know he hurt you badly, but you were both so young at the time. You've both grown and changed a lot since then, and if Rob tells you that he regrets what he did and that he still cares about you, I think you should listen to him, for once, with your heart and not your head."

"But what if it doesn't work out? What if he hurts me again?"

She sighed. "Andy, I know you've had some bad luck and you're feeling gun-shy, especially after things fell apart with Jake. But you can't turn away from a relationship out of fear that it won't work out. There aren't any guarantees, you know, but if you don't risk anything, you don't win anything, either." She paused. "Some things you've just got to take on faith, and faith alone."

"Maybe you're right," I replied. "I spent a long time nursing a grudge, and now that Rob has taken that away from me, I don't know how to feel. Part of me—a *large* part of me—wants him around, so I guess I should just give in and go with the flow."

"Then, basically, you called just so I could tell you what you already know."

"Don't be smug with me!" I laughed into the phone. My heart felt suddenly lighter. Talking with Ernie usually helped me sort things out.

Rob came into the kitchen at that moment and smiled a good-morning at me.

"Ernie says hello," I told him.

"Hello back to her, and a big sloppy kiss on the cheek." Rob fiddled with the coffeemaker, and I wished I'd made him some coffee, he had been so good to me in recent days.

I repeated Rob's message, and Ernie giggled.

"I think it's time to say good-bye," I said, "when you start giggling like a teenager."

"Why don't you give Rob a big kiss from me?" Ernie said and then hung up before I could think of a retort.

"So what's up with Miss Ernestine these days?" Rob asked as he poured water into the coffeemaker.

Feeling lightheaded, I walked over to the sink near Rob. *What the hell, maybe Ernie was right.* He turned to look at me, and I leaned forward and kissed him on the lips.

Startled, he drew away and stared at me. "What got into you?" He grinned. "I don't care what it is—I like it." He returned my kiss.

I hugged him, and his arms felt strong and warm around me. We stood that way for a long time, then I pulled back. Our noses touched. My glasses almost slid down onto his nose.

"Can we start over?" I asked softly.

"Please," he said earnestly. "I promise you this much, at least—I won't turn away from you again. I wouldn't hurt you for anything in the world."

"I'm not a shy, naive sixteen-year-old anymore," I said. "Neither one of us is the same person we were ten years ago. Duh!" I laughed. "I'm finally beginning to understand what that means. Why don't we get to know each other again, and see where that leads us? Okay?"

"Okay," Rob said, and he kissed me again.

I pulled away from him after a brief interlude, hard as it was to do, and he tensed slightly.

"What is it?" he asked, his arms dropping. "What's wrong?"

"There's something we have to get out in the open." I leaned against the sink, watching him. "Yesterday, when I came downstairs with the dictionaries, I saw you take a piece of paper out of the pile, fold it, and put it away in your shirt. What was it? Why did you hide it?"

"Geez," Rob said, paling slightly.

I waited, afraid of what I might hear.

"I was going to tell you, at some point," he said, looking me straight in the face, no longer flinching. "I just didn't want to get into it while Maggie was here. You two are close, but I don't know her as well as you do, and there are things I don't feel comfortable discussing around her."

I nodded. That much I could understand.

"I hid that piece of paper because I had looked at it long enough to realize that it was something about me. And I thought it would be better if I deciphered it on my own."

"What did it say?" I asked.

The look of pain in his eyes haunted me. At first I thought I had caused it, by forcing the questions on him, but when he spoke, I understood the true source.

"Charlie was in love with me, or so he wrote in his journal." Rob's eyes teared up. "There I was, the last two months, like an idiot, and I never realized that his feelings for me were that strong."

"What would you have done if you had known?" I asked, my mouth suddenly dry.

Rob's eyes bored into mine. "I would have given him that trite old speech about loving him as a friend but there could never be anything more between us."

I caught some faint hint in his voice.

Or maybe it was just the jealousy (yes, jealousy!) making me overly sensitive. "Was there ever anything more than friendship between you?"

He turned pink. "Geez, Andy, you're not making this easy." He sighed. "But we should start as we mean to go on, I suppose. Yes, there once was something more between us. Charlie and I had a brief—a very brief—fling a few years ago in college. I figured out quickly that it wouldn't work, partly because I had someone else on my mind"—he looked hard at me—"and partly because Charlie was too promiscuous for my taste. Somehow, we stayed friends."

"And at some point, or maybe all those years ago," I said softly, "he fell in love with you. Poor guy. He just couldn't get it right."

Rob shook his head. "I wish I could have him back for a little while, just to tell him that I did love him, in my way."

I put my arms around him, and he rested his head on my shoulder. "Geez," he muttered, hugging me.

"You don't have anything to feel guilty about," I said before I kissed him again.

"I guess you're right." He hesitated. "Do you want to see the sheet of paper I took?"

With my stomach clenched, I shook my head. "No, I trust you." *And, please, God, don't let him betray that trust this time!*

Rob smiled his thanks and his joy. A few minutes later, breathless but happy,

I left him fixing his breakfast. I floated out the door and to my car, unable to concentrate on my errand. My thoughts kept straying to Rob, and I smiled at myself in the rearview mirror. I was lucky not to have an accident, because my attention certainly wasn't on driving.

By ten-thirty I was on the fourth floor of the library, heading straight for Dan's carrel, where he usually spent most mornings. Now that I was getting closer to the actual confrontation, I was able to focus on something besides Rob, and my stomach churned. At this rate, I'd have an ulcer before I was thirty!

Dan was practically a stranger, and here I was, about to ask him some intensely personal questions.

His carrel was empty, but the light was on, so I figured he must be around. As I waited nervously, I scanned the shelves out of habit. Dan was supposed to defend his dissertation soon, though with Whitelock's death, I wasn't sure what would happen to the professor's doctoral students. Dan had to defend; he wouldn't be considered for the post-doc at Harvard unless he completed the degree. Both Selena Bradbury and Margaret Wilford had also lost their major professor, but, as far as I knew, neither of them had jobs or fellowships lined up for the spring semester. Someone else would have to take Whitelock's place in order for them to get their degrees. Ruth McClain was the obvious choice.

My eyes roved over Dan's shelves, seeing that he had the standard works on Anglo-Saxon England checked out to his carrel. One title gave my head a funny feeling as I stared at the spine of the book. The lettering leaped out at me: *Anglo-Saxon England*. Sir Frank Stenton's book, the classic, authoritative work on the period.

Dazed, I sank down into Dan's chair, as that puzzling, elusive fragment of memory suddenly took full shape in my mind.

I had seen the Stenton book on a table just before I spotted Charlie Harper's body that morning in the grad lounge. I remembered mentally reminding myself to get it from whoever had it checked out at the time. But the sight of Charlie's body—or, more likely, the bump on my head from hitting the wall—made me temporarily forget about the book.

And now, here it was, in Dan's carrel. Did this mean that he had been the person in the grad lounge when I discovered Charlie's body? What was he doing there? Had he simply found the body, just before me, and panicked over being seen with the corpse? Or was there a more sinister explanation? Was he the killer?

That would certainly explain why he shoved me and removed the book from the room. Then I remembered Dan's phone call after I had returned home from campus that morning. He had called to find out whether I had seen him or somehow figured out that he had been in the room.

"Hey, Andy!" Dan's voice roused me from my reverie. The Southern greeting still sounded discordant in Dan's nasal Boston twang.

There he stood, dressed in blue jeans and crisp Oxford-cloth, button-down shirt—long sleeves, no less—grinning down at me.

"Morning, Dan," I said quietly as I stood up.

"What's up?" he asked as he perched on the edge of the carrel desk. "To what do I owe the pleasure of your company this morning?" He picked up on my mental turmoil and watched me expectantly. As he waited, he rubbed the tip of his right index finger across his leg, as if his finger itched.

"We need to talk about something."

"Sure." Dan frowned. "Here?"

"No. Why don't we go to a study room down at end of the stacks?"

Dan followed me, and we found one of the empty rooms and went in and closed the door.

"So, Andy, what's up?" he said again, eyeing me nervously.

For the first time, I noticed dark shadows beneath his eyes and faint lines of strain around his mouth. I was going to take a chance. I didn't have much to lose, so I decided to go for it.

"What were you doing in the grad lounge the morning I found Charlie Harper's body?"

The question obviously hit home. I had hoped all along that I was wrong about him, but, by his reaction, I knew I was right. The look of shock on his face disappeared almost in the same instant it appeared, but I had seen it.

He laughed uneasily. "What on earth are you talking about?"

I didn't reply. I stared at him, not smiling, willing him to forgo the attempt at denial. He stared back almost defiantly. Then his resolve apparently wavered. His shoulders slumped, and he put his head between his hands. The fingers clinched in the thick blond hair until the knuckles went white. When he raised his head to look at me again, he looked frightened.

"How did you know?" Dan asked shakily. "And how long have you known?"

I answered the second query first. "Since just a few minutes ago, for sure. Though, I figured part of it out last night. Rob and I discovered that you and Charlie had gone to prep school together."

He gave me a startled glance, and I continued. "Rob and I are wondering why neither you nor Charlie had ever told anybody." For the time being, I decided to leave Maggie's name out of it. "It just seemed odd, and the more I thought about it, the more it puzzled me. Then this morning I saw Stenton's *Anglo-Saxon England* on your shelf."

Dan's eyes blinked in reaction, and I continued. "I saw the Stenton book on a table in the grad lounge, just before I found Charlie lying on the couch. While I was staring at his body, someone pushed me and I bumped my head on the wall. But I had forgotten about the book, probably because of the combination of the bump on my head and the shock of finding Charlie's body." I paused. "Then, when I saw the book in your carrel this morning, it all came back to me. Now I know why you called me at home that same morning. At the time, I thought it was a little strange, but I never stopped to think how you could have found out so quickly that I'd been the one to discover Charlie. You were trying to find out if I had seen you."

He started to protest, but I held up my hand to forestall him. "I realize that's not much evidence to go on," I said, "but the coincidence was a little too noticeable. So I gambled."

I almost expected him to get up and storm out of the room. After all, there was no way I could compel him to keep talking to me. I would have to tell Herrera, if I couldn't talk Dan into talking to the police himself. The lieutenant could look up the library's records of check-outs on the Stenton book.

"And so you decided that it was I who pushed you." Dan made this statement in a voice devoid of inflection.

"Yes," I replied.

He groaned, a miserable sound, then turned to look at me pleadingly. "I didn't mean to hurt you. I was so terrified of being discovered with the body that I simply reacted before I thought. I didn't realize who you were until I pushed you." Dan's hands moved restlessly on the table between us.

I felt pity, listening to his misery-laden voice, and said, "You didn't hurt me."

"Thank God," he replied. He gave me a look of calm resolution, as though he had made up his mind to talk to me. Perhaps he had been so worried about being found out, that this was more of a release than anything else.

The timing was right to ask another question. "Why didn't you and Charlie tell us that you had been in school together?"

Dan sat up straight in his chair and gazed at some indeterminate point. When he spoke, he didn't answer my question directly. "I knew Charlie for a year, in prep school," he said. "I was a senior, and he was a freshman. I was having trouble in second-year Latin and was assigned a tutor. That tutor was Charlie. He was such a whiz at languages that, even as a freshman, he was tutoring seniors." He paused to take a deep breath, then stated baldly, "He seduced me during our first session."

Well, you could have knocked me over with the proverbial feather! It was so unexpected, I didn't know how to react.

Once he got started, Dan decided to tell everything. "We had a relationship for the rest of the school year, until I graduated." He shook his head. "I've tried to forget that year, but it never worked. I was infatuated with him. He made me feel like I was the only person in the world who mattered. Even though, God knows the kind of trouble we could have gotten into if anyone had found out. I had already turned eighteen, but he was only fifteen. I had to be crazy." He looked at me again, and the pain in his eyes made me want to shrink away from him.

"I was a textbook case, the classic situation," he continued. "My father ran off when I was two, and my mother worked so hard to keep us fed and clothed that she was too tired to give me much attention." Dan laughed derisively. "I was the scholarship kid who'd do anything to fit in—an easy mark for someone as smooth as Charlie. Even at fifteen, he was years older than I was. I didn't find out until the next year, when I was in college in New Jersey and Charlie wasn't answering my letters, that he had been sleeping with another student he was tutoring. I was sure naive!"

Feeling sick at my stomach, I was uncertain what to say. Having to witness the exposure of such painful secrets unnerved me.

"The last time I saw Charlie—before we both wound up in graduate school here—was my graduation day." Dan's tone was noncommittal. "I went through hell, getting over the way he treated me. After a long time, I began dating— girls this time." He laughed again. "One of them was just as much a barracuda as Charlie ever was. I broke up with her when I moved to Houston. I was getting along well until one day, at the beginning of school two years ago, I walked into the grad lounge, and there he was, in a roomful of new students. At first, the beard threw me off, but then I recognized him."

"That must have been quite a shock," I offered inadequately.

"Yes, it was. I approached him after everyone left. It took him a minute to place me. I knew then, all over again, just how little I had meant to him." He said it with only a faint trace of bitterness. "Charlie didn't seem at all fazed when he realized who I was. He acted like we were old classmates who had grad-ually lost touch rather than former lovers."

He turned to look at me, and I met his gaze, trying not to turn red. His inten-sity embarrassed me.

"I wanted to confront him, right then and there, and say all the things I never got to say all those years ago. I wanted to make him feel, or at least acknowl-edge, what I felt then." He shook his head. "But when the time came, I couldn't say anything. He practically *dared* me to say something, knowing that I wouldn't. He was in control, as always, and I felt just as naive I'd been twelve years ago."

"What happened after that?"

Dan closed his eyes tightly and took a deep breath. "Charlie 'seduced' me again, except this time, I knew exactly what I was doing. I just didn't care. The rational part of my brain simply shut down. The next morning, though, I called myself all kinds of idiot, even while I sat by the phone, wanting to call him and wanting him to call me. Of course, he never called. At least, not that day. And I couldn't get up the nerve to call him. When I saw him on campus, he was always friendly but distant.

"Everything was fine until the end of last semester," he continued. "Foreign languages have always been my weak spot. I was desperate to pass the Latin exam. I had already failed it twice, and I was told that I could take it only once more, even though the rest of my work was outstanding." He sighed. "I can handle Latin when I'm not under pressure, but that exam just threw me, every time. They had given me extensions, because I should have passed the damn thing before I got to the dissertation stage. They made allowances because of the rest of my work. But who ever heard of a medievalist who couldn't handle Latin?

"I was desperate," he repeated. "I went to the one person I thought could help me most, and it was one of the biggest mistakes of my life. I asked Charlie for help, and he volunteered readily enough." Dan now looked extremely uncomfortable. "This is going to put you in an awkward position."

I had discerned what probably happened, knowing Charlie as I did. "I won't betray your confidence over *this*," I promised, hoping he would understand that I meant only his confession about the Latin exam.

Dan expelled a sigh of relief. "The language exams are given on the honor system, as you know," he said. "Charlie sat with me at my carrel and dictated the translation to me." He shook his head in reluctant admiration. "I think he looked up one word, the whole forty-five minutes it took him to dictate the thing. It would have taken me that long to wade through the first two or three paragraphs."

Dan looked away from me. "Needless to say, I passed. Charlie made enough deliberate mistakes for it to seem realistic."

"And once he had you safely through the Latin exam," I supplied, no trace of emotion in my voice, "he blackmailed you, didn't he?"

CHAPTER · 23

THE WORD *blackmail* reverberated in the small, stuffy room, though I hadn't really made an accusation, more of an observation. Dan nodded in response.

"I should have expected something like that from Charlie," Dan replied. "Knowing the other sterling qualities he possessed, I shouldn't have been surprised by his taste for blackmail."

Charlie's motive for blackmail puzzled me. What could Dan have that Charlie wanted? Startled, I realized I had voiced the question aloud.

Dan snorted. "He got his kicks making people do things they didn't want to do." He scratched his head. "After he helped me with that exam, I didn't hear from him for over a month. Then one day he called and said his place was a mess and he wanted me over there that evening to clean it up for him." He laughed. "I thought at first he was drunk, and I told him so, but he just smirked and reminded me of what the department would do if they found out how I 'passed' my Latin exam."

He sat up straighter. "When I got there, the place was a wreck—purposely so. He had taken the time to make it as messy as possible. His roommate was out of town. It took me four hours to do the laundry, wash the dishes, make the bed, everything. He sat there reading the whole time, acting like I was just some person he had hired to clean his apartment." Dan's tone held a note of wonderment mixed with pain. "He was the coldest bastard I've ever known."

His face paled, and again he gazed off into the distance behind me. "There were other things he had me do, things that I don't want to go into." He laughed again, and the bitterness in his laughter chilled me. "They didn't do much for my self-respect. Cleaning his apartment and running menial errands for him were bearable, at least." He clenched his fists, and his whole face tightened up. "There were more than a few times when I wanted to bash him over the head. You can't imagine how humiliated I felt. But I thought, once I had my degree, there wasn't anything he could do to me anymore, and I wanted my degree badly enough to put up with his power trip. He had me right where he wanted me, for the time being anyway, and there wasn't anything I could do about it except bide my time."

"Until you *could* bash him over the head and get away with it?" I asked this gently, feeling compelled to do it, even though I knew how Dan would respond. If he had believed having his degree would take him beyond Charlie's reach, he was deceiving himself. Or perhaps he was trying to deceive me, downplaying it, so that I would believe he hadn't killed Charlie for that reason.

"No," Dan replied tiredly, "I didn't. But I wouldn't mind shaking the hand of the person who did." He turned to look me full in the face.

"Wouldn't Charlie have gotten in trouble, too," I asked, "if he admitted to the department that he helped you cheat on your exam? Why didn't you try to bluff him? His position wasn't any better than yours."

"I didn't have the nerve, and Charlie knew it. We might both have been expelled, of course, if he had told, but I couldn't take the chance and force his hand."

If Dan had stood up to him, I thought, chances were that Charlie, for once, would have been defeated. But maybe Dan was right. Maybe Charlie would have confessed, just to see what would happen. After all, he had money to fall back on if the situation blew up in his face. Dan didn't.

Before Dan could say anything else, I posed another question. "What were you doing that morning in the grad lounge?" Since I had no idea of the time of Charlie's death, I wondered what he could tell me.

"I was looking for the Stenton book." He took a deep breath. "I've told you everything else, so you might as well hear the worst. The night before, I got a call at home about a quarter of eleven. It was Charlie, and he insisted I come over immediately to campus. He told me he was in the history grad student lounge and needed to talk to me right away. I was furious, because I was right in the middle of the final chapter of my dissertation, finishing some revisions White-lock had suggested, and everything was going smoothly. I didn't want any inter-ruptions when the writing was going so well. When I told him that, he threatened me again and told me I didn't have any choice."

Dan paused. "You know, thinking about it now, maybe he was frightened. There was something strained about his tone while he talked to me." He shook his head. "Anyway, I dropped everything and went to campus. I decided to stop by my carrel and pick up the Stenton book to take home because there were some references I wanted to check. It was about twenty after eleven when I got there. I remember glancing at my watch before I left my carrel."

As I listened, I wondered what had really happened in the grad lounge that night. Surely, after he had denied any responsibility, Dan wasn't going to confess to Charlie's murder. "What then?" I prompted.

"I took the elevator instead of the stairs, and as I turned the corner after getting out on the fifth floor, I thought I saw someone down the hall, going away from me, but since most of the lights were off, I got only a vague impression. Anyway, the light in the lounge was off, and the door was slightly ajar." He expelled a shaky breath. "I was so angry! I thought Charlie had called me over on a wild-goose chase. It would have been just like him to summon me for no reason, then disappear."

He shook his head slowly. "I started to turn around and head to the elevator, but instead, I pushed open the door and flipped on the light switch."

I felt a chill across my shoulders. I knew just what Dan had found.

"He was lying there on the sofa," Dan continued. "I thought at first he was asleep, but then I could see that he was too still. I went over to him and touched him. He was warm—but not breathing."

Dan shuddered, and, involuntarily, I did too. The bright sunshine did little to dispel our image of the corpse.

"All I wanted," he said, "was to get out of there as quickly as possible. I had seen the back of his head and knew somebody had killed him. I checked for a pulse and couldn't find one. I didn't want to be caught with the body. I turned off the light and got out. It wasn't until I got to my apartment that I remembered the Stenton book. I must have put it down without knowing it. And by then, of course, the library was closed." He grimaced. "One of the few times I wished that the history department *wasn't* located in the library.

"I hardly slept. All I could think was that someone would find that book, checked out to me, and connect me with the murder. I made certain I was at the library the minute the doors opened the next morning so I could retrieve my book before anyone found the body. I took the stairs that open into the hallway right across from the lounge door. I saw nothing when I sneaked a look out the stairway door, so I stepped into the hallway. The door to the grad lounge had been pulled almost shut. I don't remember if I closed it the night before. I had just gotten inside the room and found my book when I heard someone coming out of the stairway."

He looked at me apologetically. "It was you, although I didn't know that until it was too late. Not that it would have made any difference, I guess, because I was in such a panic. After you noticed Charlie, I pushed you to cover my getaway." His voice trembled as he continued. "I grabbed the book and got to the stairs as fast as I could. Then, for the next hour, I stayed in my carrel and read, trying to pretend nothing was going on."

"This person you thought you saw the night before," I queried, my heart racing. "Do you have any idea who it was? Whether it was a man or a woman?"

Dan shook his head. "The light was too bad, although I do think the person was about average height. That was the only real impression I got. I was in too much of a hurry—and too annoyed—to pay much attention, I'm afraid."

I hoped whoever it was hadn't see Dan, because it was probably the murderer.

Dan evidently had had similar thoughts, for he said, "When I had time to think about it, I concluded that stopping by my carrel probably kept me from walking in on the murder. Maybe it was more good luck than bad, although I might have saved Charlie's life." A shadow passed over his face, even though earlier, he had expressed little regret at Charlie's death.

The silence lengthened. Dan was gazing at me intently, a question writ large in his face. For a few seconds I felt claustrophobic, uncertain what he expected from me and equally certain that whatever my response, it wouldn't match his expectations.

After a deep breath, I spoke my mind. "I think you should tell the police what you saw the night of the murder."

"I know that's the right thing to do," he replied candidly, "but I'm terrified about what might come out. If they find out Charlie was blackmailing me, and why, they'll make me a suspect—not to mention the trouble I'd be in with the history department."

"Dan, if they dig deep enough, they're going to find it anyway, at least the fact that Charlie was blackmailing you." There was just enough doubt in my mind that I wavered on trusting him. "I can't tell you how I know, but I do know you weren't the only person he blackmailed. If you go to the police of your own free will, they're going to be less suspicious than if they have to haul you in for questioning when they discover you're involved."

"I suppose you're right," he admitted nervously, "but that doesn't make it any easier." He brightened, as a sudden thought struck him. "You know, I could tell them I had gone into the lounge that night to leave a note in someone's box, saw the body, panicked, and ran, and they'd probably never know the difference."

That gambit was so old, it was hairless, but I wasn't going to tell him. "That's your decision," I replied in a neutral tone. "I can't make you tell them the truth, but I think you should. You don't know—maybe you saw something that will help solve the case." I had no idea what that something might be, but the police needed to know.

He shrugged. "Maybe so." He stood up, a look of regret on his face as he turned to me. "I know I've put you in a difficult position," he apologized, "but I can't tell you what a relief it is to talk to someone. I promise I'll think it over and come to a decision soon, if you'll give me at least until tomorrow."

"Dan, right now I can't promise you anything, despite what I said earlier. What you've told me is rather difficult to absorb, all at once. I need some time to think myself." I shook my head. "I appreciate the fact that you trusted me enough to tell me all this. Ordinarily I would never betray your confidence, but this is an extraordinary circumstance, and I'm just not certain." I took a deep breath. "But I don't think it's *my* decision, do you?"

"No, not really," he replied softly. He looked at me, then got up, opened the door, and walked out of the study room.

Watching him weave through the narrow stacks on the way to his carrel, I ruminated on the previous day with Rob and Maggie. Remembering the strained expression on Maggie's face when we talked about Dan, I wondered if she hadn't already suspected something. Perhaps she had sensed Dan's turmoil over his sexuality. Obviously he was still troubled; the relationship with Charlie had been difficult. No wonder the guy was confused. Perhaps that was why Maggie had backed away—wisely, it seemed now—from going out with Dan more than a couple of times.

If Charlie were still alive, I would have had great joy in telling him, at great length, just how disgusting and reprehensible he was. It was the living who suffered; the dead were beyond reach, at least beyond the reach of this world. The thought of demons tormenting Charlie in the netherworld gave me some satisfaction. The pain he had wrought in other people's lives hadn't died with him, but maybe he was finally paying for it.

I stood up tiredly and went to my own carrel. It was nearly eleven o'clock. Now would be a good time to talk to Dr. Farrar about what she heard the afternoon of Whitelock's murder. During the day, she never wandered far from her office.

I came to an abrupt stop as I remembered what Dan had told me about the mysterious figure he saw before he discovered Charlie's body. Was that person really Charlie's murderer? Or had Dan invented this person to convince me that he was innocent? If this person had really been there, could he or she have seen Dan, before or after Dan had killed Charlie?

I was inclined to think Dan innocent of Charlie's murder, because I could think of no reason for him to murder Whitelock. Dan was a student of Whitelock's, but I couldn't think of another connection between the two. As far as I knew, Whitelock had confined his extracurricular activities to partners of the opposite sex. There was certainly no hint in Charlie's journal that Dan could have been involved in Whitelock's sexual hijinks.

Then another thought hit me. What if the mysterious person was Whitelock, and he had stumbled into the lounge while Dan was murdering Charlie?

CHAPTER · 24

I SAT DOWN in my carrel and stared blindly at the postcards of English cathedrals I had taped on every available surface. Could Dan have murdered both Charlie Harper and Julian Whitelock? As I relaxed in my chair, I sketched a scenario in my head.

Dan had found Charlie alive in the grad lounge, they started arguing, and Dan, his temper fuelled by the humiliation and anger of his situation, picked up the commemorative statue and hit Charlie on the back of the head. Whitelock, who often worked in the library until it closed at midnight, could have heard the sounds of an argument as he was on his way out of the building.

I carried the scene a few steps further. Whitelock, curious about the noise, decided to investigate. He walked into the grad lounge as Dan struck the fatal blow, or immediately after. Whitelock wouldn't have been too sorry to find Charlie put permanently out of his way, and he wouldn't have threatened Dan with the police. Perhaps they had come to some sort of agreement, an agreement which fell apart after Rob confronted Whitelock with his knowledge of Charlie's blackmailing efforts. Made nervous by what he probably construed as a threat on Rob's part, Whitelock contacted Dan and disturbed him sufficiently that Dan felt forced to silence the professor in order to protect himself.

I mulled it over for a few minutes, and, though it sounded plausible, the theory didn't seem all that probable. There were too many *if*'s. *If* Whitelock had walked in on the murder. *If* he had been able to persuade Dan he wouldn't turn him in. If, if, if. Dan was an excellent suspect in Charlie's murder, but since the two murders had to be closely connected, I'd have to find a better motive for Whitelock's murder to include Dan seriously as a suspect. Unless there were two killers? But I dismissed that notion. It was too complicated.

Coming out of my reverie, I gave my favorite cathedral, York Minster, a long look, then got up. How I wished I were there, soaking in the tranquillity and timeless magnificence of that great structure. But I was stuck in Houston in the middle of a murder investigation, and gazing at postcards wasn't getting me anywhere. A talk with Dr. Farrar might clear up a few things, and I should get on with it. I was hoping that the eccentric professor might have heard something— *anything*—on the afternoon Whitelock was murdered.

Once on the fifth floor, I went straight to Dr. Farrar's office. Her door was slightly ajar, and I paused for a few seconds to determine whether anyone was with the professor. Hearing nothing except the sound of rapid typing, I knocked, then pushed the door open.

Dr. Farrar typed a few more words, then turned to face me. A distracted smile lit her homely face when she saw who it was. "Hello, my dear, how nice to see you." She tended to call everyone "my dear," since she had a hard time with students' names. She shuffled a few papers on her desk, looking vainly for her appointment calendar, which was tacked up on the wall behind her chair. "Did we have an appointment?"

I bit my bottom lip to keep from smiling. She could never remember where her calendar was. "No, ma'am," I replied. "But I did hope you might have a few minutes to talk to me about something important."

Though her eyes strayed wistfully toward her typewriter, she responded, "Of course," after only slight hesitation.

Closing the door behind me, I sat quickly in the chair beside her desk and apologized for interrupting her work. Interpreting the gleam in Dr. Farrar's eyes as a signal that she was about to launch into a lengthy account of her current project, I hastily outlined the reason for my visit.

My explanation elicited such a furious glare from the woman that I thought at first I had offended her somehow. But when she was able to master her temper enough to speak, I realized that her anger was not directed at me.

"That man was the most inconsiderate creature it was ever my misfortune to know." She slapped a hand down on her desk and dislodged a stack of note cards, which slid slowly over the edge of the desk. While I watched in fascination, the cards continued down onto a pile of books beside the desk, before they came to rest on the floor. Dr. Farrar never even noticed.

After the last note card fluttered to a stop, I realized that the professor was still speaking, giving me a catalog of her disputes with Julian Whitelock. After about ten minutes, she finally got to the day he was killed.

Hoping to focus her overflow of information, I interposed a question. "What did he do that particular afternoon?"

Dr. Farrar paused in mid-sentence, blinked at me, then wrinkled her nose as she considered her reply. "If you are referring to the afternoon upon which he met his timely end," she replied tartly, "he disturbed me with all that arguing." So absorbed was she in her recriminations that she failed to notice my head snap to attention as I concentrated on what she was telling me.

"That afternoon, from about one-thirty onwards, I had little of the customary quiet that a *true* scholar needs in order to concentrate. For nearly two hours," Dr. Farrar complained, "each time I thought the argument was finished, it would resume. These walls, such are the standards of construction, are much too thin; and even if one cannot hear the actual words, the sound of loud, inconsiderate voices is sufficiently disturbing."

She pounded again on her desk, but this time nothing moved. "That man had no consideration for the persons in this department who are actually carrying on scholarly work. He sat there, year after year, and did nothing except write book reviews, and had the nerve to be jealous of anyone who was actually working. He was unbearable."

The accusations were partially justified, but now was not the time to address her sense of grievance over Whitelock's high-handed behavior. I ventured a question. "When you say there was an argument, do you mean that there was only *one* which lasted almost two hours?" I knew this couldn't be correct, but I wanted to know whether Dr. Farrar realized it herself. If she had been unable to distinguish any difference in the persons arguing with Whitelock that afternoon, her evidence might not be helpful after all.

"Goodness, no," she responded, surprised at my question. "I should have expressed myself more accurately. It certainly *seemed* like one continuous argument to me, but of course it wasn't." She frowned in concentration, then ticked off something silently on her fingers. When she had touched the fourth finger, she looked triumphantly at me. "I believe there were four different arguments in all. Two of them, I'm positive, were with women, and two of them with men."

I thought quickly. Bella and Rob should account for two of the four. Who was the other woman? Was there actually a second woman? And what about the second man? Perhaps there had been only the two arguments, with Bella and Rob, and Dr. Farrar hadn't heard clearly enough to distinguish. The order of them should settle my doubts.

"Could you tell me," I asked carefully, "just how things happened that afternoon?"

Dr. Farrar blinked at me, and I feared she wasn't going to respond.

"Well," she replied, "I returned to my office after a late morning tea break. I rarely eat a regular meal at midday. By then, it was perhaps half past noon, and I settled down to my work. I have been transcribing some copies of microfilms of Victorian manuscripts, and the task is quite painstaking," she explained.

I nodded my commiseration, having worked with similar copies that had strained my eyes and my patience.

"I keep my office door just barely open," the professor continued, "because it helps the air to circulate. It can be terribly stuffy in the afternoon. Anyway, all was quiet until around one-thirty. I had heard Julian's door open and close a a few minutes earlier, but I thought little about it until the voices grew loud."

She frowned. "I tried to shut out the sound, but fortunately this particular disagreement didn't last that long. I heard Julian's door close somewhat forcefully, then all was quiet for a while."

In response to my hasty query, Dr. Farrar replied, "It was a man, I'm certain." She leaned back in her swivel chair before she continued. "There was a nice, long period of quiet from next door. Then, around three, Julian's door opened again, and another argument sprang up not long after. This time it was a woman. This argument became loud rather quickly.

"I am somewhat vague about the actual time of day," Dr. Farrar apologized, "and I didn't look at the clock again after that, although that argument seemed even shorter than the first one. Not long after the second argument ended, Julian's door opened and closed a third time, and for the third time, I heard an argument begin." She frowned fiercely at me. "The visitor this time was also a woman." Dr. Farrar anticipated my question and said, "I know it was a different woman, because the tone of voice was much more shrill, more piercing."

Bella Gordon had a deep voice for a woman. Azalea Westover, on the other hand, had rather a piercing quality to her voice, which was fairly high-pitched. But that second female voice could have belonged to Selena Bradbury, Wilda Franken, or Margaret Wilford. I tried to concentrate and capture an aural memory of their voices. With Selena, it wasn't too difficult, and I decided she was a strong possibility. The same went for Wilda. I couldn't be sure about Margaret, because I just hadn't heard her that much.

"Then," Dr. Farrar fairly snorted in her disgust, and I called myself sharply to attention, "as if all the preceding hullabaloo wasn't enough, as soon as that argument was over and someone slammed the office door, I barely had five minutes of precious silence, when I heard Julian's door bang open once again. This time, another man set in with a rather loud tone of voice, and I decided I was ready for a cup of tea, so I left my office while Julian and that man continued to argue. It must have been around three-thirty, perhaps a little after, by then."

"You're positive the third person was a woman and that the fourth person was a man?" I asked gently and was relieved to see the firmness with which the professor nodded.

"Was the second man you heard the same as the first man?"

"Oh, most definitely not," Dr. Farrar assured me. "The first man had a higher voice. The second man had a voice that was a good bit deeper, much more rumbling."

Rob, because of the time factor, was obviously the first man in Whitelock's office that afternoon. He had a pleasant tenor voice, but Dan Erickson's voice was deeper, as was Bruce Tindall's. Which one, Dan or Bruce, had been the second man to argue with Whitelock that afternoon? Or was it someone else entirely? I thought the first woman had been Bella, because of the time; she had told me and Rob that she had an appointment with Whitelock at three. She could have returned a little later and bashed him on the head, though.

"Could you identify any one of the four voices?" I asked with some hope but not much expectation.

Dr. Farrar shook her head regretfully. "The police asked me the same thing, but I had to tell them no also."

I was happy to hear that the police knew about all this, if only for the fact that they might keep an eye out for the professor's welfare. The fourth person she had heard enter Whitelock's office was probably the murderer. Unless, of course, a fifth person had sneaked in afterwards, once Dr. Farrar had left her office, which was entirely likely. Either way, the dotty professor's life just might be in danger if the murderer had any idea that he—or she—had been overheard.

I wondered how to warn her. "Did you see anyone when you left your office?"

She shook her head. "The police asked me that, too, because they were afraid I might be in some possible danger, but I told them I didn't see anything or anyone. I can't imagine that anyone would have any reason to harm *me*," she said airily. "All I wanted at that point was some hot tea and some intelligent conversation, but I had to settle for tea alone."

I responded with a puzzled frown, for I sincerely hoped the professor hadn't been talking about having a conversation with the teapot. Seeing my expression, Dr. Farrar explained, "Anthony Logan and I usually have tea together in the afternoons, before he leaves campus around five. But since he wasn't there, I had tea on my own."

So she didn't have a talking teapot after all.

"And when you got back to your office, did you hear anything more from next door?" I asked.

"Not a sound," she said.

Then she looked wistfully at her typewriter again, and I took the hint and got to my feet. I remembered one more thing, however, that I wanted to know.

"Would you mind telling me," I asked diffidently as I loomed over her desk, "about the night of your lecture?" Seeing the professor's look of inquiry, I hastened to amplify the question. "I mean, did you return to the library afterwards? And did you see or hear anything?"

Dr. Farrar considered this. "Actually, I did come to my office for a few minutes. I had forgotten some papers I meant to take home with me, and I came up here to collect them."

"Did you see anyone else on the fifth floor?" I prompted.

The professor frowned in concentration. "As a matter of fact, I saw Julian's office light on, though, of course, I didn't make any effort to talk to him. And I believe there might have been someone in the graduate student lounge, as well. I thought I heard voices as I waited for the elevator."

"Did you happen to notice what time it was?" I inquired softly.

Dr. Farrar shook her head. "No. I believe it was sometime after ten when I finally left the lecture hall. There were quite a few questions afterwards, you know, and it took me some time to get away." She shrugged. "Perhaps it was around ten-thirty when I was in the library. I was here for about fifteen minutes. That would put my departure at around quarter till eleven. Does any of this help?" she asked kindly.

"Yes, I believe it does," I responded. I was thankful that Dr. Farrar was so anxious to return to her work that it never occurred to her to ask just *why* I wanted to know all these things. I expressed my thanks for the time she had given me.

I hadn't even reached the door before I heard the tapping of the typewriter keys. I glanced back to see the professor absorbed once more in her research, before I pulled the door nearly closed.

I needed someplace quiet, like my apartment or my carrel, before I could fully digest what Dr. Farrar had told me. But that would have to wait. I'd had several ideas during my restless night, and now was the time to put them into action.

I headed to the department office, where I intended to consult some reference tools that were kept there. The American Historical Association periodically published a listing of dissertation topics submitted by graduate students, as a way of protecting their rights in a given topic, and I hoped to find Philip Dunbar's listed. If I could find a title, and even a brief description, which was all the register usually contained, that would be sufficient to give me a start in determining if Margaret was attempting to use Dunbar's work as her own.

Azalea was out of the office when I entered, and I breathed a sigh of relief. Despite the fact that I had told her off a few days earlier, I wasn't eager to confront her again. Offering a quick good-morning to Thelma, I moved to the bookshelves in the corner to begin my search, praying that the department policy was to keep back issues readily available.

I soon found what I sought. Dunbar had been dead about three or four years, and he had probably begun work on his dissertation a couple of years before that, so I began my search with the issues dated 1985.

The first year yielded nothing, so I moved on to 1986, and there it was. Thank goodness he had been the methodical sort who registered his topic. Not everyone did.

The entry under the name Philip Q. Dunbar was brief, consisting of a title and one sentence that described the dissertation's contents: "*Alfred the Great: A Reinterpretation of the Myth and the Man.*" Well, that was certainly a provocative title. The description read, "This dissertation offers a reassessment of the life and accomplishments of Alfred the Great, with significant attention given to Asser's *Life of Alfred.*"

I returned the thin booklet to its place on the shelf and considered what I had learned. The description gave me only the most general idea as to the subject of Dunbar's dissertation, but it promised to be controversial. Anyone attempting to reassess the life of Alfred the Great would be taking on generations—no, make that centuries—of Alfredian scholarship. Margaret, or anyone else for that matter, could write on the same subject and offer a different interpretation of the evidence, or even the same interpretation, and no one would be the wiser. If Dunbar had mentioned some matter of interpretation, some startling new theory about Alfred's life and times, I might have something concrete to go on, but as it was, I had merely a general topic as my guideline.

Everything seemed too tenuous whenever I tried to push a piece of evidence toward a conclusion. "If, if, if," I muttered. If only I could figure out some way to find out more about Dunbar's dissertation. Surely there had to be a way to dig up something.

Hearing my name called in a low and urgent voice, I came out of my fog of deep thought and walked over to Thelma, who had been trying to attract my attention. Her eyes were round with excitement.

"What is it?" I asked curiously, for I could see how eager she was to talk.

After an apprehensive glance at Azalea's empty desk, Thelma crooked her finger, and, obliging, I bent over.

"Guess who got into trouble for slapping a graduate student?" she whispered gleefully.

"Really?" My tone was suitably amazed. I had hoped that it would happen, but I hadn't expected it. Most of the time, graduate students were on the low end of the scale, no matter what, and I hadn't thought anyone would reprimand Azalea for what she had done to Rob.

Thelma's cheeks split even further as she grinned. "Old Pooter tore Azalea up one side and down the other when he found out. We could hear him in here, he was yelling so loud."

The chairman's office was directly across the hall from the main office, and Dr. Puterbaugh did have a carrying sort of voice at the calmest of times.

"Well, well," I said, pleased that Azalea had gotten some of what she deserved.

Thelma laughed. "Yeah. Miss High-and-Mighty isn't so perfect after all."

A voice from behind startled us. "You little bitch! You'd better mind your own business!"

CHAPTER · 25

THELMA AND I had been so intent on sharing her news, we hadn't heard the two women come up behind us. Thelma paled when she saw Azalea standing beside her desk. Selena hovered, frowning, right behind Azalea.

"What do you mean by spreading tales like that?" Azalea demanded harshly.

Thelma's thin face flushed dark red as she stammered a reply, "N-n-nothing, Azalea. I was just talking to Andy."

Thelma's bravado had disappeared quickly in the face of Azalea's anger. Azalea may have gotten a dressing down by the boss, but she was still in charge of the office, and she could make Thelma's life miserable. That was probably nothing new from Thelma's point of view.

I wanted to laugh, not at Thelma's obvious discomfiture, with which I sympathized, but at Azalea's haughty attitude. The woman wanted to deny the truth of what her assistant had told me, but she knew she couldn't. Even with Selena standing beside her, she didn't dare push the issue too far.

"You'd better quit gossiping and get your mind on your work!" Azalea ordered huffily. She marched over to her desk on the other side of the room and picked up a stack of files, then stalked toward the door, where she paused. She didn't bother to say anything to me. Strangely enough, she seemed a little afraid of me.

I didn't mind that one bit. As I smiled to myself, she flounced out of the room, Selena close on her heels.

I turned back to Thelma, amused to hear the imprecations coming fluently, and quietly, from her innocent-looking face.

Azalea's departure gave me an idea. I leaned conspiratorially over Thelma's desk, as she ran out of names to call her supervisor. "Thelma," I said quietly, "I need your help, but Azalea would have a fit if she knew." I felt guilty about manipulating her, but I knew this was the only way to get what I needed.

Thelma tossed her head. "I don't care what that bucktoothed bitch thinks! What can I do?"

I looked around the office. I didn't want anyone sneaking up behind us again. "I need to see a student file. Not a current one," I assured her, as her eyes grew round. "I need to look at the file of a student who died about four years ago."

If I could look in Dunbar's file, I might find something more substantive about his dissertation or papers he had presented at conferences, or anything he published. Something to give me a line to pursue.

Her face cleared. "That's okay, then," she replied. "I'll do it, but I can't right now. I'll have to wait until Azalea goes to lunch. Lindy's out sick today, so Azalea'll have to leave me in the office while she's gone to eat. Somebody has to be here to answer the phones." Thelma grinned wickedly. "That means she's gotta leave me her keys, too, and I can get into the file room without any hassle." She looked at her watch. "Come back in about half an hour."

"Thanks!" I couldn't believe my luck. I scribbled Philip Dunbar's name on a piece of paper, which Thelma tucked underneath her desk blotter. Deciding not to tempt fate and all her shining teeth, I left the office after receiving a wink from the now-cheerful woman.

I checked my watch; it was nearly eleven-forty-five. Ruth McClain was probably in her office now, and there were a couple of questions I wanted to ask her.

The door of Ruth's office was slightly ajar, so I pushed it open with one hand while I knocked with the other.

"Come in," she called distractedly. Her dark head was bent over some pages of manuscript. She looked up from her reading and smiled in greeting, as I sat in the chair beside her desk. With a sigh, she put down the papers, then rubbed her eyes. "This is just what I need," she laughed tiredly. "With Julian gone, I have to serve as dissertation director for a field which is not my direct specialty. And not on just one dissertation, or two, but three!"

My nose almost started quivering. Surely Ruth meant Margaret, Selena, and Dan, who were in their final semester. This was better luck than I had a right to expect, having Ruth bring up the subject of Whitelock's students on her own. But before I could ask anything about Margaret's dissertation, the author herself appeared in the doorway of Ruth's office.

"Hello," Margaret said. "I hope I'm not interrupting." She stood diffidently just inside the door.

"Not at all," I responded, though, in fact, she'd given me a start. "I'm not here for any special reason."

"Good," she replied pleasantly. "We're coming down to the wire with my dissertation, and Ruth has been an enormous help." She turned to the professor.

"I can't imagine what Selena and I would have done without your assistance. You're certainly more approachable than Julian ever was."

There was a brief uneasy silence, for neither Ruth nor I had any idea how to follow this remark. Margaret stood there, smiling in friendly fashion, unaware that she had disconcerted us with her intended compliment. I envied the woman's cool self-possession. Maybe if I dressed like a successful lawyer, I'd feel some of that calm. Somehow, though, I rather doubted it.

"I've waited for this moment for such a long time," Margaret continued. "My degree will finally become a reality, and that will make all the waiting—everything—worthwhile."

"I'm looking forward to that day myself," I responded. "But I think some of my family members are even more impatient than I am. Sometimes I think this is more their degree than mine, they're so eager to have me finish school." *At least my mother, my cousin Ernie, and my brother Cary*, I amended silently. My father and my brother Joey didn't seem to care anymore what I did.

Both women smiled at the note of wry amusement in my voice.

"I know the feeling," Margaret said. "My father certainly never expected me to finish, however, since it's taken longer than anticipated. And he wasn't the most encouraging father in the world, in the first place."

Ruth spoke up, a slight note of disapproval in her voice. "Anthony has always seemed very proud of your work, Margaret. At least, in his conversations with me." She looked coolly at Margaret, and I got the inkling that she didn't hold much affection for her student. Certainly Ruth didn't make remarks like this in the normal course of conversation.

Then what Ruth said hit me. I goggled at Margaret. "Do you mean that Dr. Logan is your father?" Even to my own ears, my voice sounded insultingly incredulous, but Margaret was either completely insensitive to the tone, or she had terribly thick skin. She seemed so graceless when compared to her charming and genial father.

She looked at me, as if trying to remember who I was. "Yes," she laughed, a little impatiently, "it's no great secret that he's my father. He might have wanted to deny the fact on occasion, but he can't. Of course, my working on my Ph.D. in this department has made things a little awkward for him, but I can promise you that no one took it easy on me because I'm Anthony Logan's daughter."

That last part I could certainly believe, for many professors would delight in making things rough for the offspring of a fellow professor. I mumbled something in reply, and Margaret dipped her head apologetically in my direction. "I'm afraid we should be going," she said to Ruth. "I have to be back to work downtown by one-fifteen."

Thwarted of asking my questions, but relieved to get out, I said good-bye, throwing a commiserating glance in Ruth's direction. I left them on their way to lunch at the Faculty Club. I certainly didn't envy Ruth an hour in Margaret's company. From what little I'd seen of the woman, she had about as much natural charm as a stuffed iguana.

Just because Margaret was the daughter of one of the professors in the department, I didn't see how that had any bearing on the case. What was more important was the fact that she had been around long enough to have been a peer of Dunbar's. How to prove that the pair had had a close connection—close enough to get her hands on his dissertation—was another matter.

Looking at my watch, I saw that I had about twenty minutes before time to meet Thelma. I went to the student center, purchased a Diet Coke and a dry ham sandwich, and wolfed them down as I walked back to the library.

Thelma and Azalea were gone when I entered the office. I waited nonchalantly by Thelma's desk, and before long, she came to the open door of the file room and nodded and winked in my direction. Two minutes later, she slid a file folder onto her desk. "Read it as quick as you can," she hissed in a loud stage whisper. "Then get it back to me pronto." She seemed pleased with her efforts, for she smiled delightedly as she pushed the folder toward my shaking hands.

I snatched up the folder and fled the office. I didn't relish the idea of being caught reading a student file, so I went into the bathroom, chose a stall, and locked the door behind me.

I got situated and delved into the contents of Dunbar's folder. I scanned the personal information, finding nothing unusual. He had performed well in all of his classes, undergraduate as well as graduate. The only grade I saw anywhere on the two pages of college transcripts was "A."

Dunbar's application for graduate work had received high recommendations from every member of the history department's graduate studies committee, and his record after his entrance into the program was a list of one success after another. No wonder Whitelock had been intimidated by his graduate student. Dunbar certainly made me feel a little on the inadequate side.

Finally I found what I needed. I had thought someone as bright as Dunbar might have published something that would hint at the subject of his dissertation before he completed his graduate work. He had published two articles in 1987. One article, judging by its title, was apparently something he had written for a medieval literature class. I doubted that a paper entitled "The Education of Geoffrey Chaucer: A Revisionist View" would be helpful in my present quest, even though the subject interested me. His second article, published in the

Medieval Quarterly, sounded promising. Its title, "Asser's Life of Alfred: A Step Toward Reassessing a Primary Source," certainly fit within the scope of his proposed dissertation topic.

I sat there a moment, irresolute. Then I closed the file, stood up, and let myself out of the stall. No one had come into the bathroom during the few minutes I had been reading.

I hurried back to the department office. Peeking cautiously inside, I was relieved to find only Thelma, engrossed in her typing. I went in and slipped the file on the desk while she pretended not to notice me. My whispered "Thanks!" went unacknowledged except for a quick wink, as she continued the steady rhythm of her typing.

My stomach churned as I contemplated the next step in my campaign. Before I lost my nerve, I walked quickly to Ruth's office. Without glancing around, I opened the door, which she usually left unlocked during the day. There was enough illumination from the open windows for me to complete my task. No need to advertise my guilty presence with a light.

I stood before Ruth's desk and contemplated what I was about to do. Ordinarily I would never have considered snooping through the papers on someone else's desk, but I needed desperately to know something about Margaret's dissertation. Looking at Ruth's copy without her knowledge, as distasteful as the idea was, seemed to be the most expedient solution to my dilemma.

The manuscript lay on her desk, where she had left it earlier. I despaired at the size of it. There must have been between three and four hundred pages! I'd never be able to find what I wanted before Ruth and Margaret returned from lunch. Besides the stack in the middle, I could see several other piles of manuscripts on another table in the corner of Ruth's office. I'd never manage to get through enough of them to be certain about anything. Well, maybe my luck would hold, and this pile of papers on her desk would be what I needed.

I picked up the stack of pages that Ruth had turned face down, hoping to find the beginning of the dissertation. Maybe Margaret had included a contents page that would give me some help.

No such luck. There wasn't even a title page or an acknowledgement page. In his journal, Charlie had seemed so certain that something was fishy about Margaret's dissertation, and he knew Whitelock's older doctoral students better than I did. So I'd be willing to bet that this was Margaret's dissertation. I scanned the first couple of pages in the stack, numbered 15 and 16.

Yes, this had to be it. The two pages discussed the long-held views of Alfred the Great, led by Sir Frank Stenton's interpretations of key Anglo-Saxon historical documents. Shuffling through the manuscript, I looked for the beginnings of chapters. Each one of them had a title. I scanned faster, looking for some hint.

Finally! My luck was holding, after all. Chapter Five was entitled "A Critical Reassessment of Asser's *Life of Alfred*." I skimmed this chapter as quickly as possible, skipping over narrative passages, looking for points of interpretation which I could compare with Dunbar's published article. I had always been able to read and digest material swiftly, an ability which had stood me in good stead in graduate school. This worked in my favor now, since this chapter was a long one.

For nearly fifteen minutes I read, listening anxiously for the sound of footsteps out in the hall as I turned each page. With great relief I came upon the final page of the chapter and returned it to the pile.

Margaret wasn't much of a stylist. Her work read remarkably like Whitelock's leaden prose. *Like master, like student,* I thought. Hurriedly putting the manuscript back as I had found it, I mulled over what I'd learned from my rapid reading.

I slipped unnoticed into the hallway, then quickly made my way to the first floor, where I looked up the *Medieval Quarterly* in the online catalog. My luck still held. The university library possessed a complete run of the journal.

Now for the next step in the chase. I took the elevator to the third floor, where I hunted through the stacks until I found the shelf that contained the journal.

I pulled out the bound volume of 1987 and thumbed through the first few pages until I came to a table of contents. Finding the beginning page number of Dunbar's article, I turned to it and began to read.

Fifteen minutes later, I was convinced that Margaret Wilford had stolen her dead friend's work.

C H A P T E R · 2 6

I REPLACED THE VOLUME on the shelf, convinced that Margaret was a plagiarist. She had taken some slight pains to alter Dunbar's writing style. His work had flowed beautifully, and I admired how he wrote clearly and vividly. Margaret's version had been less colorful, flatter in tone—in other words, typical historian's prose. The arguments which he had used to make his points about the reliability of Asser's *Life of Alfred* were repeated with no change. As well as I could remember from my hasty—and guilty—perusal of the chapter in her dissertation, Margaret offered the same interpretation, point by point, of the evidence which I found in Dunbar's article.

He had argued for a major reassessment of the reign of Alfred the Great by calling into question what had been, heretofore, a source considered almost sacrosanct by the world's Anglo-Saxonists. Dunbar had had balls, that was for sure. If his work had gotten wider attention, he would have definitely caused a stir. As would Margaret's work, if it ever got published in book form.

One chapter did not necessarily make a charge of plagiarism stick, I reasoned. Margaret could possibly claim that she had been influenced in her ideas by Dunbar's article—she might even have cited it, for all I knew, since I hadn't looked over her bibliography—but this radical reinterpretation of one of the key sources of Alfredian scholarship had to have influenced her whole dissertation. I was willing to bet that the rest of it went hand in hand with what I found in this article. It must have been all Dunbar's work, to be consistent to the theory proposed in the article. Otherwise, Margaret was one hell of a historian.

How did this all tie in with the murders, though? My mind slipped relentlessly to the most pressing question. Had Charlie run across Dunbar's article, then made the connection with Margaret's dissertation? Surely he must have. He was in and out of Whitelock's office frequently, and he could have seen a copy of Margaret's dissertation lying on the professor's desk. Charlie would certainly have had few scruples about reading the manuscript without permission.

The point that bothered me most was Whitelock's compliance with Margaret's plagiarism. He had stooped to plagiarism himself, but that was a slightly different case, since Charlie had never published any of the results of his research, whereas Dunbar had, even though it hadn't been in one of the more prominent medieval historical journals. And even if Whitelock had been little involved in Dunbar's dissertation, he surely must have known the subject of an article published by his star student.

Margaret must have had something on Whitelock, something she could use to force his compliance. She must have been one of his many "companions," because she fit the physical type that he seemed to prefer. Otherwise, why would he go along with this gross academic fraud?

If that was the situation, then Margaret had evidence of Whitelock's sexual indiscretions and could have threatened to expose him if he didn't allow her to call Dunbar's work her own. Of course, betraying him meant incriminating herself, as well. If she hadn't been convincing enough to make Whitelock believe she would go through with it, she might have been desperate enough to murder him, after getting Charlie out of the way first. She might have had to kill Charlie because he wouldn't lose anything by exposing her. He would have looked like a hero for bringing to light one of the worst of academic sins, plagiarism.

I had a lot to think about. Margaret had shaped up—in my mind, at least—as the prime suspect in both murders, but the evidence was all circumstantial. I needed to think things through. I decided to go up to my carrel, where I could sit in relative quiet and gather my wits. I was pretty certain that I had the answer to the murders, but the question remained of what to do with that knowledge.

On the way up the stairs to the fourth floor, I thought about the fact that Anthony Logan was Margaret Wilford's father. Could that have any bearing on the whole situation? Surely not, I argued to myself. I simply couldn't see that courtly, amiable man involved in this. But something niggled at the back of my mind. Something I had just heard. What was it?

I had barely gotten comfortable in my carrel before the inevitable happened. Whenever I wanted some quiet time there, Bella always seemed to appear, Bruce tagging along right behind. Damn! Just like the drive-through window at my bank—I invariably got in line behind someone who had a complicated, protracted transaction. Bella was the main reason I ended up doing most of my studying at home.

"Hi, Andy!" she said brightly, echoed by Bruce. They stood, almost on top of me, hemming me in; Bella leaned up against the side of the desk, while Bruce leaned against the shelves behind my head.

"What's up, you two?" I asked. This crowding made me nervous, but that was the kind of thing Bella ignored.

She gave me the benefit of the smile that had dazzled the New York and Paris photographers for four years. "I ought to be asking *you* that, you rascal," she said, her dimple peeking out to chastise me.

What was going on? Surely she knew I was immune to any kind of vamping from her. Now, from Bruce, I might be tempted. I grinned at that thought.

"We should have been pooling our efforts right from the start," she continued, as ever oblivious to the look on my face.

Since I couldn't see Bruce without craning my neck backwards, I concentrated on Bella. "I'm afraid I don't quite follow you," I said, truly in the dark.

That smile blazed at me again. "Playing detective, you fathead," she replied, smiling affectionately to take the sting out of the epithet. "Bruce and I have been trying to solve the murders to keep your bony little ass—and Rob's—out of the fire. What did you think I was talking about?"

When it hit me, I couldn't help myself. Only the hurt look on Bella's face finally stopped my laughter. I had to take my glasses off to wipe my streaming eyes. All that time, we had thought Bella had been involved with Whitelock, but she and Bruce were playing detective.

"Lord, Bella," I wheezed at her, "you can't be serious."

Wounded Dignity at her most condescending, Bella nodded.

"Look," I said, my laughter under control, "you just caught me off guard. I didn't realize Nancy and Ned were on the case." She looked puzzled at the reference, and I almost burst out laughing again. She had to be the one person in America who'd never read Nancy Drew.

"You don't seem very grateful," she hissed.

"Sorry," I apologized. That cryptic entry in Charlie's journal made sense now. Bella hadn't been one of Whitelock's companions after all—she had been trying to play detective, and of course, Bruce had to go along with it to keep her out of trouble.

Taking my apology at face value, Bella settled down on the edge of the desk again. I strained my neck to look up at Bruce, and he winked at me with his left eye, which Bella couldn't see.

Frankly, I was relieved. Despite everything, I did like Bella, and I hadn't wanted to believe her capable of murder, or guilty of any involvement of the kinky sort with Whitelock.

"What have you found out then?" I asked.

"Precious little," she replied, disgusted. "*You* certainly weren't any help, the times we talked to you and Rob. I wanted to be subtle and not let you realize what we were doing, because I didn't want to alarm you." She frowned, and I thought Maggie could give her lessons on the withering look. "I never really believed that Rob killed Charlie, and I certainly didn't think Rob killed White- lock. I had suspected for a while that something odd was going on with White- lock, and I wasn't terribly surprised when something happened to Charlie."

"On Rob's behalf, then," I said, "let me say thanks. I know he'll appreciate your faith in him." And the laugh he was going to have over this would cheer him up. "But what do you mean when you say that you suspected that some- thing odd was going on?"

"Like I told you before; I heard things every once in a while in Whitelock's office, and I also overheard him and Charlie a couple of times while I was wait- ing out in the hall for an audience with His Majesty." Bella preened over her abil- ities as an eavesdropper. "Plus, I got Charlie up in a corner once, and he gave me a few hints. That was a day or two before he died."

"What did he say?" In his journal Charlie had mentioned that he had given her a clue to keep her busy. Was it something which I would find of use?

Bella shrugged. "Well, he didn't make much sense. You know how he was."

I nodded sympathetically to encourage her.

"He said, 'I'll give you two clues, "drone" and "whale." It's up to you to figure out what I'm talking about.'" She frowned again. "I didn't know what he meant, but that's all he would tell me. I still haven't figured it out."

I knew what Charlie meant by those two references, or at least I thought I did, but the clues only confirmed the identities of two women I suspected of being Whitelock's mistresses. I figured "drone" referred to Margaret, who worked a boring day job compared to the others; and "whale" had to mean that ridicu- lous earring that Wilda wore sometimes. Bella might guess the former, but since she was more concerned with her own clothes than with those anyone else wore, I doubt she had ever paid attention to Wilda's jewelry.

But I wasn't ready to let her in on the secret. "Gosh, Bella, you're right," I said in my most innocent voice. "I wonder what Charlie meant by those clues?"

Before I thought about it, I had looked up at Bruce again, and he winked. He was a lot more sensitive to what went on around him than Bella had ever been. Thank God he kept her out of serious trouble, I thought, and for once, I sym- pathized with our dear mayor.

"Well, Andy," Bella said, staring at me, "what about you? I know you've been playing detective, too. What have you found out?"

I couldn't resist. I leaned forward, thrusting my face toward hers, and she leant down to me, her eyes sparkling.

"Well, for example," I said, trying to seem studiedly nonchalant, "did you know that Margaret Wilford is Anthony Logan's daughter?"

Bella snorted in disgust. "Lord, Andy, if that's the best you can do, you'd better give up and call in the Hardy Boys." She grinned sourly at me. "Of course I knew that!" Her tone inferred that I was a moron and that everyone except me had known about the relationship.

"Well, Bella," I said, not realizing how loud my voice had become, "I can't say anything much right now, but Rob and I *have* uncovered some evidence that Charlie left—"

"Evidence!" Bella squealed in delight, interrupting me.

As my cousin Ernie would say, I'd let my big mouth overload my skinny butt; I realized it as soon as the words were out.

"What kind of evidence?" she asked. "Are you going to turn it over to the police?"

I should have just picked up a heavy book and pounded myself over the head. Most of the fourth floor had heard Bella, I was sure. I should have known better. Why did I say such things to a person with no subtlety? But, she was an American historian, after all. We Europeanists were more sophisticated.

"Hush!" I hissed at her. "Do you want the whole university to hear you?"

She looked properly abashed, but she was still excited. Bruce coughed suspiciously behind me.

I got up, deciding to get away from the two of them before I wound up deeper in trouble. I turned off the light in my carrel and said, "Look, you guys, I've got things to do. I think the less said about this right now, the better. After all, the police wouldn't like it if they knew I had spilled anything to you."

"Sure, Andy." Bruce spoke for the first time since telling me hello. "Come on, Bella." His voice was, for once, stern, though he did sound like he was trying not to laugh. Bella frowned at him, but she went without arguing.

I stood there and watched them disappear through the stacks. Then I went to the elevator and punched the DOWN button, with no particular destination in mind. As I waited for the elevator, I heard someone move, from somewhere behind me. A hand or a knee, perhaps, had come in contact with the edge of one of the sets of metal shelves, and there was a faint pinging sound.

Curious, a little uneasy and not sure why, I abandoned the elevator and walked between the carrels on my left and the stacks on the right. Had someone been eavesdropping? Most of the history graduate students had carrels on the fourth floor, and it could have been any one of them, or some nosy bystander. Bella and I had offered some entertaining tidbits to the person who had been listening.

As I moved through the stacks, I glanced casually to my right, trying to catch whoever it was. The floor was quiet. When I reached the fourth range of shelves, there was suddenly a flash of movement. In the dim light shining down through the stacks, I caught a glimpse of blond hair.

I ran back toward the elevator, but whoever had been there, eavesdropping in the stacks, had gone, possibly by the stairs or another elevator at the other end of the floor. I thought about who it might have been. Blond hair meant practically everybody involved in the case, and that wasn't much help.

On a hunch, I went upstairs to the history department office. I wasn't sure what I hoped to see, but I began walking down the hall. I could at least get some idea of who was on the fifth floor, because the eavesdropper could easily have come up.

As I turned the corner, I saw Azalea ahead of me, just coming out of the department office. Margaret was with her. Since they didn't appear to have noticed me, I trailed them casually.

They stopped at Wilda's office. After knocking, Azalea opened the door, and she and Margaret walked in.

I scurried quickly down the hall and was almost in front of the door before I realized that it was open wide enough for me to see inside, and the occupants of Wilda's office were able to see me as I skidded to an ungainly stop outside the door. Trying to appear innocent, I smiled at the four women in the office, as their blonde heads turned almost as one in my direction.

Her face blank, Margaret closed the door quietly in my face, as Wilda, Azalea, and Selena turned their backs.

CHAPTER · 27

I STOOD THERE in the hall for a moment and called myself twenty-seven kinds of stupid. One of the women in that room was probably a double murderer. I was convinced of it now. And, in my usual graceless way, I had advertised my presence at the most inopportune time. I was willing to bet also that one of them had been down on the fourth floor, listening in on my conversation with Bella and Bruce. The fourth floor was where much of the library's history collections were shelved. The eavesdropper could have been any one of them, even Azalea, who often read history, particularly books by faculty members.

But that conversation would probably alarm only one of them unduly. I just couldn't believe that this was a conspiracy by the four of them. Three of them were innocent, I thought, innocent at least of the two murders, and maybe those three didn't realize that the fourth was the culprit.

I decided to move away from Wilda's office door before one of them came out and found me still there. I lumbered down to the history office, lost in thought, and almost ran into Dan Erickson.

We both mumbled "sorry" to each other. I stopped, but Dan brushed on by me and rounded the corner. Actually I was relieved, because after our conversation that morning, I didn't feel up to talking to him again for a while. I hoped he had already contacted Herrera. If he hadn't by the next day, I'd have to tell the lieutenant myself what Dan had told me.

It might be a moot point by then, anyway, if what I suspected about the two murders was true. I went on into the office and smiled casually at Thelma, who winked at me once again. Her small act of espionage had clearly cheered her up—or perhaps it was the fact that Azalea was not in the office.

I picked up one of the phones and punched in my home number, anxious to talk things over with Maggie and Rob. My phone rang and rang, but no one answered. I disconnected, then asked Thelma for the department's list of home numbers. I found Rob's and dialed it. After four rings, the answering machine picked up. My stomach did a couple of flip-flops as I listened to Charlie's voice prompt me to leave a message. Rob obviously hadn't thought about the answering machine the past few days.

"Rob, it's me," I mumbled, trying to keep my voice from Thelma's eager ears. "I'm on campus, and I've found out a lot of things we need to talk about. I think I've got it figured out, so you and Maggie come on over as quickly as possible. I'll be in my carrel."

Once again I disconnected, then I punched in Maggie's home number. When the answering machine picked up, Maggie's voice invited me to leave a message. I repeated the message I had left for Rob, then hung up.

Thelma was staring at me unashamedly, but I didn't want to stick around and face any questions. I bade her good-bye, then escaped out into the hall.

From the periphery of my vision, I caught a flash of movement, as if someone had just ducked out of sight around the corner. I stood still, listening. Muted sounds of conversation came from an office nearby, and the fluorescent lights hummed faintly above me. I couldn't hear any footsteps.

I shrugged off my vague feeling of disquiet. Hearing Charlie's voice on the answering machine had unsettled me to the point that I was imagining things.

I turned and walked the other way down the hall, toward Ruth McClain's office. I thought the time had come to take her into my confidence and ask what she knew about Margaret's dissertation.

The door of Ruth's office was closed, but the lights were on. I started to knock, but then I heard voices and realized she must be talking to someone. I checked my watch, then peered at the small typed card taped on the door. This was during her regular office hours. I'd have to wait until whoever was with her finished.

I leaned against the wall beside her door and tried to let my restless mind slow down the turmoil of thoughts. I had to concentrate and think through all this information rationally.

Philip Dunbar's dissertation seemed to be the key to the whole problem. I found it hard to believe that all existing copies of it had been in his car when he was killed. I was convinced that he must have had another copy somewhere.

Then, when he had died so tragically, an opportunist had seized the chance to take possession of what could be a valuable property. If Dunbar's dissertation had been of the quality of his article, then the full-length work would have been valuable indeed. The article demonstrated his abilities both as a scholar and as a writer. Not only would an outstanding dissertation, published as a book, bring its possessor an excellent reputation in the competitive world of academia, but it could bring money from the popular market as well. Dunbar's writing style was lively and interesting, and I could see easily where his work would appeal to an audience larger than that of the scholarly community. Writers like Barbara Tuchman, with fewer historical credentials than Dunbar would have possessed, had hit the best-seller list with works of history that were both scholarly and entertaining. Finally, with the academic job market so difficult to crack, some persons might be willing to commit murder to get ahead.

Stealing the dead man's scholarly efforts, therefore, could pay off handsomely for the person cool enough to gamble on it—and patient enough to wait an appropriate length of time. Was Margaret cool enough and patient enough to fit the scenario I had sketched out? She would have had to do something about her writing style, however. But maybe she had written her dissertation that way on purpose, to mask her theft.

She certainly seemed cool enough, I thought, based on that conversation earlier in Ruth's office. She hadn't seemed the least bit grieved over Whitelock's death, had actually sounded pleased that Ruth was so much easier to work with. But if Margaret had been having kinky sex with Whitelock, no wonder she was happy to have him out of the way.

That would certainly explain why Whitelock was willing to let one of his students plagiarize the efforts of another of his students. Briefly I wondered whether Charlie's main motive in blackmailing Whitelock had been to get *his* hands on Dunbar's dissertation. I was convinced that Charlie had figured out that someone had the missing dissertation, and his attempts to put pressure on Whitelock might have been directed toward obtaining the dissertation for himself.

Charlie had miscalculated badly, however, because whoever had the dissertation and planned to use it had murdered to keep it. Once Charlie was out the picture, though, Whitelock must have panicked, and the killer decided to take him out of the picture, as well, counting on the fact that the whole dissertation angle seemed so unlikely that no one would ever figure it out.

I smiled grimly as I shifted my weight from one foot to the other. The killer had reckoned without my nosiness and my loyalty to Rob. I don't know whether the killer had had any idea that Rob could shape up in the police view as such a good suspect, but Rob had two hidden assets, as it had turned out—Maggie and me.

Rather pleased with this picture of Andy Carpenter as Nemesis, I entertained myself with the mental picture of the newspaper headlines. "Brilliant amateur leads police to murderer" sounded pretty good.

Then I brought myself back to earth. This was not the time to indulge my adolescent fancy of being a famous amateur detective. There were still a number of loose ends to tie up before I could call the case solved, and I wasn't going to settle anything by fantasizing.

I glanced at my watch. Almost two o'clock. I hoped Maggie and Rob would get my message soon. I wanted to talk to them after I talked to Ruth. I stared at her door, willing whichever gabby student was with her to finish up so I could have my turn.

My attempts at mental telepathy came to naught, so I settled back against the wall once more and contemplated some of those loose ends.

What, for example, was Anthony Logan's connection, if any, to the murders? Granted, I now knew that he was Margaret's father, but I couldn't figure out whether that was supposed to mean anything. I made myself slow down, and I concentrated on recalling that long conversation Logan and I had had the day Rob and I discovered Whitelock's murder.

Logan had taken some pains to tell me stories to Whitelock's discredit. That tale about the young woman, sent to Europe by her parents to get her away from Whitelock, was a good example.

What if Logan had been talking about his own daughter? That would certainly explain the bitterness he had seemed to feel toward Whitelock. The story would also strengthen Margaret's connection to Whitelock. Maybe she had had an affair with him years ago, when she was an undergraduate. Then she returned to the university as a graduate student and ended up working with her former lover. They resumed the relationship at some point, and Margaret had plenty of blackmail material to force Whitelock to go along with her plans to use Dunbar's work as her own.

Whitelock would have had to cooperate. He could have exposed Margaret, but that would have destroyed him, as well. So he had to support the whole thing.

But what if Whitelock had panicked after Charlie's murder? Margaret had killed Charlie because he was threatening exposure, and with him out of the way, she might have figured that Whitelock would be more easily controlled. But maybe Charlie's murder had backfired, made Whitelock more nervous, more anxious to confess and take whatever the consequences might have been. That could have prompted Margaret to murder him.

I thought then of my conversation with Dr. Farrar. She had heard Whitelock argue with four different people the afternoon of the day he had probably died. Two men, two women had argued with him. Bella and Rob accounted for two of the people. Who had been the other man and woman?

What if the other woman had been Margaret? Surely the police could check easily enough whether she had been at work that afternoon. If she had been arguing with Whitelock, she could have stormed out of his office and gone right down the hall to her father's office.

The more I thought about it, the more excited I became. Anthony Logan could have been the other man who had argued with Whitelock that afternoon. What was it Dr. Farrar had said about Logan?

He often had tea with her in the afternoon, but that particular afternoon, after she left her office in disgust at the noise coming from Whitelock's office, she stopped by Logan's office, and *he wasn't there.*

I was sure those were her exact words. *He wasn't there.* She hadn't said he'd already gone home for the day, just that he wasn't there. Because, I thought, my elation mounting, he was in Whitelock's office at that very moment, arguing with him.

I developed the theory further in my mind. Logan and Whitelock were arguing in Whitelock's office. Logan, having heard the whole sordid story from his daughter, tried to reason with Whitelock. Whitelock, of course, probably refused to listen. Then, angrily, Logan picked up the ashtray and bashed Whitelock over the head. Stunned at what he had done, Logan left quietly, Whitelock dead or dying on the floor. Probably no one noticed him leave Whitelock's office.

I mulled it over for a moment longer before I spotted one flaw in the scenario—I assumed that there were two murderers. Logan had killed Whitelock to protect his daughter, but he hadn't killed Charlie.

Or had he?

Maybe Margaret had come to her father with her problems *before* Charlie had been killed. If that had been the case, then Logan could have killed Charlie *and* Whitelock. Charlie first, because he was the most direct threat. Logan could have assumed that Whitelock would be more pliant than Charlie, with more to lose. Then Whitelock was killed when he panicked and threatened to give everything away. Someone would have to prove that Logan had known about all this before Charlie's death, however.

My head was beginning to hurt, plus I was feeling a little ashamed of myself. I was still having trouble seeing Logan as the murderer. I had to admit that the need to protect his daughter was a powerful motive, especially for a man who seemed to have hated Whitelock. Margaret was just as capable of protecting herself, though, as she was of asking her father to do it for her. There was no need for her to have involved him at all.

That was enough for the moment, I thought grimly. Before I tried to carry this much further, I had to talk to Ruth and confirm that Margaret was using what I suspected was really Philip Dunbar's work. Ruth could at least tell me more about what Margaret's dissertation actually contained than my hasty perusal had allowed. And, I brightened at the thought, Ruth might actually know a little something more about what Dunbar had written.

Then, almost as if on cue, Ruth's door opened, and an undergraduate popped out.

I checked my watch; she'd been in there at least half an hour. She smiled uncertainly at me, and I'm afraid I probably glowered at her before she skittered nervously away.

I could almost tell the length of the young woman's visit by the look on Ruth's face as I closed the door behind me.

"Isn't advising undergrads fun?" I asked cheerily as I sat down across from her.

She shot me a dark look. "Full of laughs," she muttered, running a hand tiredly through her hair. "What can I do for you today, Andy? I'm afraid I don't have a lot of spare time the next few days." She indicated the manuscripts on her desk.

I took a deep breath. "Actually," I began, "that's what I need to talk to you about."

"These dissertations?" she asked, the puzzlement obvious in her voice.

I nodded, trying to figure out the best way to proceed. "You already know that I've been nosing around, trying to figure out what's going on," I stated, and Ruth smiled in affirmation. "And you warned me to be careful, and I've tried to be. But I think I've finally got things figured out, and I think you can help me prove it."

She regarded me with something approaching polite disbelief. "What do I know that could help you? How do these dissertations relate to anything?"

Well, I could either launch into a long story and try to convince her, or I could cut to the chase and simply ask what I needed to know. The explanations could come later.

"Selena Bradbury and Margaret Wilford were supposed to defend their dissertations this semester, and I'm assuming, from what I observed earlier today, that you're going to be taking over for Dr. Whitelock." I waited for Ruth's confirmation, and after she nodded, I continued. "I need to know the subjects of their dissertations."

She stared at me for a long moment. "I cannot, for the life of me," she said, her voice dry as dust, "understand what their dissertations have to do with this whole mess. But I assume you think you have a good reason for asking."

"Yes, I think so."

Ruth grinned. "The great detective obviously isn't going to explain things to me, so I suppose I'll go along. There's no great secret, as far as I can tell, about their dissertations. Selena has done a new study of the Frankish laws and actually translated them into English. It's an excellent work of legal history. I've been pleased with the whole project."

My heart started beating a little faster. I hadn't given much thought to Selena as a viable suspect, and it now seemed that she was truly out of the running. A dissertation on the Frankish laws was quite different from Dunbar's work. I could see the noose beginning to tighten around Margaret's neck.

"And Margaret Wilford?" I prompted eagerly.

"Margaret surprised me a little with her choice of topic. She's working on the Norse invasions of the Frankish kingdoms, focusing on the military aspects. You know," she mused, "I hadn't realized Margaret was so interested in military history."

Dumbfounded, I stared at Ruth. "Are you sure?" I croaked.

"Of course I'm sure, Andy," she said and thumped one of the piles on her desk. "Here's her dissertation." She pointed over to the corner, and I saw another pile of papers on a table. "That one is Selena's." Then she put her hands on a pile near the center of her desk—the one I had been reading through earlier. "This one is Dan Erickson's."

"Dan's?" I managed to ask. "What's his topic?" I had never heard him talk much about the subject of his dissertation, just that damned post-doc at Harvard! The more I thought about it, the more I realized how odd that had been.

Watching me carefully, Ruth responded to my query. "Dan's work is very interesting. Anglo-Saxon England isn't my period, of course, but I know enough to realize that he's offering a major reinterpretation of the life of one of the seminal figures of the period, Alfred the Great. He's going to cause quite a stir with this. I was astonished at the quality of it."

I stared wordlessly at Ruth. It had been Dan Erickson all along.

C H A P T E R · 2 8

I FELT LIKE an utter fool. I had focused so intently on Margaret that I hadn't thought seriously about Dan, even after his so-called confession putting him at the scene of the crime. He had known Philip Dunbar; he had been around at the time of his death. He had as much to gain as Margaret or Selena by stealing Dunbar's work. That junior fellowship at Harvard would be worth killing for—at least for some people. Dan had certainly put me off the scent, at least for a while, with his confession. Did he think he had convinced me of his innocence?

"Goodness, Andy," Ruth's voice broke through my chaotic thoughts. "You look dumbstruck. What does this mean?"

I felt I owed her the truth. As the person who would have to sign off on the dissertation, Ruth would be in a difficult position if Dan's work was proven to be plagiarism. But I wasn't completely certain what the truth was. I had to have a little time to assimilate this new information and review my obviously flawed reconstruction of events.

"Well," I said shakily, "at the very least, I should tell you there's a good chance Dan's dissertation isn't his work."

"That's a serious accusation," Ruth warned. "What proof do you have?"

I looked at her for a long moment, and I saw the concern—and the fear— in her eyes. Spotting a pad of paper and a pen on her desk, I reached over and picked them up. I started scribbling while she watched with growing irritation and concern.

"I'm going to give you a citation," I told her as I wrote, "to an article you should check out. You read it, compare it to Dan's work, then you tell me." I handed the piece of paper over to her, and she examined what I had written.

Ruth studied my face, as comprehension dawned in her eyes. She had known Dunbar, and she was certainly astute enough to make the connection.

She slumped back in her chair. "I *thought* there was something vaguely familiar about that chapter on Asser's *Life of Alfred*."

"Look, Ruth." I leaned forward in my chair. "I think I've finally got it figured out, and I'll talk with the campus police when I'm ready. Then they can handle it. I don't want to run the risk of getting anyone, you and me included, in trouble."

She sighed. "I suppose you're right about turning it over to the police, but I'm still having trouble understanding why a dissertation could be a motive for murder. It's by far the best work by a graduate student that I've read, but is it worth killing for?" She shook her head.

"I know it all seems like a bizarre nightmare," I said, "but I believe this is the key to the whole thing. After all, a postdoctoral fellowship at Harvard is riding on this work."

Ruth nodded. I could see that, against her will, she was coming to believe in the truth and strength of Dan's motives for murder.

"The only thing I can't figure out," I said, "is how he got hold of it. According to the story I heard, nobody could find a copy."

"If I remember correctly," she said slowly, "they were sharing an apartment."

That clinched it, as far as I was concerned.

I stood up. "Please don't say a word about this to anyone, except maybe Maggie or Rob. I'm going down to my carrel to wait for them. I want to talk this through with them first, before we talk to the police." I grinned to reassure her, and myself as well. "Maybe, by tomorrow, this whole thing will be over."

Ruth shook her head. "It won't be quite that easy, but I'll do as you suggest." She shot me a look. "And you be very, *very* careful until you talk to the police. Thank God I don't have an appointment with Dan today or tomorrow." She shivered. "Maybe I ought to go home and lock all the doors and close the blinds, or maybe I should just lock myself in here."

Both sounded like good suggestions, I said, and I promised that I would be careful. When I left, Ruth was still shaking her head, staring at the piece of paper I had written upon. The hallway outside her office was quiet as I made my way to the stairs. Down on the fourth floor, I headed to my carrel.

I switched on the light and sat down. Staring at the postcards of cathedrals, I wondered where Maggie and Rob were. There was no note on my carrel, so I supposed they hadn't made it to campus yet. If I headed home, I'd probably miss them. Surely they were on their way.

I tried to focus on the implications of what Ruth had told me. I unlocked the desk drawer in my carrel and pulled out a pad of paper and a pen and began to jot down notes.

Dan was the one who had stolen Dunbar's work. Ruth should be able to confirm that partially, once she compared Dan's dissertation to Dunbar's article. After that, it would be up to the police to connect Dan to the murders. Would they believe that he would kill just so he could pass off someone else's dissertation as his own?

I had no idea what kind of evidence the police had, like time of death and forensics, but perhaps they had something which could link Dan if they were aware of his motives. Up till now, the police had no reason to connect him to the scene of the crime.

Then I cursed myself for an idiot. I had played right into Dan's hands. I had tried to be magnanimous and honorable, to allow him the time to go to the police on his own, because I had been certain that Margaret was the thief. There was no telling what Dan could be up to now. An hour earlier, I had seen him upstairs, and then he had gotten away from me quickly. He could be headed for the airport now to catch a flight to anywhere.

Should I call Herrera and tell him everything? Would he think I was a crazy, interfering busybody, still trying to deflect attention away from Rob and myself?

I had a sudden prickling at the nape of my neck, as if someone was watching me. I stuck my head out of my carrel and looked up and down the stacks. I didn't see anything, and all I could hear was the hum of the lights. Trying to control my nerves, I settled into my chair again.

Dan had manipulated me so easily. He had told me a convincing story of seduction and blackmail, which had steered me completely away from his real motive. I didn't know if Dan had told me the truth about his relationship with Charlie, but the story had definitely served its purpose. I had set him aside as a viable suspect, despite the fact that he had told me he was at the scene of Charlie's death. I decided to call Herrera and tell him what I knew—or was it what I *thought* I knew?

A dark shape fell across my desk, startling me, and I almost banged my head on the metal shelf behind me.

"Thank God you're finally here," I said quietly to Maggie and Rob, my heart hammering away in my chest. "You startled me, but, boy, am I glad to see you." I got up and peered through the stacks at Dan's carrel and was relieved to see it dark.

Rob pulled a chair from the carrel next to mine, and Maggie perched on the edge of my desk. Sensing my excitement, she asked, "Okay, Andy, what's going on?"

I described my conversations with Dan Erickson, Dr. Farrar, and Ruth McClain. As I related Dan's story, I could see the distaste in Rob's face and something I couldn't identify in Maggie's. Maybe Dan hadn't been making up everything he told me; obviously there was something to my speculations earlier about his ambiguous sexuality. Perhaps Maggie would enlighten us once I finished.

The telling of my fact-gathering took about thirty minutes, and neither Maggie nor Rob interrupted. I had to remember to keep my voice down so that I didn't broadcast to the whole fourth floor. By the time I got to my conversation with Ruth, I was hoarse and my throat longed for water.

"Well, Andy," Rob replied, "I have to hand it to you. I think you're right. Dan has to be the murderer. If he's trying to pass off someone else's work as his own, then he might be willing to kill to keep it a secret. If anyone accused him of plagiarism, he would lose any chance of being considered by Harvard."

Maggie nodded. "I agree with Rob. I don't think any of us would pass up a chance like that easily." She paused, and a shadow passed briefly across her face. "Besides, from what Dan told me, he had it pretty rough growing up in Boston, and Harvard represents something very important to him."

I wanted to ask her what she thought about the validity of Dan's story about Charlie, but I couldn't rake up the nerve to do it. Almost as if reading my mind, however, Rob jumped in.

"You know," he said, "I never knew about any connection between him and Charlie, but I did wonder if Dan was gay. Then, when Maggie started dating him last year, I decided I was wrong. But from what you've told us, Andy, I guess I was right all along."

I glanced quickly at Maggie. She nodded. "That's why Dan and I went out only twice," she said. "I picked up on a lot of uncertainty from him. Plus, I caught him cruising other guys. I decided that I didn't want to go through all that with him, no matter how attractive he was."

The story Dan had told me that morning could very well have been the truth. That simply intensified his motives in murdering Charlie. He needed to keep quiet the fact that he was plagiarizing someone else's work, and on top of that he was humiliated and angry over the way Charlie had treated him. Whitelock had gotten caught in the crossfire, though I in no way considered him blameless. I couldn't help but believe that Whitelock knew that Dan's dissertation was really the work of Dunbar. But in Whitelock's eyes, the fact that his doctoral student was heading off to a fellowship at Harvard more than compensated for the immorality of the situation.

Seeing that Maggie and Rob were waiting for me to say something, I quickly said aloud what I had just been thinking, and they agreed with me.

"But now what are we going to do?" Maggie asked. "Shouldn't we be on the phone to Herrera right now?"

Both Rob and I nodded vigorously. "Now that we've talked it through," I replied, "and neither of you thinks I'm crazy, then I feel better about calling Herrera. He can track Dan down and settle this whole thing."

I stood up, and Rob shifted his chair. I looked out into the stacks and caught a glimpse of blond hair and the flash of a long-sleeved shirt. Someone was hiding and listening to us. I nudged Maggie and nodded toward the spot. Casually, she stood and took a step to the left, where she was in a position to see down the aisle.

She tensed, and Rob and I watched, immobilized. We could hear the thump of footsteps on the worn linoleum as someone started running through the stacks, away from us. It was Dan, and he had been listening, for who knew how long.

"After him," Rob said as he began to run.

Maggie reacted immediately, cutting through the stacks to my right, in the direction of the front staircase on the south side of the building, trying to head Dan off before he could get out.

I felt frozen to the spot as I watched Maggie and Rob rocket off on the chase. Then I got my legs in gear and followed Rob. Once my legs started functioning, my brain did the same, and I suddenly had an idea where Dan might be headed, if Rob hadn't managed to head him off at the pass, so to speak.

The eastern end of the floor had a staircase rarely used by students because of its inconvenient location and poor lighting. It had been the scene of an attempted rape several years earlier. The convenient feature of this staircase— convenient at least for Dan's purposes, I thought grimly—was an emergency exit in the basement entrance. He could get out that way, rather than through the front door.

Ahead of me, Rob suddenly veered off through the stacks, and I thought he must have seen something, but I couldn't believe that Dan would run around in circles on the fourth floor. I had almost reached the door to the stairs, and I pounded the last few steps to it. If Rob needed me, he'd give a holler. In my flight, I had barely had time to notice that a few carrels were occupied. Wonder what their occupants thought about this race through the stacks?

I yanked open the door to the stairway and stepped inside. Over my own heavy breathing, I could hear feet running lightly somewhere down below me. They had to belong to Dan. I yelled, "Stairs, Rob!"

Then I was off at breakneck speed. Though my face was streaming with sweat and my glasses had begun to slide, I managed, by some minor miracle, to keep them on. One hand on my glasses and one hand on the railing, I almost flew down the steps, my feet barely touching the treads.

When I reached the bottom of the stairs, I had so much momentum that I couldn't stop, and I literally hit the door. If Dan wasn't already out of the building, he certainly knew that someone was behind him. I jerked the door open and plunged into the murky shadows of the basement.

I paused to get my bearings. The door from the stairs opened onto a small room maybe four feet square. Opposite the stairway door was an opening out into the basement stacks. To my right was another opening; this one led down a short hallway with storerooms off either side. At the end of the hallway was the emergency exit.

I peered through the dim light to the end of the short hallway. The exit sign glowed feebly in the gloom, and I could see a bunch of boxes piled in front of the door. The fire department wouldn't like that. Certainly this wasn't the first time the building had failed to come up to code, but for once I wasn't complaining.

My breath quickened again. Those boxes in front of the door meant that Dan was still inside somewhere. He might have had time to get out of this hallway and out into the basement stacks, but he couldn't run up the stairs to the first floor. Maggie was surely there by now, and I figured she'd probably had someone call the police. Dan must realize that he couldn't get out that way.

I took a deep breath and began moving cautiously down the dark hallway. The storage rooms didn't have doors, and their openings were shrouded in the dark. I stuck to the center of the hallway, which was only about five feet wide, and tried to listen for sounds of movement or breathing.

I heard nothing as I moved closer and closer to the pile of boxes in front of the emergency exit. As I stood next to the pile, I thought I heard a sound behind me. Someone grabbed my left arm and twisted it savagely behind my back. My glasses almost flew off my head from the impact.

CHAPTER · 29

PAIN SHOT THROUGH MY ARM and nearly took my breath away. I tried to turn to get a look at Dan's face, but he twisted my arm brutally, and I gave up. His ragged breathing matched my own.

We stood there for a moment, then Dan forced me into one of the storage rooms. Once we got past the darkness of the doorway and into the interior of the room, I could see the glimmerings of light from windows high on the wall. He pushed me up against the wall underneath one of the windows, and there was enough illumination to see his face and the room around us. He let go of me, and I subsided against a shelf, rubbing my arm, which had gone numb from the force of Dan's grip.

Full bookshelves lined the walls, and I could see boxes of more books in the floor, but a wide swath through the center of the room was clear. Just about anything could happen, and no one would notice for a while. There was little chance that anyone would come along to interrupt whatever Dan was planning to do. Unless, I prayed fervently, Rob had heard me and followed me down the stairs.

"Why did you have to stick your nose in all this, Andy?" Dan asked abruptly. He stood in front of me, muscular and threatening.

I no longer had the energy to try to knock him out of the way and run for it. "Did you really think Rob and I were going to sit still and let either one of us be arrested for murder?" I said, my voice raspy from all the talking I had done earlier and from the exertion of the chase down the stairs. I swallowed, but that didn't help much. "I'm afraid it's too late to go back now. You're not going to get very far if you run. You know that. Maggie and Rob have seen to it that the police are on the way."

I wondered what was running through Dan's mind. Maybe he had reached the point where he just didn't care. I was praying that I could talk him out of doing something I'd regret. Besides, unless the police had strong evidence to link him to the crimes, who knew whether a jury would convict him on the motives and evidence I had ascribed to him?

"If you hadn't been so damned nosy," Dan said furiously, "no one would ever have connected me with this. And they didn't have enough real evidence to make a charge stick against you or Rob."

"Maybe not," I responded. I stared at him through the murky light, trying to decide whether I had regained enough strength and energy to try to knock him out of the way. As I peered at him, over his shoulder I could see someone hovering in the doorway of the room. Rob was quietly sneaking up with a large book in his hands.

Dan stared at me, his eyes full of hatred. "You don't know what I've been through, what it took for me to get this far, and now you're ready to take it all away. Just like they did."

Chilled, I realized that by "they" he meant Charlie Harper and Julian White-lock. "Did it mean so much to you that you had to kill them?" I asked as gently as I could.

"You'd never understand," he said. "Everything I ever wanted, about to fall out of my hands, because Charlie couldn't leave me alone. He deserved what he got, dammit. He pushed me too far, once and for all." Dan seemed to have forgotten me, and I was afraid he'd sense Rob sneaking up on him if I didn't do something.

"One thing I don't understand," I said in as calm a tone as I could muster, "is how you could live with yourself, knowing that you stole the work of a dead man. How could you do it?"

He laughed bitterly. "A hell of a lot of good it was going to do him, wasn't it? He didn't need a good job or a good reputation. I needed it. So I took it."

I was chilled by the sheer, brutal self-interest of his actions. "Was he that much better than you, Dan?" I had to keep him distracted for a moment longer; Rob was getting closer. "Did you hate him because he was brilliant and you aren't? What will you do when Harvard finds out?"

I had gone too far. Before I could stop him, he had his hands around my throat, squeezing the dickens out of my vocal cords, trying to bang my head against the shelves behind me, all the while screaming at me.

I was beginning to have trouble with my vision as I struggled to loosen Dan's hands from around my neck. I caught a glimpse of Rob, who became a blur of motion in the dim light. At the last second, Dan sensed there was someone behind him, but he realized it too late. The heavy book in Rob's hands connected with Dan's head. The crack of head against book was so loud, I thought his skull must surely be fractured.

He toppled sideways to the floor, and I slumped against the wall, rubbing my throat gently with my right hand and the back of my head with my left. Rob dropped the book on Dan's head for insurance. After the second loud whack, Dan was out cold.

My knees suddenly gave way beneath me, and I slid bumpily down the shelves until I was sitting on the floor. Rob stood like an avenging fury over his prey, and I pulled off my glasses and wiped across my sweaty face with an ice-cold hand.

"Thanks," I tried to say, but my throat was dry and bruised, so what came out sounded totally different. I had a sudden strong urge to start giggling, though it wouldn't have done much for the pounding in my head.

"You're more than welcome," Rob said wryly. "Are you all right?"

Just then Maggie came into view, followed by two campus cops, both waving flashlights. The big beefy men were not the same officers I had encountered earlier in the week.

"What's going on here?" one of them barked, as they pushed Maggie and Rob out of the way.

Slowly I stood up, then pointed down at Dan, still out cold at my feet. One of the officers shone his light down on him. "The man on the floor tried to strangle me." I then gestured toward Rob. "If it hadn't been for him, I'd probably be dead by now."

Rob nodded in confirmation. "You need to keep an eye on him, Officer," he said, pointing down at Dan. "We think this is the man who is responsible for the murders here on campus."

"Is that so?" the policeman responded. Motioning for us to step away, he stooped over Dan and checked him out, while the other officer used his radio to contact campus police headquarters.

Maggie, Rob, and I were all relieved to hear that Lieutenant Herrera was on the way. The campus cop looked like he wanted to lock us all up.

Dan, who was coming around, began muttering and cursing. The officers got him on his feet and marched him out of the storage room, ordering Maggie, Rob, and me to follow. Rob had his arm around me, for which I was thankful. I still felt a little weak in the knees. As we headed up the stairs to the first-floor foyer, Maggie told me that she had brought the campus police down to the basement. Rob had figured that Dan would try to get to the emergency exit if he couldn't make it to the front entrance of the library. Even if Maggie and the cops hadn't found us so quickly, I wasn't that worried. Rob was obviously more

· DEAN JAMES ·

than a match for Dan. And I might have managed to get out of the situation myself. A quick knee to the crotch would probably have done the trick—if I had thought of it at the time, that is, I told myself ruefully.

There we all stood, in the brightly lit foyer of the library, waiting for Herrera. I glanced down at myself and realized what a sorry sight I must be, sweaty, smelly, and grimy. Nobody had cleaned those rooms in the basement in decades, to judge by the dust I had picked up. Rob and Maggie, of course, looked cool as proverbial cucumbers. Dan stood there stoically, his eyes closed, as if he might be trying to shut out everything. Passersby goggled at us, but no one said anything.

Lieutenant Herrera arrived, accompanied by a couple of uniformed HPD officers and two more campus policemen. He began the business of sorting out what went on. Dan remained quiet, refusing to speak until he could talk to a lawyer. Herrera and the officers from HPD conferred and decided to take us all downtown for questioning, where we spent six dreary and tiring hours.

After our mind-numbing visit to police headquarters, Maggie, Rob, and I were ready for something to eat. Back at my apartment, I enjoyed a luxuriously hot shower and changed clothes while Maggie and Rob ordered pizza. While we waited for the pizza, we broke out the wine in celebration. Though we were worn out from the events of the day, we were mightily relieved that the worst of it was over. We felt sorry in a way for Dan, though we abhorred what he had done for the sake of his career. No academic job, not even Harvard, was worth two murders.

The delivery man arrived quickly, for which he got a generous tip, and we happily gorged ourselves on pizza. None of us felt like talking. I certainly, for once in my life, felt talked out. Those six hours at the police station had been brutal. Not to mention the fact that my throat was sore.

I was burping contentedly over my fifth slice of pizza when the doorbell rang. "I'll get it," I offered, lumbering slowly to my feet.

I figured it was probably Bella, with Bruce in tow, hot to find out the juicy details, but I was surprised. At the door, looking tired but pleased, was Lieutenant Herrera.

"Mind if I come in?" he asked. "I promise this isn't an official visit."

"Sure," I responded, standing aside to let him in. "Come on into the kitchen," I invited. "We're finally having dinner. Would you like some pizza? I think there's some left."

"Thanks," he replied, slipping off his jacket and laying it across his arm. "I haven't had dinner yet myself."

He followed me to the kitchen, and Rob and Maggie fell silent when they realized who the visitor was.

— 198 —

Herrera nodded in friendly fashion at them, and I motioned for him to take the seat across from Rob. "Wine?" I asked him as I retrieved another glass from the cupboard.

"Don't mind if I do," he replied, helping himself to a slice of pizza. "I'm finally off duty for the evening." He chewed for a moment, then took a long sip of wine. He loosened his tie and took another sip from his wineglass. "That's much better," he announced, smiling at us.

Maggie and I smiled back at him, but Rob continued to watch him warily.

"I know you're wondering," Herrera said, "why I came here, after we all spent so much time together today." He grinned, and I could see why Maggie had found him attractive. Relaxed and friendly, he was handsome and personable.

He took another bite of pizza, and we waited politely for him to continue. He wiped his mouth and said, "We've charged Dan Erickson for both murders."

"That's a relief," Rob said, his eyes still intently on Herrera's face. "Did he finally confess?"

"No, but with what Andy told me, and other evidence we collected, I think we have more than enough to make a strong case against him." He paused for more wine. "By the way, had you seen what was on that second videotape you gave me?"

Both Rob and I shook our heads.

"That second tape," Herrera explained, "was much like the first, with one exception. It seems that Whitelock was bisexual," he continued, "because a tall, blond man featured very prominently on that second tape. And that blond man had a distinctive tattoo on a certain part of his anatomy. By coincidence, Dan Erickson has the same tattoo on the same part of his anatomy."

Rob's face probably mirrored the shock on mine. Maggie kept her eyes firmly directed toward something on the far wall, and I couldn't read her expression.

That locked the last piece of the puzzle into place. Dan had to have something to force Whitelock into going along with his plan to use Dunbar's dissertation, and the games they played together had given him the leverage he needed.

"Besides that," Herrera added, "Erickson had a small cut on the index finger of his right hand, and I'll just bet you that when we match his blood to some blood found on the second murder weapon, we'll have him sewed up tight."

My mind quickly fastened on an image from Whitelock's office, the morning that Rob and I had found his body. I remembered the sun glinting on that ashtray, and I remembered seeing a smear of what looked like blood on one of its edges, near a nick in the glass. I guess Dan had left a trail behind him.

"Thank God it's all over," Rob said, relaxing in his chair for the first time since Herrera had come into the room. "But why the hell"—his voice had suddenly turned savage—"did you put us through all that nonsense about Charlie's will? Did you really think Andy and I killed him?"

Herrera shrugged, not offended by the heat in Rob's voice. "Hey, in my job, you have to work all the angles. I sure thought you were a strong possibility for the first murder. But you had a good alibi for the second one." He grinned hugely at Maggie, and she dimpled back at him. "I was pretty confident that the same person murdered both men, and if you couldn't have done the second one, I thought it let you off for the first one. But I couldn't take any chances."

Herrera took another big bite of pizza. He chewed for a moment, swallowed, and wiped his mouth with the napkin. "Besides, stirring up the pot a little certainly didn't hurt. I would have got there in the end, I think, but you put some of the evidence together faster than I could. Those folks up on the fifth floor were more likely to talk to you than they were to me. I figured you might get some of the good dirt that they'd never tell me." He grinned again. "But I think you should retire from the detective business from now on. You could get hurt." He nodded in my direction.

Rob just shook his head. He was still angry with Herrera, but I could understand the lieutenant's point of view, in a way.

Herrera stood up. "All of this has been off the record, of course."

"Of course," I responded, standing up also.

He looked across the table at Maggie. "Could we talk for a minute?" His voice was soft, almost pleading, quite a different tone from any I had heard him use before.

She stared back at him and stood up. "Sure, why not? Why don't we go into the next room, though?"

Rob and I watched as the two of them left the kitchen. Moments later, we could hear the rumble of low-voiced conversation.

"Well," Rob mused, "wonder what that's all about?"

"I bet he's asking her out," I laughed. "And I'll bet you she accepts."

"You gotta be kidding!" Rob was flabbergasted. "After what he put us through?"

"Oh, come on, you didn't see the way they were looking at each other? Batting eyelashes like it was mating season at the zoo?"

Rob just shook his head. "Then she's welcome to him, if that's what she wants."

"Oh," I said, "Maggie always knows what she wants. And she usually gets it."

"Good for her," Rob said, amused. "But what about me? Do I get what I want?"

"That depends," I said. "What do you want?"

"Oh," Rob said airily, "a certain ditzy blond who seems to have a knack for getting into trouble." He took a step closer to me.

My world had shifted quickly over the past week. Having Rob this near me set my pulse racing, and my heart had taken over from my head. I wanted him now as much as I ever had. The intrusion of murder into our lives had probably put certain things into perspective much faster than would have happened otherwise. Hanging on to my anger didn't seem so important any longer. It was time for me to take some chances. Rob was waiting for an answer.

"Oh, yeah?" I said. How clever of me. I swallowed hard. "Thanks, by the way, for saving my life."

"You're welcome." He took another step closer.

"My hero," I said.

"If you'll be mine," he said. Then he kissed me.

ALSO BY DEAN JAMES

CRUEL AS THE GRAVE

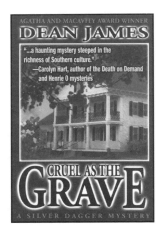

Maggie McLendon should be at home in Houston, studying for her Ph.D. qualifying exams, but a letter from her great aunt arrives, bearing bad news. Maggie's grandfather, Henry McLendon, whom she has never met, is seriously ill in Jackson, Mississippi. Maggie's father, English professor Gerard McLendon, has been estranged from his family since Maggie was an infant, but now there is perhaps one last chance for the McLendons to be reunited. The family welcomes Maggie and Gerard to Jackson, and Gerard has a chance to reconcile with his father. But a murderer strikes, savagely, and Gerard McLendon looks like the chief suspect. Maggie must sort out decades of family secrets, including the puzzle of her grandmother's death twenty-five years before and its relationship to the present crime, to arrive at the truth. But not before the killer strikes a second time. Could Maggie or her father be next on the list?

"In *Cruel as the Grave*, Dean James brings to life a family burdened by dark secrets. Determined sleuth Maggie McLendon peels away layers of hidden sadness to find the truth of her heritage in a haunting mystery steeped in the richness of Southern culture."

—Carolyn Hart

"*Cruel as the Grave* is an engaging, literate novel of family secrets and skullduggery. With a clever plot and appealing characterization, Mr. James has created the perfect English drawing room mystery set smack in the middle of steamy Mississippi. It is a witty and solid debut that will leave mystery readers clamoring for more."

—Earlene Fowler

"*Cruel As The Grave* exposes the underbelly of a Southern family, where secrets and skeletons lurk, cloaked in every imaginable guise. Well-written, deftly-plotted, and highly recommended for fans of Faulkner and others who zeroed in on the dysfunctional social structure that, to this day, continues to be concealed by superficiality and faded magnolia blossoms."

—Joan Hess

Trade Paper ISBN 1-57072-127-0 $15.00
Hardcover ISBN 1-57072-111-4 $24.50

ALSO BY DEAN JAMES

CLOSER THAN THE BONES

Recently retired from teaching high school English, Ernestine Carpenter freely admits that she's more than a bit nosy. She is also good at solving problems, and she's let it be known that she's willing to take on interesting jobs. Mary Tucker McElroy, well known as a patron of the arts, hires Ernie (as she is called by her nearest and dearest) to help her figure out which of her circle might have murdered one of their own. The group had gathered at Idlewild, Miss McElroy's ancestral home in Mississippi, and one guest, writer Sukey Lytton, turned up dead in the pond, an apparent suicide. Six months later, Miss McElroy is convinced that Sukey was murdered, and she wants Ernie to help her find the guilty party. Ernie finds danger lurking in unexpected places at Idlewild, as the killer continues to strike.

"Big-city PIs would envy Ernestine Carpenter's intimate knowledge of small-town relationships and how family secrets can fester into murder. Dean James writes with equal intimacy and knowledge of those relationships, and in crafting another thoughtful problem for Ernie to solve, he gives us a compelling mystery in the Carolyn Hart tradition."

—Margaret Maron

"The traditional mystery is not dead. Thanks to Dean James, it takes on new life in the New South, where (just like the Old South) ladies of a certain age are noticeably quirky, everyone is hiding a guilty secret, cooks know their way to your heart, and murderers are . . . almost . . . impossible to detect. James's *Closer Than the Bones* is a fine variation on a fine tradition, and enjoyable from start to finish."

—Charlaine Harris

"If you can't resist a story with all the traditional trappings, including an elderly spinster sleuth, you're going to love *Closer Than the Bones*. Dean James has plotted a classic puzzle with enough suspects and secrets to keep even the most astute reader busily guessing."

—Toby Bromberg

Trade Paper ISBN 1-57072-183-1 $13.95
Hardcover ISBN 1-57072-182-3 $23.95

TAKE A STAB AT THESE MYSTERIES
COMING
SOON